Murder in Madden

Raegan Teller

D1502099

Pondhawk Press
Columbia, SC
www.PondhawkPress.com

Murder in Madden/ Raegan Teller 1st ed.
ISBN 978-0-9979205-0-5

Dedicated to my mother, who taught me determination.

Dora Bryant
(1911–1997)

"It's impossible," said pride.
"It's risky," said experience.
"It's pointless," said reason.
"Give it a try," whispered the heart.

—Unknown

CHAPTER 1

Ten Years Ago

Rose Marie Garrett studied her reflection in the mirror and smiled with the realization that today could change everything. She examined her makeup and then wiped the dark eyeliner from her eyes with a wet washcloth. The soap stung and she blinked several times until the image of her young face appeared again. She wanted to impress the man at the insurance agency, not seduce him. Somehow she had to convince him she would be a hard worker and that she desperately needed the money.

She went to her closet and pulled out the step stool she kept hidden in the corner behind her winter coat. Rosie got the wool coat for her seventeenth birthday a few months ago, but she had never worn it. Winters in Madden were mild. Rosie stepped onto the stool and stretched overhead to reach a wooden panel that opened to the small attic. She pushed the flimsy square of plywood to one side and stretched as tall as she could until she recognized the familiar feel of the wooden box. She tugged at the corner of the box until she could get a grip on it.

The top was covered in dust, and she brushed it off carefully so she wouldn't soil her dress clothes. She laid the box on her bed and shut the bedroom door. After taking the cover from the box, she gently removed a worn envelope and pulled out two handwritten pages of a letter. The creases were nearly torn through from repeated use and age, but Rosie didn't want to put tape on the precious paper. That might ruin it. She read the letter slowly, as though this were the first time she had seen the familiar words. She refolded the letter and returned it to the box. A small roll of mostly dollar bills was in the corner of the box. She took the rubber band from the roll and counted the money. And then she counted it again. Not enough to get her to Mississippi, even on a Greyhound. She rolled the bills and put the rubber band back around them, but the rubber had become brittle and snapped.

She folded the bills and tucked them in the bottom of the box, and then pulled out another envelope. Rosie gently opened the one-page typewritten document and ran her trembling finger across the information typed in the blanks near the top of the page. She sighed and returned the envelope to the box with the letter, her meager cash, and a few other items, touching each one reverently. Myra would be in soon to tell her she was going to be late, so she stepped on the stool and stretched to return the box to the small dark hole in the top of her closet.

Rosie was brushing some dust from her hands when Myra knocked on the door and walked in. "You're going to be late." Myra held out her hand. "Here's a few dollars in case you need them." She continued to hold out her hand toward Rosie. "Are you sure you don't want me to take you?"

Rosie reached out and took the money. "I got a ride."

"With who?"

Instead of responding, Rosie put the money in her small purse and walked out the bedroom and down the hallway.

"Just remember to be polite and answer Mr. Barton's questions," Myra called out.

Rosie threw up her hand in acknowledgement and walked out the front door, slamming the screen door behind her.

Myra walked out onto the porch and watched Rosie walk away until the big evergreen bushes growing at the edge of the neighbor's yard blocked her view. Myra said a silent prayer for Rosie's soul and asked God to forgive and protect her.

Myra turned to open the screen door to go back inside, and a gust of wind tugged it from her hand, knocking the screen against the house. She pulled the screen shut and looked at the sky to see if a storm was coming. Even in the late-summer humidity, Myra shivered as a chill came over her.

CHAPTER 2

The Present

Enid tapped her hand on the stacks of paper on her desk trying to find her vibrating cell phone. She longed for the days when her co-workers popped into her office to ask a question instead of texting her. She pulled the phone out from under a file folder and read a text from Jill. She was being summoned to the boss' office. Enid had been expecting this conversation because the bank was going through yet another reorganization. The office buzz was that at least half of their jobs would be eliminated when they merged with the larger bank that had acquired them.

Enid walked the short distance down the hallway and tapped on Jill's partially opened door.

"Come in," said Jill. The tall willowy blonde in a navy pantsuit motioned for Enid to have a seat in the chair across from her large glass and metal desk. "We're both busy, so I'll be brief." She leaned forward and locked eyes with Enid. "You're one of my best employees, and I want you here. But, I've got to be honest and tell you that your job is being eliminated."

Enid started to speak but was interrupted.

"Before you say anything, let me finish." Jill walked over to the office door and shut it. Sitting back down, she continued, "There's another job I want you to post for. A promotion. It will require you to travel a good bit, but it's a great opportunity for you." She handed Enid a typed document from her desk. "Here's the new job description and requirements."

Enid skimmed the job posting. "Thanks. I'll read it more thoroughly tonight."

"You'll need to make a presentation before the selection committee next Monday. I'll be glad to give you some tips on what they're looking for." She stood up and walked to the door, holding it open for Enid to leave. "This is the promotion you've been working for. I know everyone here is nervous about all the changes, but this is a big break for you." She smiled, showing a perfect set of teeth. "I've already put in a good word for you."

* * *

Enid sat in her BMW SUV on the sixth floor of the concrete parking deck. Dozens of workers swarmed from elevator doors and scurried to their cars. Most of them were checking their cell phones for messages and hurrying home or to wherever they would spend their brief time away from the office.

Enid ran her hand across the smooth leather seats. A few months ago, buying a BMW seemed like a reward for her hard work and a way to forget her mother's protracted, agonizing death. Now the long-term loan was a huge stone around her neck.

Enid sat in the car, listening to the hypnotically repetitive click-clack of the metal expansion joints in the parking deck as cars drove over them. One by one, the cars filed out until there were only a few left. Enid wiped away the tears that spilled down her cheeks and drove toward the red exit arrow.

At this time of day, the roads in Charlotte, North Carolina, were congested with irritated, impatient commuters. Charlotte was an exciting, growing city, but the congestion made the three miles from her office at the bank to the grocery store a thirty-minute ordeal. By the time Enid finally pulled into the grocery store's parking lot, she was irritable, just like everyone else.

Inside the Harris Teeter supermarket, a young man in tan slacks and a golf shirt nudged her aside to grab a ready-made salad, while talking on his cell phone. Enid was familiar with the weekday ritual of quick take-out meals, checking messages, and then several hours of work before going to bed and starting all over again early the next day.

Enid walked back to the seafood section and got a pound of large shrimp. The price of seafood was exorbitant, but tonight she needed to talk to Cade, and she wanted him in a good mood. Maybe his favorite shrimp and grits dish would do the trick. After picking up a bottle of Chardonnay and a bunch of fresh flowers, she got in line at the checkout counter. She never thought of these things as luxury items, but the money she had spent taking care of her mother had depleted their savings. More than once, she had assured Cade she would rebuild their nest egg. He hadn't complained, but things between them had changed, and she felt guilty.

As she swiped her credit card to pay for the groceries, Enid tried to shake off the sense of doom that had fallen on her after the conversation with Jill. In a loud voice, the young female cashier told her the card had been declined. Enid glanced over her shoulder, embarrassed to think that someone might have overheard.

"I forgot we canceled that card," said Enid. She pulled out two twenty-dollar bills that had been tucked away in her wallet to pay for the dry cleaning items several weeks overdue for pick-up. The grocery clerk handed her the change and shifted her attention to the next person in line.

* * *

At nine thirty that night, Enid blew out the candles and put away the unused dishes and silverware. The shrimp and grits, now congealed to a solid clump in the pot, went into plastic storage containers in the refrigerator. She cleaned the kitchen and poured the last of the Chardonnay in her glass. After checking the doors to be sure they were locked, she glanced at her phone once again to check for messages from Cade. He had not returned her calls.

Before getting into bed, Enid ran her hand across the framed photo of her mother on the nightstand. The picture was taken in her mother's younger, healthier days. "I love you," she said aloud. She wanted to take comfort in the fact that her mother was no longer in pain and withering away, but the cloud of those final days darkened her memories.

As she lay in bed, waiting unsuccessfully for the wine to put her sleep, the squeak of the front door opening startled her. Regretting that she had left the alarm off, Enid tiptoed to the bedroom door and peered down the dimly lit hallway. She peeped around into the kitchen and was relieved when she recognized Cade's profile in the light of the open refrigerator door. There were many things she wanted and needed to say to him, but tonight wasn't the time.

Thirty minutes later, Enid was still awake and staring at the ceiling when she heard the guest room door shut.

CHAPTER 3

The next morning, Enid was making a second cup of tea when Cade came up behind her and put his arms around her waist. She stiffened and remained silent. Cade released her and sat down at the small glass table at the window overlooking the backyard.

"I'm sorry about last night," he said.

"I was worried about you. Why didn't you return my calls?"

"I was with some of the guys. I should have called."

Enid sat down in the chair beside Cade and stared into her teacup, wondering if the few stray leaves in the bottom held any answers for her. "I wanted to talk to you about a decision I have to make."

Cade sat down beside her, a look of concern on his face. "Are you okay? What's going on?"

"I want to quit my job." Enid continued to stare at the bottom of her cup and could feel Cade looking at her.

"Quit your job? I thought you loved it."

Enid spoke louder than she intended to. "No, you love my job. I hate it."

"What do you want to do? Work for a different bank?"

"I want to write again," she whispered. *And keep the promise I made to Mother.*

"Write? You mean like a book? Or do you want to be a journalist again?" Cade put his hand on her leg and stroked it gently. "Look, babe, I know your mother's death has you confused about your own life. You've been through hell. But, don't make any hasty decisions you might regret." Cade pulled his hand away and sat up straight. "Besides, we've got to stay focused on the big picture." His tone was sharp.

Enid turned to look at him. "What does that mean?"

"It means I may lose my job, that's what." Cade stood up and walked to the kitchen for another cup of coffee. When he returned, he said, "I'm sorry. I shouldn't have snapped at you."

"Is this another downsizing?" asked Enid. "Pretty soon there won't be any investigative reporters left in the country."

"That's the excuse they're giving me, but in reality, I pissed them off on the senator's bribery piece."

"I thought they told you to drop that story." Enid ran her hand through her hair, and sighed. "But you didn't, did you?" She reached out and took Cade's hand. "I can't be upset when you're doing what we said we would do as journalists." When Cade didn't respond, she withdrew her hand. "The timing is bad, that's all."

Enid got up to put her cup in the sink and went to the bedroom. She was putting her makeup on when Cade came in. "I'm sorry about all of this. Really, I am. We'll figure something out." He kissed her cheek and turned to leave. From the hallway, he called back to her. "Oh, I forgot. We're going to Mother's for lunch Sunday." She heard his footsteps on the hardwood floor. "We'll talk more later. Love you," he called out.

After Enid heard the front door close, she sat back down on the bed and buried her face in her hands.

CHAPTER 4

The smell of a perfectly roasted hen engulfed Fern Blackwell's house. No doubt, the woman could cook a great meal.

"My baby boy!" said Fern as she walked from the kitchen and gave Cade a big hug.

"Hello, Mother," said Cade, gently holding her at arm's length.

"Well, you look comfortable today," Fern said as she surveyed Enid head to toe. "But then I guess there's no point in dressing up on Sunday if you're not going to church." In contrast to Enid's slacks and casual top, Fern wore her typical Sunday uniform: a navy sheath that showed off her trim figure and a beloved set of pearls, a gift from her late husband.

The dining table had been set with the formal china, a Victorian rose pattern Enid detested for its prissiness. A pressed white linen napkin was beside each plate, along with seven pieces of flatware at each setting. She never understood Fern's formality for family meals. Enid tried to imagine Fern eating a messy tuna salad sandwich, with mayo and pickle juice dripping down her arm while standing over the kitchen sink. But the image wouldn't materialize.

The usual small talk accompanied lunch, mostly about the weather and the ladies garden club activities. "You need to eat more if you want to stay healthy," Fern announced to

Enid, while playing with the meager bits of food on her own plate.

Enid didn't bother to reply. Over the years, she had learned to pick her battles with her mother-in-law.

Fern didn't expect or wait for a reply and began talking about Reverend Adams' sermon that morning, which apparently centered on idle hands being a straight pathway to hell.

Fern turned to Cade who was busily putting butter on a hot roll. "So, what are you going to do if you lose your job?"

"I haven't decided yet." Cade glanced at Enid. "Enid and I haven't decided yet, I meant."

"I just don't understand why you kept pursuing that story about that old senator, even after your boss told you to let it go. You always were hard-headed, even as a boy," said Fern.

"I think you should be proud of Cade for not giving up on the story. After all, journalism is about searching for the truth," said Enid.

"Well, the truth doesn't always set you free," said Fern. She looked at Enid. "Pass the salt, please. I try to avoid salt in my cooking since you and Cade think salt is as evil as sin, but I just think these green beans need a bit, don't you, dear?"

"Mid-thirties is a bit late for me to become a doctor or a lawyer, if that's what you're hoping for," said Cade. "I'm going to start looking around, and then we'll decide what's best for us." He avoided looking at Enid.

Fern dabbed the corners of her mouth with the napkin and smiled tightly. "Yes, of course you will. Anyone ready for coffee and a slice of coconut cake?" she asked, rising from the table.

When Fern was out of hearing range, Enid said to Cade, "I can't believe you told your mother you might lose your job. I wish you had waited until we could talk about it."

"I'm sorry, it just came out when we talked the other day. You know I wouldn't give her the satisfaction of catching you off-guard intentionally. Please, let it go for now. We'll talk when we get home."

Fern reappeared with giant slices of coconut cake on a silver serving tray. "Here you go. I know this is your favorite, Cade."

Enid had come to accept that Fern used her cake recipe to signal whether female members had been accepted. If a woman marrying into the family got the recipe, she was in. If not, then she was still on trial, by Fern at least. As far as Enid could tell, she was probably the only woman in the Blackwell family who did not have the family's secret recipe, and she was doubtful that she would ever have that dubious honor. She knew buttermilk was a main ingredient, but otherwise, she was clueless as to how to take all those ingredients and create a perfect cake. As much as Enid hated to admit it, Fern's coconut cake, along with everything else she cooked, was absolutely delicious, whereas her own cooking was only tolerable.

"Thanks," said Cade, as he stared at the cake on his plate.

"I'll wrap mine and take it home with me," said Enid.

"I don't know why you're always watching your weight. Especially since you're always working out at that gym. Seems like you should be able to eat what you want to," said Fern. "All you do is go to work and to the gym. What kind of life is that?"

For once, Enid agreed with Fern, although she wouldn't give her the satisfaction of acknowledging it. She glanced at Fern's plate and saw that she had picked a little at everything but had eaten only a few bites.

Cade tasted the cake and remained silent, while Enid drew a design in the creamy icing with her fork. Fern finally broke the silence. "I found some old photographs the other day you might want to see." She turned to Enid. "Dear, can you check the top drawer of the console in the entrance hall and get them. They're in a big brown envelope."

Anxious to escape, Enid went to search for the photos, even though she dreaded what would follow. She found the big brown envelope lying in the drawer and wondered how many prints were in it. Enid knew Fern could talk about a few photographs for an hour or more, filling in every detail of the story, as if she were telling it for the first time.

Enid pulled the envelope out of the drawer and was thankful it seemed light. Maybe there were only a few photos inside. She opened the metal clasp and pulled the contents out: several yellowed newspaper clippings, but no photos. The articles were dated 2006, all neatly cut from the *Madden Gazette*. Enid recalled that Cade had lived in Madden with his parents until he left home to study journalism at the University of South Carolina, where she met him.

Enid could hear Fern chattering away in the dining room about her brother and his upcoming gall bladder surgery. Feeling a little guilty about snooping, Enid skimmed the articles quickly. All of them were about a seventeen-year-old girl named Rose Marie Garrett that had been found dead on the outskirts of the small town in South Carolina. One of the articles said "foul play is suspected," although the cause of death had not been determined. An article with a later date said Rose Marie had "apparently been strangled."

Fern called out from the dining room, "Enid, dear, do you need help finding those photographs?"

"No, be there in a minute," said Enid. She looked in the drawer again and found another large brown envelope. This one contained a stack of old photos. Groaning in anticipation of the endless conversation ahead, Enid decided to take the clippings back to the table also.

"Sorry, I apparently opened the wrong envelope and found these articles," said Enid, as she settled back down at the table.

Fern's coffee cup stopped midway to her mouth and her face tightened. "It's not nice to snoop in other people's things, now is it?" asked Fern. "Just let me have those, and I'll put them back where they belong. They were in the trunk with the photographs. It's old stuff that needs to be thrown out."

"Who was Rose Marie?" asked Enid.

Cade glanced at Enid with a "let it go" look she knew well and which made her even more curious. She would question Cade later.

"I actually don't remember much about her," said Fern. "And besides, it's not important. Ancient history." She reached out her hand across the table. "Here let me have those."

"I'd like to read them. If you don't mind, that is," said Enid.

Fern straightened up in her chair and squared her shoulders. "Fine, but I'd prefer you not bring up that topic again. Some family matters are best buried and forgotten."

CHAPTER 5

Driving home several hours later, Cade was quiet. Enid finally broke the silence. "How are you related to Rose Marie? I know Garret was your mother's maiden name."

"Rose was my cousin. Everybody called her Rosie." Cade kept his focus on the traffic as he drove down John Belk Freeway, which was unusually busy for a Sunday afternoon. "Everybody except Mother, that is."

"Why didn't you ever mention her murder to me?"

"Like Mother said, it's ancient family history." Cade reached down and turned up the volume on the radio. Garrison Keillor was on NPR talking about life in Minnesota.

Enid turned the volume back down. "Did they ever find out what happened or who killed her?"

"As far as I know, it's still unsolved." Cade glanced in his rearview mirror and put on the turn signal. "Idiot!" he screamed at the driver who cut in front of him.

"Was she really strangled?" asked Enid.

"Yes."

"Aren't you even curious about what happened? And why?"

Cade looked in the rearview mirror and changed lanes. "Several years ago, I did a little checking on it. But, you know how small town police departments are. They have limited resources and not much was done in the way of investigation. Rosie was involved with some unsavory types and did some drugs, so the police pretty much wrote her off."

"That's so sad. No matter what, she deserved better."

Cade just nodded.

"The article mentioned Rosie was living with someone named Myra. Was that her mother?" asked Enid.

"No, Myra was Mother's cousin. She raised Rosie."

"Where was Rosie's mother?"

"Aunt Wynona was Rosie's mother. I assumed she must have been dead, since Myra was raising Rosie. I saw Aunt Wynona a few times when I was a child, but she moved away from Madden, and I never saw her again. Mother never mentioned her after that, other than to say they had never been close."

"What about Myra? Where is she now?"

"Myra died several years after Rosie's murder. Mother said Myra died of a broken heart."

"Today at lunch, why didn't Fern want to talk about Rosie?"

"It's not a pleasant topic for her. I think Mother would just like to forget it ever happened."

"One day, not long after we had married, you called and said you were going to a cousin's funeral somewhere out of town. I offered to go with you, but you said there was no need. Was that Rosie?"

"Yes."

"You had just started with AP as a reporter. Weren't you curious about what happened?"

"Of course, but she was family, not an assignment. We were told the Madden police was investigating."

"But they never caught the killer?"

Cade shook his head. "There were no leads, little evidence, and no enthusiasm by the Madden police force to pursue it."

"So you dropped it?"

"There was nothing I could do." Cade turned up the volume again, and Enid leaned back against the headrest and closed her eyes. "Now, can we please change the subject?" he said.

CHAPTER 6

Enid woke to find Cade packing his suitcase. "Good morning. I tried not to disturb you," he said.

"Where are you going?" asked Enid. She rubbed her eyes. "I don't remember your saying anything about traveling today."

"I'm going to Montana," said Cade.

"Montana? To do interviews for a story?" Enid sat on the edge of the bed.

"An interview. For a media relations job," said Cade without looking at her.

"Don't you think we should have talked about this first?" She stood up to face Cade, but he continued packing. "What if you get the job? Are you expecting to just up and move to Montana?"

Cade kissed her cheek and picked up his suitcase. "It's just talk right now. I won't commit to anything without discussing it with you first." He walked out the bedroom and called over his shoulder. "Love you. I'll call later."

After Cade left, Enid tried to eat a bowl of oatmeal but couldn't force it down, so she spooned the cold clump into the garbage disposal. She glanced at the clock. Her presentation for the search committee was less than an hour away.

* * *

After her presentation and interview for the promotion at the bank, Enid sat at her desk, staring out the window at the world nine floors below her. Late summer thunderstorms were moving through the city, and streaks of lightning blazed across the sky. A light tap on her open office door brought her attention back to work.

"Hi, Jill, come on in."

Jill sat in a chair and glared at Enid. "I'm going to sit here until you tell me what that performance was all about."

"I'm sorry. It wasn't my best effort."

Jill sat upright in her chair. "It was *no* effort." She relaxed a bit and sat back. "I wouldn't be so upset, except I know you're the best candidate for the job." Jill lowered her voice and leaned forward. "And you blew it."

"I'm sorry I disappointed you." Enid paused. "It's just that I'm not sure this position is right for me."

"Well, when you figure out what is right for you, please enlighten me," Jill stood up to leave. "You do understand your job is being eliminated next month?"

"Yes, I know." Enid felt like a school child who had failed a test. Jill headed to the door. "Wait, I . . ." Jill sat down again, and Enid continued. "I need to take some time off. To handle some personal matters."

"Your timing isn't great, but do what you need to. Just make sure your staff handles everything while you're out." She leaned over Enid's desk. "Get your shit together and then let's talk again."

As Jill stormed out the door, Enid turned back to the window and watched the storm dumping rain on the city.

CHAPTER 7

Enid looked to the other side of the bed, expecting to see Cade asleep beside her, until she remembered he was in Montana. She picked up her iPhone on the bedside table and checked her messages before she realized she wasn't going to the office. Her staff was experienced and could easily handle the work without her for a week or two. In fact, one of her most experienced employees had seemed eager to prove she was worthy of stepping into Enid's shoes.

A good night's sleep was usually enough to give her a clearer perspective, but this morning she still felt a heavy uneasiness about her conversation with Jill. Even though Enid had plenty of paid leave available, taking time off now probably wasn't a good idea, given her tenuous situation at the bank.

The phone rang, pulling her from her thoughts. "Hello."

"Hello, this is Fern. If you don't mind, could you drop those articles by here on your way to work. I'd prefer to hold onto them myself."

"Good morning, Fern." *Nice of you to call.* "I can drop by around ten o'clock if you'll be home then."

"Aren't you going to work today?"

"I can stop by later if that's inconvenient for you."

"Ten o'clock is fine." With that, Fern ended the call.

After a long, hot shower, Enid climbed the stairs to the walk-in attic space Cade had converted to her private retreat.

The walls were shiplap, stained a warm brown, and a slightly frayed oriental rug covered most of the hand-scraped hardwood floor. She sat at the large wooden desk and tried to remember the last time she enjoyed her work. Like Cade, she appreciated the paycheck and the security the bank job had brought them, but the cost of that security was steep.

Enid reached into her large leather tote bag that served as purse, briefcase, lunch bag, and, at times, overnight bag. Cade had given the buttery-soft, Italian leather tote to her when he was promoted to staff reporter for the Charlotte bureau of the Associated Press. On their meager salaries, the expenditure had been extravagant. Now, it was still a treasured, if well-worn, possession, and she was rarely without it. Cade jokingly called it her survival tote, because she carried everything from Band-Aids to roasted nuts to a tape measure in it.

She pulled the big brown envelope from her tote, and being careful not to tear the brittle, yellowed news clippings, she pulled them out and spread them across her desk. One by one, she placed the articles on the flatbed scanner and ran off copies, and then placed them back in the envelope to return to Fern.

* * *

Before Enid could ring the doorbell, Fern's housekeeper opened the front door. Without speaking, she nodded to Enid and motioned her inside. Fern was standing in the hallway. "I won't invite you to sit down, since I'm sure you're in a hurry to get back to work." Fern reached out for the envelope in Enid's hand.

"Actually, I'd like to sit a minute. That is, unless you're busy." With a housekeeper and gardener in Fern's employ, Enid wondered what her mother-in-law did all day.

Fern turned to the housekeeper, who was holding the door open, waiting for Enid to leave. "Get us a tray, please." The housekeeper closed the front door and disappeared down the long hallway.

Enid followed Fern into the living room, where she sat on the sofa, and Enid sat in the one of the chairs across from her. Enid handed Fern the envelope of newspaper articles.

"Thanks for letting me read these. May I ask you a few questions about Rosie?"

Fern busied herself clearing a place on the table for the tray. "What do you want to know about Rose Marie, and why?" she said without looking up from her task.

The housekeeper brought the tray in and put it on the table. She put milk in Fern's cup, poured the tea, and added a single sugar cube. She then poured a cup for Enid, placing a slice of lemon on the saucer.

"Thanks for remembering the lemon," said Enid. The housekeeper nodded and left the room.

"Now where were we? Oh, yes. Why are you asking about Rose Marie?"

"It's not every day that you find out your husband's cousin was murdered. And that the case has never been solved."

Fern methodically stirred her tea, gently tapping the cup with the silver spoon. "Oh, I'm pretty sure we all know what happened." She paused and sipped her tea, a stalling tactic she often used to signal she was in control of the conversation. There was no way to rush her, so Enid sipped her own tea and waited.

"Rose Marie, I always liked that name. Anyway, Myra did a superb job raising her with the right values. But, in spite of Myra's efforts, Rose Marie turned into a rebellious teenager and fell in with the wrong crowd."

"What do you mean?"

"She started taking drugs, and doing Lord knows what else." Fern put her teacup back on the tray. "Now, if we're finished, I need to work on the menu for our garden club meeting. It gets harder and harder these days to please everyone. You know, gluten-free, low-fat, or whatever the current craze is. Fresh, simple food—that's all anyone needs to worry about." She dabbed the corner of her mouth with a linen napkin. "Well, thank you for bringing these articles back. Give Cade a hug for me."

"They never found out who killed her?"

Fern, clearly annoyed at continuing the conversation, replied, "I'm certain it was one of her friends, if you can call them that, or one of those thugs she bought drugs from." She added in a softer voice, "That girl was raised better than that. May she rest in peace. Now, let's leave her that way."

As Enid stood up to leave, Fern added, "We're clear on that, aren't we, dear? I don't want to talk about this matter again. And I expect you to respect my wishes on this topic."

CHAPTER 8

As Enid sat at her desk in her attic office, something about Fern's demeanor was tugging at Enid's thoughts. She just couldn't put her finger on it. Why was Fern so eager to sweep her niece's murder under the rug? Why was Fern adamant that Enid forget about the articles?

Enid laid out the copies of the articles on her desk. The first one simply stated that the body of an unidentified young woman had been found at the edge of town. Cause of death was unknown. The second article gave more information.

Murder Victim Identified as Rose Marie Garrett
Jack Johnson, Senior Staff Reporter

The young woman's body discovered at the edge of town has been identified as Rose Marie Garrett. According to the county coroner, Garrett died of strangulation and also suffered a severe blow to the head. Her death has been ruled a homicide, although no suspects have been identified at this time.

A spokesperson for the Madden Police Department said Garrett's body was discovered by a local man walking his dog in the woods, just inside the Madden city limits. The man, who asked not to be identified, said, "She looked so peaceful, like she was just sleeping. But then I looked again and could tell something wasn't right. That's when I called the police."

According to Police Chief Richard Jensen, "We are pursuing several leads in this case and hope to have an arrest soon." Jensen added his department was investigating reports that Garrett regularly purchased illegal drugs from dealers passing through Madden. In recent years, Madden's drug trafficking problem has increased. In a recent town council meeting, Jensen attributed this rise to Madden's proximity to interstate highways and network of unpatrolled rural roads, making transportation of drugs harder to detect with the police department's limited resources. Jensen told the council, "I intend to do what it takes to keep these outside influences away from Madden and to keep them from corrupting our children."

Garrett's closest relative, Myra Edmonds, a resident of Madden, told police that Garrett left the house two days ago to go on a job interview but never showed up. Edmonds said she had not reported Garrett's disappearance prior to the discovery of the body, as she thought Garrett would return on her own. Edmonds declined an interview.

There were only five articles on the murder, and most gave little information, other than to say the investigation was ongoing. The last article was the most disturbing to Enid.

Murder Investigation Goes Cold
Jack Johnson, Senior Staff Reporter

Two months have passed since the body of Rose Marie Garrett was found in a wooded area near the edge of Madden. When asked about the investigation, Chief Richard Jensen of the Madden Police Department replied, "We've followed a number of leads, but none have led to a viable suspect. However, we are committed to finding Miss Garrett's killer and bringing him to justice."

Before her death, Garrett resided with Myra Edmonds, a relative and resident of Madden. Edmonds has been unavailable for comment since the incident. A neighbor, who asked to remain anonymous, said Edmonds left town several weeks after the murder and has not returned. A family spokesperson, Fern Blackwell, issued a statement saying "the family would not discuss the matter further" and that they are "confident the Madden Police Department is doing all it could to solve this horrific crime against our family." Blackwell lives in Madden with her husband, Samuel Blackwell, who owns a commercial real estate development company.

After reading the last article, Enid pushed back in her chair and thought about Rose Marie Garrett, the young woman whose life had been taken from her, and who death was now a cold case. *Forgotten.*

Each article had been written by a Madden Gazette staff reporter named Jack Johnson. A Google search on Johnson produced a short article announcing his retirement from the *Madden Gazette* about ten years ago, shortly after Rosie's death. She checked online for a phone number and found numerous listing for the name, but none in Madden. She then looked up the number for the *Madden Gazette* and called.

"This is the *Madden Gazette*. How can I help you?" The woman spoke with a deep Southern accent.

"I'd like to speak with Jack Johnson."

"I'm sorry, hon, but he left here several years ago. I can connect you someone else that can assist you."

Before Enid could reply, she was put on hold. Shortly, another voice answered. "Hello, how can I help you?"

Enid repeated her request. "I'm trying to locate Jack Johnson who used to be a reporter there."

"Oh, my, yes! Jack was such a nice man. I really hated to see him leave."

"Yes, I'm sure he was. Do you have a number where I can contact him? Or at least an address?" asked Enid.

"I'm so sorry, but we're not allowed to give out personal information," the woman said. "Can someone else help you?" Enid had not expected them to tell her, but it didn't hurt to try.

"No, thanks. I'm calling about some articles he wrote, and I need to speak directly with him. Does he live in Madden? Can you at least tell me that?" Enid regretted the sharp tone that had crept into her voice.

"Well, technically, he doesn't live in Madden." The woman paused, sounding unsure whether to continue. "That is, since his place is outside the city limits."

Enid tried to ease into the meandering cadence of the conversation. "What city would he be listed in?"

"His mailing address probably is Madden, but I'm not real sure. He drops in the office from time to time. If you want to leave your name and number, I'll get him to call you. How about that?" The woman sounded pleased with herself, but Enid doubted she would ever hear from Jack Johnson.

Enid gave the woman her cell phone number and thanked her. Again, Enid read each article and made a note of the key information and a list of questions. Why had Myra left town and where did she go? Why was Fern speaking for the family? And most disturbingly, why had the family not pushed for answers instead of shutting down communications? Were there more articles? The *Madden Gazette* was a small-town, weekly newspaper, and it was doubtful that decades-old papers were on microfilm. She would likely have to search the paper's print archives for past editions.

The questions, along with Fern's behavior about the articles, nagged at Enid. What bothered her most was the fact that Rose Marie Garrett's murder seemed to be more of an embarrassment for the family than a tragedy. Even Cade didn't want to talk about it.

Enid glanced at the clock. If she left now, she could be in Madden by noon. She sent a quick text to Cade and told him she was going on a short trip out of town and would call him later. While it wasn't a lie, she tried to remember the last time she had withheld information from Cade. On the other hand, he hadn't told her about Montana until this morning. Besides, what was the harm in being curious?

CHAPTER 9

Following the instructions from the navigation system's disembodied voice, Enid took the next exit off I-77. She drove down the two-lane state road for close to ten miles until she saw a small sign on the side of the road welcoming her to the town of Madden. A speed limit sign warned her of the thirty-miles-per-hour limit, so she braked slightly, not wanting to fall victim to a small-town speed trap. A few cars were parked along the street, but she didn't see anyone on the sidewalks.

On the left side of the small street were a few retail stores: hardware, drugstore, ladies dress shop, and a small diner. On the right side stood the post office and the *Madden Gazette*. Beyond the newspaper office, a sign in front of a one-story cinder block building identified the Madden police station.

Enid pulled into one of the empty parking spaces in front of the Post Office. There were no parking meters, only a rusty metal sign on the sidewalk indicating a two-hour parking limit. She walked into the post office, admiring the two large planters on each side of the door with red geraniums spilling over the sides. Inside, she approached the lone clerk who was busy putting mail in postal boxes.

"Hi, I'm trying to find Jack Johnson," said Enid. "I understand he lives near Madden, but I wasn't able to find him online. Is there a local directory I might use to find him?"

The clerk continued to stuff boxes, and Enid wasn't sure the woman had heard her. Enid glanced around the post office, waiting for the clerk to acknowledge her presence. In several places, bare wood showed through the worn linoleum floor tiles. Sun filtered through the opaque glass windows, sunning several African violets on the window sills. The purple beauty of the violets offered a stark contrast to the dingy, yellowed walls. Overhead, large metal fan blades cut through the humid air, creating a warm breeze.

Finally, the clerk turned to look at Enid and chuckled slightly. "You're looking at the local directory." She scanned Enid from head to toe. "He know you're looking for him?"

Caught off-guard, Enid replied, "Well, no. I mean, not exactly." Enid gave the woman her most charming smile. "Please, if there's any way you can help me I'd appreciate it. I'm here to get information about some articles he wrote about ten years ago."

The clerk tilted her head down and peered at Enid over the top of her reading glasses. "What's your name? I'll give him a call and see if he wants to be found."

Enid dug down into her tote bag for one of the business cards she ran off on the printer this morning and handed one to the clerk. She listed her title as writer. "Here's my cell number."

The clerk studied the card. "Wait here." She disappeared into a small office behind the service counter, shutting the green metal door behind her.

While Enid waited, she walked over to a large bulletin board on the wall. Most of the notes were local items for sale. One person wanted to buy a trailer for hauling hay.

Enid read several more before she spotted a flyer at the bottom of the bulletin board. It showed a beautiful white mansion on a lake. "Glitter Lake Inn" was printed at the bottom of the flyer, along with an address and phone number. As Enid jotted down the information, the postal clerk called out, "Ms. Blackwell?"

Enid walked back to the counter.

"He'll be down at Sarah's 'round three today," said the clerk as she turned to walk away.

"Wait. Where does Sarah live?" asked Enid.

The clerk pointed to a small building across the street. "We call it Sarah's Diner around here, but she prefers the fancy name."

Enid read the sign painted in deep pink, script-style letters on the big glass window: "Sarah's Tea Shoppe." "Oh, I see it. Thanks."

* * *

Enid glanced at her watch as she left the post office. It was close to twelve-thirty now. She walked down the street to the Madden police station, a few blocks away. The small brick building had been painted white at one time, but most of the paint was now peeling or gone. A long wooden sign over the door read, "Madden Police Department, Richard Jensen, Police Chief."

Enid opened the door and walked in. A bell on the back of the door announced her entrance. The plump woman, middle-aged woman sitting at the front desk looked up. "May I help you?"

"Yes, thank you. I'm Enid Blackwell from Charlotte, and I'm doing some research on an incident in my husband's family." The woman's expression remained unchanged as Enid continued. "A girl named Rose Marie Garrett, a relative, was murdered."

The woman stood up, straightened her stiff-pressed khaki slacks with her hand, and headed to a coffee pot in the back of the room. Glancing over her shoulder, she asked, "Coffee?"

"No, thank you."

The woman sat down and stirred her coffee. "My name is Molly. Molly Anderson. I manage the front desk, do most of the paperwork, and dispatch. Our staff is pretty small, as you can see."

Enid smiled, although her charm hadn't been effective in Madden so far. "Do you have some information on the murder?"

Molly stirred her coffee again. "That's a pretty old case. Probably ten years ago, maybe more, I'd guess."

"Yes, that's about right," said Enid.

"As I recall, that's still an open case, so I can't give you a copy of the file. Why do you need this information?"

Enid reached into her tote for one of her business cards. Before handing it to Molly, Enid glanced at it to make sure the ink had not smudged.

"You're a writer, huh?" Molly turned the card over and read the back of it. "You writing about this particular murder? Rosie Garrett, I mean?" Molly sipped her coffee.

"At this point, I'm just doing some research for a possible article. Rosie is my husband's cousin, and I am intrigued by her life."

Molly tucked the business card under the pad on her desk. "And by her death, I imagine." She paused briefly. "Well, there's not much to tell. Rosie was doing drugs and hanging out with the wrong crowd. Don't mean to speak ill of your family, but she was bad news. Always in trouble."

"I am aware of Rosie's involvement with drugs. That doesn't diminish the sad circumstances of her death and the need for some kind of closure on this case. I'm sure you agree."

Molly stood up. "What makes your family need closure now, after all these years?"

Enid squared her shoulders. "I'd like to talk with the police chief." When Molly didn't respond, Enid added, "At his earliest convenience."

"Chief Jensen is out on a call. Your number on the card here?" Molly studied the card again. "Okay, I see it. I'll have him call you."

Realizing she had been dismissed, Enid said, "Thanks, I'd appreciate that. Please tell him it's important that I speak with him in person." She added, "I'll be checking in at the Glitter Lake Inn this afternoon."

"I thought Cassie was closed for renovations."

Enid put her tote on her shoulder. "That's my cell number. He can reach me anytime," she said as she left. Enid hoped Molly was wrong about the inn and decided to try it anyway.

CHAPTER 10

When Enid got her first glimpse of Glitter Lake, she knew how it had gotten its name. The sun shimmered on the surface of the water, creating glimmering gems of light. She pulled onto the dirt road by the sign and drove up to the big white mansion with green shutters. On one side of the house, workers were on a scaffold scraping paint from the wooden siding. From the back of the house, she heard the high-pitched whine of a power saw. Molly had been right about the renovations.

The front door was open, so Enid walked inside. She gazed around the high-ceilinged room and looked at the massive staircase, soaking in the beauty of the old house. Dark wide floorboards shone with a mellowness that came from decades of wax and loving care. The tall ceilings were defined by deep, ornate molding around the perimeter. She walked over to the front desk and ran the bell, as instructed by the small, hand-painted sign. The faint scent of lemon polish reminded Enid of her mother's house.

She waited a few minutes before ringing the bell again. A woman's voice came from the back of the house. "Hold on. I'm coming." The woman was drying her hands on a towel as she walked into the room. "I'm sorry. I was in the back and didn't hear you come in." She extended her hand. "I'm Cassie, the innkeeper."

"Hi, I'm Enid Blackwell. I was hoping you could rent me a room for a couple nights."

"I'm so sorry, but we're closed for renovations. An old place like this, seems like we're always having to do something."

"Molly, the lady at the police station, mentioned you were probably closed. I was hoping she might be wrong."

"I know Molly well. She's worked for Dick Jensen, the police chief, for at least twenty years."

"Is there another place in town I might stay?" asked Enid.

"Madden is pretty small, as you can tell. We're the only place around. Columbia is about forty miles from here, but it's not a bad drive. Or there's a bed and breakfast in the next town."

Enid looked around the room. "This place is beautiful. How old is it?"

"More than 150 years old. It was a cotton plantation back in the day. Been in my family for generations, although I just became the innkeeper about fifteen years ago. The only way I can keep it is by taking guests. The upkeep is staggering."

"The inn is very charming," said Enid.

"Would you like some iced tea and fresh-baked cookies? I need a break, and I'd like the company."

"That would be nice. Thanks."

Enid followed Cassie to the inn's library. Mahogany bookshelves stuffed with an odd assortment of leather bound volumes, contemporary novels, and paperbacks covered three of the walls. At the back of the room, two tall glass doors opened onto a screened porch overlooking the lake.

"Oh my, what a gorgeous view. How can you resist sitting out here all day?"

"I hate to admit it, but I forget how wonderful this place is until my guests remind me. Yes, it is beautiful here." Cassie invited Enid to explore the library's books while she prepared their snack. "I'll bring the cookies out here to the porch. Shouldn't take but a few minutes."

* * *

Cassie returned with a large silver tray holding the tea pitcher, two glasses of ice, and a plate of cookies. She placed the food on the white painted table near the rocking chair where Enid was sitting. "Do you have relatives here?"

"No, I'm doing some research in Madden."

"Sounds interesting."

"I'm beginning to wonder if this was such a good idea. Coming to Madden without planning my trip, I mean," said Enid. "I'm usually not this impulsive." She finished her tea and put her glass back on the tray. "I'm sorry to have bothered you. Anyway, I have a meeting at Sarah's in Madden, so I need to go soon. I don't want to be late."

They chatted a few minutes, and then Enid reached for her leather tote and stood up. "Thanks so much for your hospitality. I can't imagine how the food or the company at Sarah's can be any more enjoyable than this has been."

"Sarah is a good friend, and she has a charming place. You tell her I said to take care of you," said Cassie.

"I will, thanks." Enid started to walk away and then turned back to Cassie. "I bet you know a good deal about the town and its people."

Cassie laughed. "What happens at the inn, stays at the inn, but the rest of the town is fair game."

"Would you mind if I come back tomorrow and ask you a few questions?"

Cassie's smile faded slightly. "I'm trying to be polite and not ask you what your research is about. But now that you're asking me to get involved, I think I need to ask."

"Fair enough," said Enid. "I promise to fill you in. I'll need to find a room somewhere in Columbia after my meeting this afternoon, so I'll call you tomorrow before I come to make sure you're available."

Cassie tilted her head slightly to one side. "Tell you what. If you don't mind a little hammering and the smell of fresh paint, I can open one of the guest rooms for you. Heaven knows, I could use the company. It does get a bit lonely here."

"Are you sure? I don't want to be any trouble."

Cassie laughed. "I'll see you later this evening. The doors are unlocked until dark, so just come on in. I'll leave your room key at the front desk in case I'm in the middle of something."

"Oh, I forgot to ask you how much the rooms are." Enid looked around, trying to estimate the cost. "This place is elegant, and I appreciate your willingness to let me stay here, but I'm on a pretty tight budget. I probably should check out something less fancy in Columbia."

Cassie put her hand on her hip and appeared to be sizing up Enid. "I was going to ask around town for someone to house sit for me from time to time. I've got some shopping and things to do to get ready for the re-opening in a few weeks. If you'd like to stay here, keep me company and watch the inn when I travel, we'll just call it even. If I didn't have workers here, I wouldn't worry about leaving the inn unattended. I won't be gone more than a night at a time, and you'd be more like family than a guest, if that works for you."

Cassie's offer made her feel a little better about coming to Madden. After thanking Cassie again, she left and checked her messages in the car. Cade had left her a voice mail telling her he needed to talk to her. He didn't sound too happy, so she decided to wait and call him after her meeting with Jack.

CHAPTER 11

Walking into Sarah's Tea Shoppe was like stepping back in time several decades. An old brick wall lined one side, and on the opposite side, shelves of big glass canisters held various assortments of tea. Expecting to see silver-haired ladies, Enid was surprised when she saw two men sitting at the only occupied tables. One man wore tan trousers and a blue sport coat. A large brown accordion folder sat on the small table in front of him where he was jotting notes on a legal pad. The man at the other table had on jeans and a golf shirt. One of his legs stretched out into the aisle, and Enid noticed the intricately cut leather on his western-style boots. The man stared out the window and appeared to be deep in thought.

She turned back to the man making notes, "Mr. Johnson?" The man looked up, but she heard her name called out from the opposite side of the room.

"Ms. Blackwell?" asked the man in the boots.

Enid turned to face the man who stood up. "Yes, I'm Enid Blackwell. Are you Jack Johnson?"

The man extended his hand. "Just call me Jack." He pulled out a chair. "Please."

Enid sat down at the small table, just as a woman appeared. She focused her attention on Enid. "Welcome to Sarah's. We have some wonderful blackberry tea today. And the apple cinnamon scones are fresh out the oven."

"You must be Sarah. Cassie at the inn told me to say hello."

"Yes, I am. Are you staying at the inn? I didn't think Cassie was taking guests during renovations."

Enid was amused that everyone seemed to know the inn was closed, but in a small town, she figured that the only place to stay being closed was probably big news. "Cassie was kind enough to let me stay—if I promised not to be any trouble." Enid extended her hand. "So nice to meet you."

"Bring us a pot of tea and a couple of those scones," said Jack. After Sarah walked away to get their order, Jack turned to Enid. "Cassie is good people. I've known her ever since we moved here."

"Do you live in Madden?"

"I live on a small horse ranch just outside of town." Jack turned his head and gazed out the window. "My wife loved that place, before she died, that is."

"I'm sorry about your wife's death. Do you have other family around here?"

"No kids, and my only family is back in Chicago. My wife and I were too busy working and traveling to settle down. By the time we starting thinking about slowing down a bit, the doctor told her she had six months to live. Unfortunately, it turned out to be only three." Jack appeared to force a smile. "But, enough of that. How can I help you?"

"This may sound a bit crazy to you, but I'm curious about a series of articles you wrote about Rose Marie Garrett. She was my husband's cousin."

Jack's face showed no reaction. "What would like to know?"

"I just found out about her murder, and … well, actually, I'm just curious at this point."

"Your card says you're a writer, are you planning on doing a follow-up on her?"

"Well, I am looking for a good story to write, but at this point, I'm just doing some research. Since you were no longer at the paper, I assumed you weren't interested in doing anything further on the story."

Jack nodded. "You are correct. You might say I took early retirement."

Jack looked out the window at the newspaper office across the street. Enid couldn't determine if he was sad or merely thinking, so she just waited. Finally, he turned his attention back to her. "You related to Cade Blackwell?"

Caught off-guard, Enid replied, "Yes. I am. I'm his wife. Are you a friend of his?"

Jack chuckled. "We worked a few stories together back when I was with the *Tribune* and he was with AP. When I first met Cade, he was a stringer, jumping at any chance to write stories." Jack scratched his ear. "He with you? Here in Madden, I mean?"

Enid reached down and picked a speck of napkin lint off her pants leg. "No, he's not here."

"I don't mean to jump into your personal stuff or strike a nerve. I found out Cade was Rosie's cousin when I did the articles. That's all."

"It's just that, well, Cade doesn't know I'm here. At least not yet. I will tell him, but he's in Montana for a few days on business, and I don't want to distract him right now. He's got enough on his mind."

Jack took a bite of scone. "Look, what you tell Cade, and when, is your business. But I don't want to get involved in family matters, especially since I know Cade and don't have any idea what I'm getting into." He leaned back in his chair. "Why don't you tell me why you're really here and what you want from me. Then we'll see where we are."

"Fair enough," said Enid. "I was a journalist myself at one time. That's how I met Cade. We were young and idealistic. Both of us thought we'd change the world with our stories."

Jack laughed. "Show me a journalist that doesn't start out that way."

"Cade is a great investigative reporter." Enid picked at another bit of white lint clinging to her dark pants.

"And you?" asked Jack.

"My first job was reporting local business news for the *Charlotte Observer*. I got some recognition for a few stories where I explored the human impact of business decisions. Later, I was promoted to cover broader stories and report on the banking industry. Banking is big business in Charlotte. My stock was rising as a reporter, and Cade and I talked about my trying to get on with the Associated Press. That's what I always wanted to do—the kind of investigative reporting Cade does." She then added, "Or at least what he was doing. Then my mother was diagnosed with cancer. She ran through her insurance limits pretty quick. I wasn't making enough money to pay our own bills, much less take on her medical expenses. I helped her as much as I could, but we were broke."

"So you left journalism for a better paying job."

Enid stiffened. "I didn't have a choice. Cade landed a staff position with AP, and he was so excited. I couldn't ask him to take another job to help pay our bills. I used my banking contacts to land a job in corporate communications."

Jack leaned in toward Enid. "Look, I'm not judging you. You're not the first or last reporter to leave the profession because she couldn't live on the meager wages."

Enid relaxed her shoulders. "I was lucky to get a position at the bank. I worked hard and got several promotions. Mother lived another five years after I left journalism, but even with the extra income I was making, we wiped out our savings." Enid poured another cup of tea. "I'm not resentful of the choices I made." She blinked back tears. "I cherish those last years with her."

"But . . ." Jack paused. "It's not enough. Is that what you're saying?"

"I want to write again." Enid took a deep breath. "I'm not that same idealistic girl I was the first time around, and I know I'm rusty. Most of my contacts and friends in journalism have moved on, and I've lost touch with them."

Sarah came back to the table with a small gift bag, the handles tied together with pink ribbon. "Here, take these scones to Cassie. Tell her to come have lunch with me sometime."

"Thanks. I will," said Enid. Sarah left and Enid continued. "I want to try freelancing and see how it goes, but I need a good story. That's why I'm doing research on Rosie—to see if this is it."

"I know a thing or two about being forgotten and losing contact," said Jack. "When my wife got sick, I went on leave from the paper. After she died, I didn't go back. Didn't have it in me. Most of my friends were still working, and we didn't have anything in common any more. Didn't take long for us to drift apart."

"You're still young enough to go back. Why don't you?"

"There was nothing for me at the *Madden Gazette*. I told myself I left for my wife, but the truth is I was also fed up with small town politics and a spineless editor."

"Did I strike a nerve?" Enid smiled.

Jack laughed. "You might say that. But, let's get back to you. Why attracts you to *this* story?"

"When I read your articles, they touched something in me. I don't know why, but I can't get Rosie out of my mind. I keep thinking of her tossed in the woods, left alone." She paused, momentarily lost in thought. "You know how it feels when you find the right story to write about? How the hairs on your neck stand up? Well, that's how I felt about this one from the minute I read those old clippings." She paused. "This story may be exactly what I was looking for."

Jack sat back and studied Enid. "What is it you want from me?"

"I want to write about Rosie's life. Maybe if people can understand her better, they won't be ashamed of her."

"What makes you think the family was ashamed?"

Enid pulled out a copy of the article with the latest date. "Did you write more articles after this one?"

Jack looked at the copy she handed him. "No, that's the last one. My editor told me to 'wrap it up' and move on to the next story."

"In that last article, you seemed to focus on Fern Black-well and her family's standing in the Madden community. What were you trying to say between the lines?"

Jack read the article again and handed it back to Enid. "Nothing, at least not consciously. I wrote that one in about five minutes. I was frustrated and pissed off, so that's probably what's you're reading between the lines."

"Did you get the impression the Blackwell family was try-ing to sweep the murder under the rug?"

"Oh, without a doubt. But that's not unusual. Rosie was a troubled girl from a fairly prominent family."

"You asked what I want from you. As I said, I'm rusty and have no contacts, especially not here in Madden. I'd like to do some research on Rosie's life and see if there's a story to be told. If you want to do the story yourself as a follow-up, I would be happy to share the byline, with your name first, of course. What do you think? Would you work with me?"

"You know this is an open case? And you'll be writing about your husband's family, which will complicate things."

"If you think I'm trying to play detective, I'm not. It's the human interest angle I'm interested in. Why did she turn to drugs and who was she before she became rebellious? Why did the family want to move on and forget her? Besides, her murder was more than ten years ago, and I'm sure whoever did it is either dead or in prison for something else. Most certainly, he's long gone from this area."

"Maybe. As far as I know, the only killings in Madden since Rose Marie were a drunken brawl where a gun acci-dently discharged and a farmer who killed the insurance agent who was having an affair with the farmer's wife." Jack rubbed his chin and looked away again. When he turned back to Enid, his expression had changed. "Don't take this the wrong way, but I think you might be getting into something you didn't bargain for."

"I don't understand."

"Randy Travis had out a song years ago called 'Diggin' Up Bones.' Ever hear it?"

"I vaguely remember it. But what are you trying to say?"

"Just that some things are best left buried. That's all."

"Now you sound like my mother-in-law."

Jack threw back his head and laughed. "Cade used to keep me in stitches talking about his mother's garden club ladies."

"You've got a good memory."

"I always remember good stories." Frowning again, he added, "There's a reason that writers stay away from crime stories involving open cases."

"You wrote about them all the time, in Chicago, at least. I read your bio. So does Cade."

Jack chuckled. "Not quite the same thing. A reporter's job is to snoop around in open cases and find that one story that might lead to a Pulitzer." He smiled. "Working for a newspaper or news service also gives a reporter some protection from lawsuits. You'd be on your own, at least while you're snooping around."

Enid wiped the corner of her mouth with her napkin. "You think I'm being foolish. And if I am, well, you, Fern, and Cade can all line up later and tell me 'I told you so.' But I'm going to at least do my research and then decide if there's enough for a story." Enid threw her napkin on the table. "I think Rosie's story has a lot of potential as a follow-up to your articles."

When Enid tucked a lock of hair behind her ear, Jack smiled. "You remind me a lot of my wife. Same red hair and hard head." He motioned for Sarah to bring the bill. "I need to go pick up a few things, but if you'd like, I'll bring my file and notes over to Cassie's tomorrow and show you what I've got. In the meantime, I'll give your request some serious thought."

Enid smiled. "That would be wonderful." She chewed on her bottom lip. "I'm sorry for being so defensive. I'm going through a rough patch right now, and finding a story like this one could be my break."

"I'd feel better about all of this if you'd tell Cade I'm helping you." When Enid started to speak, he raised his hand. "I'm saying this only because I know Cade. I don't want him to think I'm doing something behind his back. That's all."

"As I said, Cade is in Montana, but I'll talk with him to-night." Enid stood to leave. "I appreciate your offer to help."

"I'll take care of the bill. You can go on," said Jack. As Enid was leaving, he called out to her. "Don't do anything until we can talk further. There are some things you need to know about Madden before you go snooping around."

CHAPTER 12

The next morning at the inn, Enid was getting dressed after her shower when she heard a knock on her bedroom door. "Come on in, I'm decent."

Cassie cracked the door open slightly. "I've got eggs and bacon ready if you're hungry."

Enid opened the door wider and motioned for Cassie to come into her room. "I don't want you to feel like you need to feed me. I know you're busy with the renovations, and I promised not to be any trouble."

Enid was caught off guard when Cassie gave her a hug. "I told you I needed some company. You're no trouble." Cassie turned to leave and then called out over her shoulder, "Food's getting cold. Come on down."

Enid finished her makeup and walked downstairs. She had forgotten how the smell of bacon could arouse an appetite. She heard Cassie's voice. "I've got everything set up on the library porch."

Enid sat down with Cassie, who was sitting at a small table covered with a pristine white tablecloth. "I'm not used to this kind of service." Enid gazed across out at the lake. "Just look at that view. The water is like shimmering glass. It's so peaceful out here."

They ate breakfast and talked about the shops and restaurants in Charlotte. When the conversation was winding down, Enid said, "I hope you don't mind, but Jack Johnson is going to stop by later today to discuss the story I'm writing. I should have asked you first, but he's the one who suggested meeting here."

Enid noticed Cassie blushing. "Well, of course it's okay. He's always welcome." Cassie stood up and began clearing the table. "We have a housekeeper, but she wanted to visit her relatives in Savannah while we are closed. So, it's just you and me." Cassie smiled. "You can meet with him in the library if that's okay. They're doing some plaster repairs in the living room, so it'll be messy in there."

"Thanks. That would be great. Here, let me at least help you with this." Enid put the last dish on the large serving tray. After Cassie left with the dishes, Enid went upstairs to her room. She checked her cell phone, hoping Cade had returned her calls from yesterday. No messages. She started to call him again, but stopped. She threw her phone, notepad, and a pen into her tote bag and went back downstairs. Cassie was walking down the hallway with a load of laundry in a basket.

"Going out?" she asked Enid.

"Yes, I need to check something out. Maybe you can help me. I'd like to go to Pinewood Cemetery."

Cassie set the basket on the floor. "Pinewood? Why do you want to go there?"

"I know I promised to tell you why I'm here, and I will. But can we do that later?"

Cassie put her hands on her hips. "Pinewood is not a place you want to go by yourself. I think you need to take Jack or somebody with you." She hesitated. "I'd go with you myself, but I'm meeting a plumbing contractor here shortly."

"I don't want to involve you or take advantage of your hospitality. I'll be fine." Enid smiled. "It's broad daylight."

"Alright, but be careful and pay attention." Cassie gave Enid directions, about two miles away. "When you get to the cemetery, there's a narrow dirt road that you'll have to follow for about a quarter mile before you get to the cemetery. It's pretty isolated. I haven't been there in, gosh, at least ten years. No telling what kind of shape it's in by now."

"Thanks, sounds pretty easy to find."

Cassie bent down to pick up her laundry basket but left it on the floor and stood up to look at Enid. "I'm not trying to pry in your business here, but do you know the history of Pinewood Cemetery?"

"No, I want to see a family grave there."

"Pinewood is for people who don't belong to one of the churches here. Madden still clings to the old Southern traditions. The first thing people ask newcomers is where they go to church. When folks die that don't have a church affiliation, they're buried in Pinewood." Cassie started to say something else but stopped. "Be careful. Like I said, it's pretty isolated at Pinewood."

* * *

Enid followed Cassie's directions and soon saw a wooden sign reading "Pinewood Cemetery" and an arrow pointing down a narrow dirt road. She drove slowly to avoid the pot holes, dodging the biggest ones the best she could. In her rearview mirror, dust clouds swirled behind her, so she rolled up her windows. Ahead, a large tree limb sprawled across the road.

She got out to see if she could pull it aside. She grabbed the limb at one end and starting dragging it to the side of the road. A hornet buzzed across her face and sweat trickled down between her shoulder blades. The rough bark cut into her hand, and she wiped the scrape on her jeans, getting blood on them. Her white shirt, a favorite, was covered in dirt and dust. Regretting her decision to come here, she considered going back to the inn, and said aloud, "I doubt Cade would let a tree limb stop him from covering a story." The smallness of her voice against the solitude of the surrounding woods reminded her of Cassie's warning. She gave the limb one last tug and decided she could drive around it now. She walked back to her car, cursing herself for not bringing a bottle of water. Turning the air conditioning up as high as it would go, she continued down the dirt road.

A short distance further, another dirt road, almost as narrow as a path, veered off to the right. Deciding not to chance getting stuck on the narrow road, she parked and started walking.

A rotted wooden fence enclosed the small cemetery. The gate hung off the hinges and partially blocked the entrance. She stepped over the gate and surveyed headstones nearly obscured by tall weeds in the overgrown field. After surveying the number of graves, she decided the odds were pretty good at finding Rosie's, even if she had to inspect each one.

"Rosie, where are you?" she said as she walked to the first row of graves.

After looking at each grave and working her way to the middle of the cemetery, Enid leaned down to wipe the dirt off a simple granite marker. Her hand tingled as she ran her finger across the words, "Rose Marie Garrett." She wiped another row of writing and read the girl's birthdate and year of death.

Enid stood over the grave. It had sunken a few inches and several beer bottles and a used condom, brittle from exposure to the sun, were resting in the indented earth. Enid kicked the debris aside and stooped down to pull the weeds away from the headstone. After a few minutes, she realized the futility of trying to clean the grave without proper tools, so she wiped her hands on her already stained jeans and placed her hand on the headstone.

"Rosie, you don't know me. My name is Enid. I'm married to your cousin Cade."

A crow sitting on a nearby headstone screeched in protest to Enid's intrusion. She glanced around before continuing her conversation with Rosie.

"I'm so sorry you've been forgotten. I want to tell your story. Who were you? What did you want to do with your life?"

The crow flew away and startled Enid. She looked around again and saw a cloud of dust close to where her car was parked. She shaded her eyes with her hand and tried to see who was coming. And then she heard the sound of a motorcycle. Her heart was pounding as she assessed her escape route and discovered there was no way out other than the way she came in.

She brushed the dust from her clothes and stood tall. *Don't be afraid.* She silently cursed Cassie for putting fear in her head. *Maybe he's just out for a ride.*

As she began walking back to her car, she turned her ankle on a small rock and leaned down to check her foot. The sound of footsteps behind her made her stand up quickly and turn around.

A man with a bandana around his head smiled. A large Bowie knife protruded from a worn leather sheath on his belt. His shirt sleeves had been roughly cut away making the shirt sleeveless. His muscular arms were leathery from years of sun exposure but, surprisingly, his arms had no body art.

"Well, well. What we got here?" said the bandana man.

"I came to visit a family grave, but I was just leaving." Enid started walking away and tried not to wince when a pain shot through her ankle.

The man whistled and two men on motorcycles drove over the fallen wooden entrance gate and headed toward Enid, stopping just a few feet away. She coughed as dust filled her lungs. She surveyed the men and stood tall, hoping to hide the fear that gripped her. She took a step forward, and one of the men moved his bike to block her path.

"I apologize if I'm disturbing something here. Let me be on my way."

The bandana man laughed. "My, my, what a fine piece of ass you are. You got spunk, too. I like that." He turned to the two other men, both of whom were shirtless and clad in faded jeans and leather vests. "Don't you?" They nodded in agreement. Bandana man looked over at Rosie's grave. "This here your family?"

Enid tried to speak but her voice cracked nervously. She managed to say, "Yes. That's my husband's cousin."

"That's the gal that got herself killed, ain't it," he said, more like a statement than a question.

Enid cleared her throat again. "Yes, she was murdered here about ten years ago." She added, "Here in Madden, I mean."

"That's a shame, it surely is." He walked back over to Enid and put his face close to hers. "Hate to see bad things happy to such a sweet, pretty ass." He spat on the ground by Enid's foot.

She recoiled involuntarily as the brown liquid splattered on her shoe and fought the bile rising in her throat. "Did you know her? Were you friends with Rosie?"

"Don't recall." He looked at the other bikers. "You friends with her?" Both shook their heads without changing their expressions. Bandana man then grabbed Enid's arm so suddenly, she yelped. He laughed. "I'd get me some of your ass today, but I got me some business to take care of." He whispered in her ear, "Later," and let go of her arm.

Enid gasped for air and tried to control her breathing.

Bandana man walked back to where his motorcycle was parked and kick-started the loud motor. When he left, the two other bikers raced their motors and followed him out of the cemetery.

Enid watched them ride down the road in a swirl of dust. Feeling dizzy from the heat and fear, she leaned over and tried to tell herself she was safe now. Her ankle had begun to swell and she felt sick to her stomach. She felt a hot sting on her leg and looked down to realize she was standing in an ant bed. She slapped her jeans, trying to kill the ants crawling up her pants leg, desperate to stop them before they made they made their way further up her body.

When Enid finally made it back to her car, her ankle was throbbing, her throat was parched, and her leg was stinging from the ant bites. She managed to turn the car around and headed back to the main road toward the inn. Cassie's warning kept playing in her head. *Be careful.*

CHAPTER 13

After showering and changing into fresh clothes, Enid put ointment on her ant bites. She realized she had not returned Cade's earlier call, and she had promised Jack she would talk to Cade. It would be two hours earlier in Montana, but she decided to call anyway.

Cade answered on the first ring. "Hello."

"Hi, it's me. Sorry I didn't call you back right away. How's the interview going?"

"Pretty good, actually. I've done a couple one-on-ones, and today they're going to do a panel interview with me, with the team I would be working with."

"Sounds pretty serious then."

"I like what I see so far. How's things in Charlotte?"

Enid hesitated. "Well, I'm not in Charlotte. I'm in Madden."

"Madden? What the … what are you doing there?" Cade said, raising his voice.

"I took a few weeks leave them from the bank. Since you were gone, I decided to do some research on Rosie." Enid braced herself, waiting for Cade's reaction.

"What is there to research? I told you not much had been done. Shouldn't we have talked about this first?"

"Like we talked about your going to Montana to interview for a job?"

Cade didn't reply, and since there was no point in hashing this out over a long-distance phone call, she continued. "I think there's potential for a follow-up story on her. In fact, I met with the reporter who originally covered her murder."

"You mean Jack?"

"Yes, he asked about you."

"He's a good guy. Tell him I said hello. Does Mother know you're there?"

"No, and I'd appreciate it if you didn't tell her, at least not yet. I haven't decided anything yet."

"She's not going to be happy."

I'm sure she won't. "How long will you be in Montana?"

"I haven't decided yet. I'll let you know. How long will you be in Madden and where are you staying?"

"I'm house sitting in exchange for a room. Not sure how long I'll be here." Enid chided herself for withholding information because of Cade's evasiveness. When had they become strangers? "By the way, was there something you wanted to tell me when you called earlier?"

"It can wait. I need to get ready for this panel interview thing, so I'm going to run. And … and, please be careful. I don't feel good about you being there. Let me know if you find out anything interesting. Love you, 'bye now." He hung up before Enid could reply, which was just as well.

* * *

When Enid walked downstairs to the library, Jack and Cassie were laughing together. As soon as they realized she had come in, they stopped talking.

"Sorry, I didn't mean to interrupt you," said Enid. She walked to a chair across from the sofa where Cassie and Jack were sitting, trying not to limp on her sore ankle.

Cassie stood up and moved away from Jack. "Oh, you weren't interrupting anything. I've got to get busy with some paperwork." Before leaving the room, Cassie turned back to Jack. "Good to see you."

Enid poured herself a glass of iced tea from the tray on the table. "If I didn't know better, I'd say you two had something going on," Enid said, grinning at Jack.

"Cassie was a good friend to me and my wife. Later, Cassie and I became friends. We had dinner here at the inn a few times." Jack cleared his throat. "That's all."

Enid gazed out the window across Glitter Lake. "It seems so peaceful here, but you said I needed to understand some things about Madden."

Jack told Enid about the history of the town, which had been founded in the late 1800s. For many years, it was an agricultural town, primarily growing cotton. Later, many of the family farms were sold and then bought by city folks who turned them into boutique farms.

"So far, it doesn't sound like a very dangerous place."

"Well, I'm getting to that part. In recent years, Madden has developed a drug trafficking problem. We're close enough to the interstate highways to make the long runs, and these little country roads are the perfect place to stage local deliveries."

"You make it sound like a retail distribution system, like Walmart."

"No question about it, these dealers have a well-organized system. Once the drugs hit these areas around here, bikers distribute them to Columbia and all these little sur-rounding towns on these rural roads."

Enid felt her chest tightening. "Bikers?"

"Yes, motorcycle gangs."

"I think I met a couple of them earlier today." Thinking about the cemetery incident made her leg itch worse. She leaned down and scratched her swollen ankle.

"Where was this?"

"Please don't tell Cassie. She warned me not to go to Pin-ewood Cemetery alone. I foolishly thought she was being overly protective." Enid tried discreetly to scratch her thigh.

Jack smiled. "You must have met up with some fire ants too. They're all over around this area. The sand makes it easy for them to build mounds. Some get pretty high—a foot or more. You need to take Benadryl for the itching and put some Calamine lotion on those bites to dry them up. Oth-erwise, those stings will get nastier before they get better."

"We have ants in Charlotte but not like here. I'll run to the drug store later." After Enid gave Jack the details of her encounter with the bikers, she asked, "Are the biker danger-ous? Or just good businessmen?"

"They live by a different set of codes than you and I. Cas-sie was right to warn you," Jack said as he pointed his finger at Enid in a mock scolding. "Next time, you should listen." His expression softened again. "Years ago, I got acquainted with Eddie, the guy who's their leader now, as I understand it. He gave me some good, insightful info for an article I was writing. Of course, I had to be careful what I used so I didn't betray Eddie's trust. I promised not to implicate their gang in any way."

Jack leaned back on the sofa and rubbed his temples several times. When he sat up again, he continued. "Eddie is a good kid who fell into a bad life. His older brother, Sam, was bad to the core, but Eddie worshiped him, mostly because Sam was the only family Eddie had left. The two of them were on their own after their mother overdosed. Another brother, the younger one, got adopted while he was still a baby. Eddie hasn't seen him since the adoptive family took him away. In exchange for his helping me, I promised to find out what I could about his brother."

"Where is Sam now?"

"He got killed by a rival gang member while he was making a drug run."

"And what about Eddie's younger brother? Did you find him?"

"I haven't been able to find out anything about him. Eddie remembers calling him Little G. Without a name or any other information, it was a dead end." Jack's face tightened and the crease between his eyes deepened. "Has Cassie talked to you about her son?"

"No, she hasn't. Why would she?"

"Well, it's her story to tell, so I'll let her tell you if she wants to. But tread carefully, and don't make her talk about it if she doesn't want to."

Enid studied Jack's somber face. "You care a lot about Cassie, don't you?"

Jack's face relaxed. "She's a fine lady."

"What else do I need to know about Madden?"

Jack clasped his hands together, appearing as though he was searching for the right words. "One of the reasons the drug business is thriving in Madden is because the local police turn their heads the other way."

"Why would they do that?" Answering her own question, Enid continued, "For money, I suppose."

Jack rubbed his chin. "I can't prove it, but yes, I'm reasonably sure Chief Jensen gets paid to look away."

"Paid by Eddie and his biker gang, you mean?"

"Eddie as much as told me so, yes."

"Why doesn't someone investigate Jensen?"

"The State Law Enforcement Division, what we call SLED in South Carolina, would be the higher authority that would investigate. But they've got to have something concrete to go on, and all I have is a few hints dropped by a local thug and my own suspicions."

"Are you telling me all of this about Madden police corruption because you think it has something to do with Rosie's murder?"

Jack seemed to be weighing his words before responding. "Like I said, I don't have any proof. And pardon me for saying this, but other than the fact that you're Cade's wife, you're a stranger to me. The last thing I need is for you to go around telling folks I said the police department is corrupt. When you head back to Charlotte, I'll be left to deal with the fallout."

"I may not have a lot of experience writing about crime, but I know how to handle confidential information."

"You're right, and I didn't mean to insult you." Jack's smile faded. "There's a few other things you need to be aware of before you go off tromping through cemeteries alone and poking your nose around doing research." He rubbed his chin in the now-familiar gesture he used when he was deep in thought. "Chief Jensen's son, Ray, was a friend of Rosie's."

"You mean like dating?"

Jack sat up in his chair. "Oh, good Lord, no. Or at least not openly. The Jensens are like royalty around here. No offense, but Rosie wasn't in the same social strata."

"What do you mean then? They were platonic friends? Or did they meet secretly? For sex, drugs ... both?"

"I realize this is painful for you to hear. It's hard to be objective about family."

Enid thought before she spoke. "I appreciate your concern, but she is Cade's family, not mine. I never knew her. And, as a journalist, I can make myself be as objective as I need to be. I just want to know more about her." She sighed. "At least I'm beginning to understand why Fern didn't want me digging into Rosie's life."

Cassie knocked on the door and came in. "You two look way too serious." She smiled. "Anything I can bring you?"

Jack stood up. "No, I was headed out." He handed Enid a file folder. "Here. Read this. It's my notes and interviews. And then let's talk some more."

Jack kissed a blushing Cassie on the cheek as he walked out the door.

CHAPTER 14

Enid was sitting on her bed at the inn when her cell phone rang. From the number, she could tell it was a local caller, but one she didn't recognize.

"Hello," said Enid.

"Hi, Enid, this is Molly. You know, Molly Anderson from the Madden Police. The chief will meet with you at his office tomorrow afternoon at two o'clock. That is, if you're available then."

"Yes, of course. Thanks for setting it up."

"He said to tell you he won't have but a few minutes."

"I'll try to be as brief as possible. Thanks, Molly."

Before Enid could end the call, Molly said, "If you're not busy tonight, I'd like to invite you to dinner. My daughter, Rachel, is coming over. I thought you might like to come, if you're free."

Caught off-guard, Enid hesitated before answering. "Well, yes, of course. I'd love to come."

* * *

Molly smiled when Enid handed her the bouquet of fresh flowers Cassie had given her from the inn's garden. When Enid told Cassie about Molly's invitation, Cassie had assured her that Molly loved to cook and often invited people over to her house. Taking flowers was Cassie's idea.

"Thanks. It's been a while since anyone gave me flowers." Molly motioned for Enid to come in.

"And it's been a while since I've been invited to anyone's house. Seems like most of my friends in Charlotte are from work, and we're usually too busy to get together—other than for a quick lunch at a restaurant."

Cassie took Enid's tote bag and put it on the hall table. "Come on in the kitchen. I'm just finishing dinner. Rachel is setting the table." Molly stuck her head in the dining room door. "Rachel, honey, come meet Ms. Blackwell."

Rachel walked into the kitchen and smiled. "Hi. Nice to meet you." She twirled a piece of hair in her hand. Her fingernails had been chewed until they were raw looking.

"Nice to meet you too, Rachel." Enid put out her hand. Rachel seemed surprised by the gesture, but took Enid's hand and then quickly released it.

Enid helped Molly and Rachel get the food to the table. Molly sat at the head of it, with Enid to her left and Rachel to her right.

"Enid here, she's a writer," Molly said to Rachel.

Rachel smiled. "That's nice. I mean it's nice to have an exciting career."

"What do you do, Rachel? Do you work?" asked Enid.

Rachel nodded. "At the convenience store." Rachel stared at the green peas on her plate and rolled them around with her fork. "Sometimes I do volunteer work with the vet over in Camden, as an assistant." She looked up briefly. "I love animals."

Molly offered to refill Enid's glass. "No thanks, I'm good." said Enid. She still hadn't adjusted to drinking the sugary sweet iced tea everyone seemed to drink in Madden.

During the rest of the meal, Molly and Enid talked about how Madden was changing. Occasionally, Rachel would join in for a brief comment. Molly was particularly concerned that family values were not what they used to be.

When Molly announced she was going to get dessert from the kitchen, Rachel excused herself. "I'm sorry, but I need to go. Got a busy day tomorrow."

Molly looked disappointed but smiled. "I'm so glad you came tonight, honey. Don't be a stranger."

After Rachel left, Molly said, "Sometimes I wish she was still a little girl. Don't get to see her much anymore." She handed Enid a huge slice of coconut meringue pie. "Here you go. My auntie's recipe. You'll love it." Enid thought about Fern's secret-recipe coconut cake.

While Enid was helping Molly clear the table, she asked, "Wasn't Rachel a close friend of Rosie's?"

Molly looked up suddenly. "Why do you ask?"

"I'm looking into Rosie's life, for the story I'm writing about her, and I wondered if Rachel might be able to provide some details?"

Molly set the stack of plates in the sink. "I'd rather you not talk to her about Rosie. That girl was trouble. God bless her soul. It was a tragedy what happened to her, but she put herself in a bad situation."

Enid threw the paper napkins in the trash can by the kitchen door. "I don't want to cause any problems, and I'm not defending Rosie's behavior. But if I tell her story, perhaps it could at least serve as a cautionary tale for other young women."

Molly put the glasses in the dishwasher. "Rosie is best forgotten. Let her rest in peace."

Enid and Molly worked in silence, except for a few polite comments about the weather and other trivial topics until the kitchen was clean. Afterwards, Enid retrieved her tote bag from the hall. "I want to thank you for a lovely meal. It was nice to meet a friend of Rosie's."

Molly showed her to the door. "I hope you don't feel I'm not being Christian when it comes to Rosie. No matter what, she was God's child, and I'll be glad to help you any way I can. It's the least I can do for that poor girl." She then added, "But leave Rachel out of it."

CHAPTER 15

Enid was driving on the state road back to the inn when she saw headlights in her rearview mirror. She slowed to let the car pass, but it stayed behind her. When Enid sped up, the car did too. Headlights flashed in her mirror. The car pulled beside her and Enid recognized Rachel behind the wheel. She motioned for Enid to follow her.

Enid drove behind Rachel until they pulled into an Exxon station near the edge of town. She followed Rachel inside to a snack bar at the back. No one else was there. Rachel sat at one of the tables and brushed crumbs off with the back of her hand. Enid sat across from her.

"Didn't mean to scare you any," said Rachel.

"Well, I'd be lying if I said you didn't. Why did you follow me?"

Rachel squirmed in her seat and looked down at her hands in her lap. "I wanted to talk to you, but I didn't want Mama to know."

Enid put her tote bag on the seat beside her. "Is this about Rosie?"

Rachel nodded.

"Your mother made it clear she didn't want me talking to you about her."

"Mama knows I'm still upset about Rosie's death. She's just trying to protect me." Rachel paused. "Rosie wasn't what everybody says she was."

"Then why don't you tell me about her."

Rachel glanced at the front door of the building. "Can't nobody know I talked to you."

"It'll be our secret. I can identify you as a confidential source." Enid reached into her tote for a pen and writing pad. "May I take a few notes?"

Rachel nodded again.

Pen in hand, Enid asked Rachel, "Who was the real Rose Marie Garrett—the person you knew? I'd like to know what she was like. What did she enjoy doing? What were her dreams?"

Rachel stared at the water-stained ceiling tiles of the Exxon snack bar as if the answers would appear there. "She liked animals, just like me. She wanted a dog, but Myra wouldn't let her have one."

"Did you and Rosie ever talk about leaving Madden and doing something else with your lives?"

"All the time. I wanted to be a veterinarian in a big city, like Charlotte, where you live." Rachel added in a low voice, "But that probably won't happen."

Enid felt sorry for the young woman sitting across from her. "Hold onto that dream. One day, you'll find a way to make it come true."

For the next few minutes, they talked about Charlotte and whether dogs or cats made the best pets. Focusing on a safe topic that she was passionate about, Rachel talked excitedly.

Enid shifted the conversation back to Rosie. "And what about Rosie? What did she want to do when she left Madden?"

Rachel's expression hardened. "She just wanted to get away."

"Small towns can be pretty confining."

"It weren't that. She just wanted to get away from Myra."

"Why is that?" Enid tried to remember what Cade had said about Myra and didn't recall anything about her being mean or abusive.

"Because Myra told Rosie her mama was dead." Rachel paused. "She wasn't."

"I don't understand. Why would Myra lie to her about something like that?"

"Myra told Rosie she was forced to."

"I'm sorry, but none of this is making sense. Who forced Myra to lie to Rosie?"

Rachel shrugged her shoulders. "She never said."

Enid couldn't decide if Rachel really didn't know or just wasn't willing to talk about it. "If Rosie's mother wasn't dead, where was she?"

"In prison." Rachel pulled a napkin from the dispenser on the table and began tearing bits of it from the edges, making a little pile.

"Why? What was she convicted of?"

"Killing Rosie's daddy in Mississippi. Her mama was in prison there."

Enid's mind was racing, trying to make sense of Rachel's puzzling comments. "Poor Rosie. She must have been upset, learning that her mother was alive and having no other immediate family. At least, I'm glad she had you as a friend." Enid knew what it felt like to be alone, without a mother, father, or siblings.

"Is Rosie's mother still in prison?"

"All I know is that Rosie found out about her mother being alive about a year before Rosie got killed. When I asked Mama later about Rosie's mama, she got mad and told me not to ask questions."

"When Rosie found out her mother was alive and in prison, is that when Rosie became rebellious and began using drugs?"

Rachel's eyes flashed with anger. "She only did that a few times, 'cause she was upset with everybody lying to her. But she weren't trash, like they called her."

Rachel was shutting down, but Enid decided to press on. "When she did buy drugs, did she get them from Eddie or someone in the biker gang?"

"Ray bought the drugs from Eddie."

Enid recalled her conversation with Jack. "You mean the police chief's son, Ray Jensen?"

Rachel nodded. "If he got caught, his daddy wouldn't have put him in jail, so he was the one that got the drugs."

"Do you think Ray had anything to do with Rosie's murder?"

Rachel appeared to be thinking before replying, "No. He liked Rosie. They were close."

"Was Ray using drugs too or just buying them for Rosie?"

"He used sometimes, but mostly he got them for Rosie and a few of his other friends."

"Did the chief know?"

"Mama caught us one time out in the back shed. Ray and Rosie were smoking pot. She tried to slap Rosie, but Ray stopped her. Mama said she was going to tell his daddy, but I don't know if she did."

Enid had so many things she wanted to ask Rachel, but she was clearly nervous and looked like she was ready to bolt any minute. "On the day Rosie disappeared, do you know where she was going?"

Rachel nodded. "To a job interview."

"Do you know where?"

"Down at the insurance agency. She was going to file and type, you know, stuff like that." Rachel wiped a few tears from her cheek. "She was saving money to go see her mama."

Enid leaned back in her seat. "You mean in prison?"

Rachel nodded. "Ray gave her some cash to get a bus ticket, but she wanted to save some more money." Rachel paused. "I don't think she was planning on coming back."

"Going back to the day Rosie disappeared, did she make it to the interview? You know, before she went missing?"

Rachel shook her head. "They said she never showed up."

Suddenly, Rachel's eyes froze on the front door. "I gotta go." Rachel ran toward the back of the store and through a door marked "Employees Only." Enid turned around to see what had startled Rachel. A man about six feet tall walked toward Enid, pausing to tip his hat to the attractive blonde at the checkout counter. His uniform fitted as if it were tailor-made, and his brown hair was streaked blond by the summer sun, with a bit of grey around the temples.

The blonde at the front register winked at the man. "Hi, Chief Jensen. How you doin' tonight?"

The man winked back with his enormous blue eyes and smiled as he walked toward Enid. "Well, hello. You must be Ms. Blackwell. Heard you were looking for me earlier, and there aren't too many red-headed strangers in town, so I'm guessing it's you. You sitting here by yourself?"

Enid put her notepad and pen in her tote. "Yes, I'm Enid Blackwell. And you must be Chief Jensen." Enid held out her hand, but he just stood there. "I was just catching up on my research notes." She stood up to leave.

Jensen glanced down at the tabletop and the small pile of torn napkin bits. Enid brushed the debris into her hand and then tossed it in the trash. As she walked toward the front door, she could feel Jensen's eyes following her.

"Looking forward to our meeting tomorrow, Ms. Blackwell."

CHAPTER 16

The weather was overcast in Madden when Enid arrived at the police station the next morning. Dark clouds hinted at an afternoon storm. She pulled into the gravel parking lot and reached over to the passenger seat for her tote.

"Hi, Molly," said Enid as she walked into the station.

Molly glanced up from her computer screen and nodded. "Good morning. Chief Jensen is on the phone. Have a seat, and I'll let you know when he's off."

Enid sat on a wooden chair against the wall in the small waiting area. The seat was covered in thick red vinyl. A piece of it had torn and the rough edge was cutting into her leg. She pulled out her notes and digital recorder from her tote.

"No recorders in here," said Molly.

Enid dutifully put the recorder back in her tote.

After a brief wait, Molly called out to her, "Chief's ready. You can go in now."

Chief Jensen remained seated when Enid walked into his office. "Well, hello again."

"Chief Jensen, thank you for seeing me. I want to be respectful of your time, so I'm going to get right to the point," said Enid.

"Good! I've got a busy day."

Enid wanted to ask what kept him so busy in a town like Madden but decided against it. "I'm writing a story about a murder that happened around here. It was about ten years ago."

"Molly told me you were asking around town about Rose Marie Garrett's death," said the chief.

"I'm curious as to why you call it a death instead of a murder, since she was killed and dumped in a shallow grave at the edge of town."

Molly walked in and reminded Jensen of his appointment with the mayor in twenty minutes. When she left, Jensen replied, "Rosie led a troubled life. Her unfortunate demise mirrored her life."

"So I've been told."

The chief sat up straight in his chair. "What's your interest in Ms. Garrett?"

"Rosie was my husband's cousin. I recently found some old newspaper clippings about the murder, and as a writer, I'm doing some research for a possible article, or perhaps a series, if I can get enough research. You know, about a young girl who lost her way and her faith in everyone around her." She paused so she could emphasize her next comment. "And how everyone just wants to forget her."

The chief failed to take her bait. "That'd be a mighty short article, since it's a pretty simple story. Girl turns into rebellious teenager, gets hooked on drugs, and then gets herself killed by some drugged-up junkie."

"Is that what you think happened? What about the bikers who sell drugs in and around Madden? Could they have killed her?"

The muscle in Jensen's jaw tensed. "You have a vivid imagination, Ms. Blackwell, but I suggest you stick to what we know, not what will make your story sell."

Enid forced herself to ignore his jabs. "I was hoping you could help me."

"What have you got so far?"

"I've got enough to make me keep asking questions."

Jensen grunted. "I think you're wasting your time."

"I appreciate your concern for my time, Chief Jensen, but I'd like to hear what you know."

The old wooden desk chair squeaked as the chief swiveled slightly from side to side. For the next few minutes, the chief described a troubled teenage girl that had come to his attention numerous times in the year prior to her death, mostly for petty theft or minor mischief. One of Myra's neighbors had also reported Rosie for yelling curse words at him.

"She sounds like a typical teenage to me," Enid said. "How long had she lived in Madden?"

"She was real young when she came here to live with Myra."

"Is that when her mother went to prison?"

Jensen got up and walked to the coffee pot on the metal table along the wall. "Want some?" he asked, holding his cup out toward Enid.

She shook her head. "Did you have any problems with Rosie when she was younger?"

Jensen sat down again in the squeaky chair. "Not that I recall."

"Why do you suppose she became rebellious later?"

Jensen put his coffee on the desk in front of him. "Why do I get the feeling you're asking me things you already know the answer to?"

Enid looked up from her notepad. "Just confirming some things I've been told."

"About a year before she died, Rosie was kicked out of school, and Rosie told Myra she wanted to work instead of going back. Myra was a good person, although a bit strict at times. I don't think she was prepared to handle a teenager, especially one like Rosie."

"I know that on the day Rosie disappeared, she told Myra she was going on a job interview. Myra and Rosie had a few words and Rosie stormed out the house to catch a ride with someone. That's the last time Myra saw her. Is that correct?"

Jensen sipped his coffee. "That's about right."

Enid recalled her conversation with Rachel the night before. Rosie must have longed for the kind of family her best friend Rachel had, but Rosie had no adults in her life she trusted. Enid's heart ached when her own mother's face flashed into her memory. Since Enid's father had died when she was a toddler, what would she have become without her mother's love and protection? Pushing those thoughts aside, she focused on Jensen.

"Where any suspects identified?" she asked.

"We checked out several people, but nothing panned out. Look, that's about all I can tell you. As I said, this is still an open case." He glanced at the large schoolhouse-style clock on the wall. "And I've got an appointment I need to keep."

"May I call you if I have any further questions?" asked Enid.

"I think we're done, don't you?" Jensen stood up. "I'm sure you're anxious to wrap up your research here and get home to Cade."

Enid stiffened. "Do you know my husband?"

"He lived here when he was younger, but I wasn't the police chief then. I only know Cade by reputation." Jensen flashed the same smile he had given the clerk at the Exxon station last night. "He's a well-known, reputable journalist, isn't he?"

"How would you know about Cade's work?"

"I'm an avid reader." He put his hands in his pocket and rocked back on his heels. "Funny that you should both have Welsh names. You're not related somehow, are you?"

Enid remembered the day she and Cade met at a campus party and laughed about their Welsh names. Cade told her he would trace their family trees before he picked her up for dinner, just to make sure they weren't distant cousins. She told him it was the most unique pick-up line she had ever heard.

"I'm impressed that you know the origin of names."

"It's a hobby of sorts. I like to study names and their meanings. For example, your name means— "

Before he could continue, Enid gathered her notes and stood up. "Yes, I'm aware that it means 'soul' or 'life.' Have a good day, Chief."

Molly watched as Enid marched out the front door of the station and slammed the door.

CHAPTER 17

Jack and Enid sat at the table in the inn's library. Jack's reporter notes scribbled more than a decade earlier were spread out in front of them.

"That son-of-a-bitch!" she said, telling Jack about her meeting with Chief Jensen.

Jack laughed. "Sounds like you and the chief hit it off pretty good." He patted her arm lightly. "Don't let him get to you. That's what he wants. You said Rachel followed you. What was that all about?"

"She wanted to talk to me away from Molly. And she had some interesting things to say."

"What's that?"

"Rosie's mother was in prison in Mississippi for killing Rosie's father."

"You're kidding. Well, that explains a few things. If it happened in another state and the family kept it quiet, the Madden paper wouldn't have run anything on it."

"Rachel said Myra was forced to tell Rosie her mother wasn't dead, but Rachel didn't know, or wouldn't tell me, who forced Myra."

"Is Wynona still alive?"

"When I talked to Cade, he assumed Wynona was dead, especially since Fern never mentioned her and Myra was raising Rosie. But Rachel made it sound like Wynona was still incarcerated. If she is, she'll be easy to find. I'll call the prison and see what I can find out."

"What else did Rachel tell you?"

"She confirmed Rosie and Ray were at least close friends, and I got the impression they were probably romantically involved."

Jack ate the last bite of one of the sweet rolls Cassie had brought them and then wiped his mouth with a napkin. "After I tried to question Ray, that's when my article got shot down at the paper, and my editor told me to back off."

"We've got to talk with Ray. Does he still live in Madden?"

Jack picked up another roll and nodded while he took a big bite of it. "These are delicious. I could eat a hundred."

Enid laughed. "I think Cassie made those just for you."

Jack ignored her comment. "Ray lives here and works for his uncle, Otto Jensen, at OJ Development."

"That's the company you said had bought up a lot of the farms around here." She jotted some notes in her pad, while Jack sipped tea to wash down the sweet roll.

Jack pushed the plate of sweet rolls to the other side of the table. "I heard he was in Europe on some kind of business trip. He's on some kind of state committee about effective land use. His trip will be in the *Madden Gazette* this week, I'm sure." He laughed. "Amazing that a small weekly newspaper can survive these days. But it's mostly local stories and events you can't get anywhere else."

Enid made a note to find out if Ray had returned. She picked up one of the documents. "Is this the complete coroner's report?"

"Rosie's murder is still an open file, so I only got what was public information. When I talked to the coroner, he confirmed Rosie had been strangled but wouldn't give me the full autopsy report or any of his notes."

Enid looked through Jack's handwritten notes to himself, scribbled in what looked like his personal version of shorthand. On one page he had written the name Myra Garrett and underlined it. From her conversations with Cade and Rachel, Enid knew Myra had raised Rosie after her mother went to prison and that Myra had died a few years after Rosie's murder. Jack's notes also included short interview notes from Chief Jensen and his son Ray. So far, she had not learned anything she didn't already know.

Enid picked up another piece of paper with the name Rachel Anderson written on it. Under her name, Jack had written "MA-NO."

Enid pointed to the notation. "What does that mean?"

"That means I asked Molly Anderson if I could talk with Rachel and she said no.'"

"After talking with Rachel last night, I can see why. I think she wanted to tell me more, but she was clearly scared to death her mother would find out. And when Chief Jensen walked in, I thought she was going to faint."

Jack sat back and looked at Enid before speaking. "To quote Yogi Berra, 'This is starting to feel like deja vu all over again.'"

"Why is that?"

Jack shook his head. "It's just that even after more than ten years, we keep running into the same brick walls. Just be careful, that's all."

Enid held up the coroner's report. "Not much in this."

"That's all that is public knowledge." He brushed some crumbs from the table and put them in his empty teacup. "Gotta go run meet with my CPA. Seems I need to diversify a bit more to secure my retirement fund."

Enid was helping Jack gather up the documents and put them back in the file when Cassie walked into the library carrying several shopping bags. "You two look busy. I don't want to interrupt you."

"No, come on in. We were finishing up here." Enid put the folder back in her tote bag.

Jack and Cassie talked briefly and then he left. Enid turned to Cassie. "If you have time this afternoon, I'll fill you in on the story I'm researching here in Madden." Enid reached out and took Cassie's hand. "You've been so kind to take me in while the inn is closed, and I feel like I've been secretive with you."

Cassie laughed. "Well, I was feeling a little left out, but my guests' business is their affair, not mine. On the other hand, if you want to talk about your research, I'd love to hear about it."

"Good. I'd like to get your thoughts on a few things."

"Just give me about fifteen minutes to put these things up." Cassie motioned toward the porch. "We'll sit out there where there's a nice breeze."

After Cassie left to put up her bags, Enid decided to look through some of the inn's scrapbooks lined up on one of the bookshelves. Each of the leather binders had a date on the spine. She picked up the most recent date, which was last year, and flipped through the photos, a few news clippings about events at the inn. Apparently, the inn hosted an annual picnic by the lake for guests, former guests, and anyone in the town that wanted to attend. In plastic sleeve protectors were some handwritten notes from people telling Cassie how much they appreciated her hospitality and great service while staying at the inn.

Enid looked at some of the photos again and recognized Chief Jensen and Molly. Jack was in several photos, talking with guests. Enid flipped through the previous year's scrapbook and saw much of the same.

As she was putting the binder back on the shelf, Cassie arrived with a tray full of sandwiches, a plate of deviled eggs, iced tea, and chocolate brownies.

"How can you pull together a meal so quickly?" asked Enid.

"When you run an inn, you have to be prepared to feed people, so I'm in the habit of keeping snacks cooked ahead for times like this." Cassie spread a small tablecloth over the white wooden table and then set out the food. "Come on, let's eat first and then we can talk. I can't wait to hear what you're up to."

CHAPTER 18

A warm breeze was blowing off Glitter Lake, and Enid brushed a strand of hair from her eyes. Cassie listened as Enid told her about finding the newspaper clippings of Rosie's murder at Fern's house, and about how Fern and Cade had both asked her to forget about it.

"So, are you telling me you're here because they told you *not* to come here?" asked Cassie.

Enid smiled. "It does sound that way, doesn't it?"

"That probably explains why I took an instant liking to you. I like women who can hold their own." Cassie's smile faded. "I used to be strong like that."

"You seem pretty strong to me, running this inn by yourself. That's pretty impressive. But I'm not researching Rosie to spite my husband or mother-in-law. I'm here because of Rosie. There was something about her that tugged at me."

"What was it? Do you know?"

"I think I identified with her, because my father died when I was young, and, like Rosie, I had no other close relatives other than my mother. And then she died. I felt so alone, even though I was married. When I read those stories, I couldn't stop thinking about Rosie being dumped in the woods, dying alone. And then nothing being done about her murder. I needed to find out more about her."

"So you're going to write about her?"

"I think so, although I'm still not sure. I was looking for a good story, but I don't want to upset Cade or Fern. I should walk away, but I can't seem to turn my back on this story, or on Rosie."

"Well, for whatever reason, I'm glad you followed your instincts and didn't let Cade and his mother bully you. You know, running an inn is easy, at least compared to living with your demons." Cassie seemed lost in thought for a minute before speaking again. "I'm sorry, I didn't mean to throw a bucket of water on the fire, but today is my son's birthday, and I've been trying to hold it together all day." Tears welled in her eyes. "He died ten years ago."

Enid reached out and put her hand on Cassie's. "I'm so sorry. That must have broken your heart to bury a child. Do you have other children?"

Cassie shook her head. "No, he was the only one. In fact, he was the last of my family."

Enid patted Cassie's hand. "I don't want to pry, but if you want to talk about him, I'd like to listen."

Cassie forced a smile and gently pulled her hand away. "Let's talk about you first, and then I'll show you a picture of my son Mark."

Enid sighed deeply. "My life is kind of mess right now. Cade and I are having problems, he's lost his job, and I've probably lost mine, too." Enid told Cassie about the bank's acquisition by a larger bank and her job being eliminated.

"What will you do? Can you get another job at the bank?"

"That was the plan, but I think I blew my chances in the interview." Memories of that day were still vivid, especially the look of disappointment on Jill's face.

"Well, we all have off days. I sure have my fair share of them," said Cassie.

Enid frowned. "I wish I could blame it on having a bad day. The truth is, I may have subconsciously botched it."

"Now, why would you do that?"

Enid laughed. "You must think I'm crazy. First I tell you I'm pursuing a story my family asked me to drop, and then I tell you I want to lose my job at the same time my husband thinks he's about to be fired." Saying it out loud made her life seem even more of a mess.

Cassie smiled. "And I thought I had problems."

"When I found those clippings about Rosie, I realized this story might be my way to get back into journalism, or at least into some kind of writing again, and redeem the career I abandoned."

"Why did you leave journalism if that was what you loved?"

Enid told Cassie about her mother's prolonged battle with cancer, and Enid's decision to work at the bank. "Mother begged me not to take the bank job. She said I would resent her for it eventually."

"Did you?"

"No. I resented the situation, but I owed it to her to make sure she got the best treatment available. She had a lot of expenses that weren't covered by her insurance. One day she called me to her bedside and thanked me for all I had done. She made me promise to return to the work I loved when she was gone." Enid pulled a tissue from her pocket and dabbed at her eyes.

Cassie took Enid's hand. "How long was that before she passed?"

"She died the next day. That morning before I left for work, she was in good spirits, and she looked radiant. Her day nurse called a couple of hours later and told me Mother had passed away." Enid wiped her eyes again. "It was so sudden. I thought she had more time."

Cassie patted Enid's arm. "Your mother must have loved you very much."

Enid nodded and tried to push the nagging doubts surrounding her mother's death from her mind. After the funeral, Enid tried to find the nurse to ask her a few questions about her mother's death, but she had disappeared. Enid later discovered the nurse had left the country, fueling even more questions. "Yes, a mother's love is very powerful."

Cassie leaned back in her chair. "So you're going to keep your promise to your mother by writing this story."

Enid nodded.

"Jack told me that being a journalist was like belonging to an exclusive club," said Cassie. "Work was important to him, and he misses being part of something meaningful."

Enid tucked an errant strand of hair behind her ear. "Jack's right. I felt left out when my husband became an investigative reporter for the Associated Press. As much as I hate to admit it, I resented him for being able to do what I wanted to do."

Cassie smiled. "Honey, don't beat yourself up. You're not the first woman to resent her husband's work. Or the first woman to put her career on hold to take care of someone else. That's what we women do." She paused. "Do you love your husband?"

Caught off guard by the frank question, Enid hesitated. "I've loved Cade since we met at college." She pulled at a loose string on her shirtsleeve. "It's just that we're growing apart, and I don't know what to do about it. It seems we both want a change, but not the same thing anymore."

Cassie got up and walked over to the library bookcase where all the scrapbooks were lined up. She pulled one from the shelf and walked back to sit beside Enid. Cassie opened the binder and pointed to a young man standing at the edge of Glitter Lake.

"That's Mark, my son," said Cassie. "He was seventeen when this was taken." The same age that Rosie was when she was killed.

Enid took the scrapbook from Cassie and looked at the photo. The handsome young man had light brown hair and a big smile. "What happened to him? Do you want to talk about it?"

"There's no easy way to lose a child, but when you lose one senselessly, it's all the harder to bear." The creases around Cassie's eyes deepened.

"Jack asked me if you had talked about your son, but he didn't give me any details."

Cassie took the binder back from Enid and closed it, holding it to her chest. "Mark was killed in a drive-by shooting at the Exxon station at the edge of town while he was putting gas in the car."

Enid felt a knot in her stomach when she realized that's where she and Rachel had met. Enid reached out and put her hand on Cassie's arm, rubbing it gently. "I'm so sorry," said Enid. "Did they catch the person who shot him?"

"It was one of the bikers. He was shooting at a rival gang member from another town, and Mark was just in the way."

"So they got the person who shot him?"

"Nothing ever came of the investigation. Our police chief has a way of looking the other way when he needs to protect his own interests. Besides, the guy who supposedly did the shooting later got killed himself." She sighed. "I guess Mark's killer will never be identified. Maybe justice was served, but it was on the street, but not by our police department."

"Jack hinted that the police chief might be taking payoffs from the gang. Do you really think that's happening?"

Cassie put the binder back in his place on the shelf. "I'm sure of it." She sat back down beside Enid. "But I can't prove it. And you won't be able to prove they killed Rosie."

Enid felt lightheaded. "Are you . . ." She put her hand to her throat. "Are you saying the bikers killed Rosie? How do you know that?"

Cassie frowned. "From what I understand, Rosie provided, well, let's just say she exchanged favors with the gang to get drugs."

"Do you know that for a fact?"

"No, I don't know it for sure, but that was the talk around town after it happened. I had moved here from Virginia several years earlier, after inheriting the inn, so I didn't know Rosie personally. But Molly Anderson, the lady you met at the police station, let it slip one day when we were talking. Please don't tell her I mentioned it to you. Molly doesn't usually talk about people like that."

Enid stood up and walked over the window to clear her head. "Did Jack tell you about my encounter with the bikers at the cemetery?"

"I wondered if you planned on telling me about it," said Cassie, making a stern face. "I warned you about going there."

"I know. I should have listened to you."

Enid's cell phone vibrated in her pocket. She glanced at the screen. "It's my boss at the bank." She put her phone back in her pocket. "I'll call her back later."

Cassie's smile faded. "You've got to be careful. Maybe you should leave Madden and forget this one. Find yourself another story."

Enid was silent.

"But you're not going to give up on this story, are you?" asked Cassie.

"I honestly don't know." Enid's shoulder slumped. "Maybe all of you are right. Maybe I should let it drop."

Cassie put her hand on Enid's arm. "I want to give you something." Cassie walked over to the desk and unlocked the middle drawer with a key from her pocket. She pulled out a .38 Smith and Wesson revolver and handed it to Enid. "Here, I want you to keep this while you're in town."

Enid pulled back instinctively. "No, I don't like guns. And I don't think that's necessary."

Molly pointed the gun to the floor and held it out for Enid. "It's not loaded." She took a box of bullets from the drawer and handed it to Enid. "Here. Please take these too. I'll feel much better. You don't know this area and could wind up somewhere you're not supposed to be. Jack can help you get comfortable with handling the gun."

"I've got a concealed weapon permit in North Carolina. Cade insisted I take lessons and learn to shoot, but I never learned to like guns." She reached out and took the gun from Cassie. "If it'll make you feel better, I'll keep it while I'm here."

Cassie leaned back in her chair and closed her eyes briefly. "After my son was killed, Molly was like a mother hen, always there when I needed her. I mentioned to her that I had dreams that bikers broke into the inn to kill me, too. I was scared to death, so she gave me that gun and showed me how to use it. I carried it everywhere for a long time. And then, one day, I stopped being scared and got mad. When Jack told me about your encounter with the bikers, I got it out to give to you." She smiled. "Yes, I'll feel much better if you have it."

Enid leaned over and hugged Cassie's shoulders. "I'm so sorry about Mark. Thanks for telling me about him. I promise I'll be careful. And thanks again for loaning me the gun, although I'm sure I won't need it."

CHAPTER 19

Enid sat at the desk in her room and Googled the Central Mississippi Correctional Facility and found a phone number. After being transferred a few times, she talked to someone who could help her. Enid explained that Wynona was her husband's aunt, and she was helping him locate her. "Her name is Wynona Garrett. She was convicted of murder. Can you confirm if she's still incarcerated there?"

"Hold while I check." In less than a minute, the woman came back to the phone. "She was here, but not anymore."

"Do you mean she was released?"

"No. She died while incarcerated, in 2008."

"Thanks," said Enid before ending the call. She then texted a message to Jack"

Enid: Wynona can't help us. She died in prison. After Rosie killed.

Jack: Sad. Another tragedy.

CHAPTER 20

Enid was surprised when Cassie told her Jack was downstairs to see her. When she went down to see him, he was
standing by the front door twirling his car keys in his hand.
"Come, let's go," he said.

"What are you doing here? Where are we going?"

"Thought this might be a good time for you to check out
the dump site."

"Dump site?"

"You know, where they found Rosie." Jack dropped his
head. "Look, I don't mean to be insensitive. I guess it's the
newspaper reporter coming out in me. Sometimes I forget
Rosie was family to you, or at least she was Cade's family."

"It's okay. I'll just be a minute." Enid went up to get her
bag.

* * *

In late summer, the trees were still green but showed signs
of summer fatigue. Soon the leaves would die and fall to
earth, and the cycle of life would continue, just as it did a
decade earlier when Rosie was killed.

Jack turned to Enid. "Do you want to get out? We don't
have to, you know."

Enid opened the passenger door. "I'd like to look
around." She got out and walked a short distance to the edge

of the woods. She looked around and then reached into her tote bag and pulled out the file folder containing copies of the crime scene photos. She held up one of the photos to see if she could determine the exact spot where Rosie's body had been found. "It hasn't changed much. A few of the big trees are gone, and there's more undergrowth."

Jack took one of the photos from her and then walked over to a dense thicket of undergrowth beneath a cluster of tall trees. "It was there." He pointed to the spot. "That's where they found her."

Enid walked over to the thicket where Jack had pointed. She kneeled down and touched the ground, picked up a handful of dirt and smelled its earthy fragrance. Still holding onto the dirt in one hand, she pointed overhead. Jack looked up at the green canopy.

"It's a cathedral of trees," said Enid. "Rosie found the peace here that she lacked in her life." Enid dropped the dirt and wiped her hand. "I can feel it too."

"Maybe we should just let her rest in peace," said Jack.

"Or maybe she's at peace because she knows she's not forgotten any longer."

Jack kicked at a wild mushroom growing at the base of one of the trees. "I'm worried that you're getting too close to this story—maybe identifying too much with her. I don't have to tell you how important it is as a journalist to keep your distance."

Enid nodded. "I know."

"But you're right about Rosie finding some comfort here. Maybe not the kind of peace you had in mind, though. This used to be a spot where kids bought drugs from the bikers."

Enid looked around the area. "It's far enough off the main road. I guess it's a good a place as any for that kind of thing."

"Like I said, it was well-known . . . and overlooked, if you know what I mean."

"You mean the Madden police knew about this place?"

"Sure they did. After Rosie's murder, the bikers moved the meeting spot with their buyers over to the woods behind Pinewood Cemetery," said Jack. "Too much attention here, I guess."

"Well, that explains why they weren't too happy to see me poking around in there."

"Far as I know, the bikers have quit selling to local kids. Not enough profit. Besides, the bikers aren't independent sellers now. They work for a bigger distribution network and mostly transport to other dealers instead of selling directly to users."

"Even if Chief Jensen and his police department turn their heads, what about the feds? It's interstate trafficking. Surely they know what's going on," said Enid. A yellow jacket buzzed around Enid's face, and she brushed it away.

"They're attracted to your perfume," said Jack. "They probably think you're just a big flower."

She swatted at another one with the file folder in her hand.

"Even if Chief Jensen wanted to stop the drug trafficking, it's bigger than his department," said Jack. "Hell, it's bigger than South Carolina. Our lovely state has become a major pipeline for transporting drugs throughout the country."

"Why is that?"

"The interstate highway system is great for moving up and down the coast. I-95 is the longest north-south-running interstate in the United States. It's the main expressway for the eastern portion of the nation, running from Maine's Canadian border to Miami."

"I just read where they did a drug bust on I-77. From the description in the news, it sounded pretty close to Madden."

"Both I-77 and I-85 have also become drug corridors. And the seaport in Charleston has always been an international gateway, and I mean for more than just cheap imports," he said.

Enid looked again at spot where Rosie's had been found. "Do you think the bikers killed Rosie?" Before Jack could reply, she added, "Why would they kill her if she was just a customer? That doesn't make any sense."

Jack swiped a trickle of sweat from the back of his neck. "The-bikers-did-it version is the one that sells," he said. "The good folks in Madden feel safer believing that it was something that happens only to 'bad' kids, like Rosie. At least that's how my editor wanted me to spin it. He always wanted me to insinuate that it was out-of-town drug dealers that were probably to blame. I did a lot of research on the national drug epidemic to shift the focus from Rosie's murder being a local crime."

"But I want to know what you think," said Enid.

"I think we'd better get out of here before one of those bees drives a stinger into your arm," said Jack. "Man, those suckers hurt when they sting, and we've got lots of them around here. If you do get stung, pull the stinger out and put a little dab of wet tobacco on the area. You know, like a poultice. It'll take the pain and swelling right out." He placed his hand on her elbow to guide her back to the car, but Enid pulled back and looked at Jack.

"Why didn't you push back and pursue the story?" she asked.

Jack sighed and put his hands in his pocket. "You think I sold out." He glanced at spot where Rosie was found. "Maybe I did. At the time, it was just another story. My boss told me to back off, and I needed to keep my job and benefits. That was my world at the time, not some seventeen-year-old drug user who fell in with the wrong crowd and got killed." Jack started walking back to the car and called to Enid over his shoulder. "You coming?"

Enid followed Jack back to the car. He got in and started the air conditioning and adjusted the vents so the cool air would blow directly on his face. "I've been here almost fifteen years and still haven't adjusted to this heat." Enid stared out the passenger window in silence. Jack checked for traffic and then pulled out onto the main road.

After driving a few miles, Enid said, "This isn't the way back to inn. Where are we going?"

CHAPTER 21

Enid and Jack rode in silence until he pulled into a parking lot in front of a small brick church. "Come on," said Jack, "there's someone I want you to meet."

Enid got out and followed Jack through a narrow wrought iron gate. The hinges were rusty, and Jack had to shove it open. He walked over to a simple, but elegant black granite headstone engraved with the name "Matilda Johnson."

Jack waved his arm toward the grave. "Enid, meet my wife, Mattie."

"I know you miss her, and I'm very sorry for your loss." Enid put her hand on Jack's arm. "But, why did you bring me here?"

Jack focused his gaze on a patch of wilted grass at the base of the headstone. "When Mattie got sick, my world came to a screeching halt. Nothing made sense any more. She was my foundation. And then she was gone." Jack cleared his throat. "At the time Rosie was killed, Mattie was dying. We had medical bills piling up, and I couldn't afford to get fired." He kicked at a rock with his foot. "Rosie was just another story." Jack looked back toward the grave. "You sold out, left journalism, and went to work for the bank to make more money. Does that make you a bad person or just a good daughter?"

"You're right. I'm sorry for judging you earlier." Enid turned and started walking back to the car.

Jack followed her and called out, "I shouldn't have lashed out at you."

Enid wiped a tear from her eye before turning around to face Jack. "We both put our families ahead of our work. I guess that makes us both pretty decent people, but bad journalists." She slapped at a mosquito sucking on her forearm. "I've got a lot on my mind right now, and I'm not being very sensitive to what you've been through. I'm sorry."

Jack motioned to a shady path near the edge of the neatly manicured cemetery. "Come on, let's walk down here a little way. It's shady and bit cooler." They walked into the wooded area on the dirt path, the earth hard as stone. The air smelled musky and slightly sweet. Jack kneeled down to pick a small flower in the midst of some weeds. "Even in nature, things find a way to go on," he said.

Enid took a deep breath. "I'm sorry to have reopened old wounds for you. Rosie was just an assignment and you had other things to worry about. I shouldn't have pulled you into all of this."

Jack smiled. "I got pissed because you pulled the scab off an old wound. Every journalist I know has that one story that got away. You know, unresolved." He paused. "Rosie was mine. After Mattie died, I decided to leave the paper. I traveled a while and then came back here to Madden. I never forgot Rosie, but I did move on."

"Why do you think your editor pulled you off the story?" asked Enid.

"You ever live in a small town?"

"No, at least not one as small as Madden," she said.

"There's a lot of good things about its small-town ways. People know and help each other. There's a closeness here, like family."

When he didn't continue, Enid asked, "But?"

"But, it's also incestuous."

"How do you mean?" she asked.

"Everybody and everything are connected somehow, so every action has a ripple effect."

"Like the butterfly flapping its wings and causing a hurricane on the other side of the world?" she said laughing.

Jack nodded. "Something like that."

"But how is this related to Rosie?" she asked.

"You wanted to know why I got pulled off the story. The editor of the *Madden Gazette* is part of the Jensen family. Chief Jensen made it clear he wanted this story buried alongside Rosie, and so it was.

"What exactly are you saying then?"

"It bothered me then, and still bothers me, that Rosie's murder was the paper's biggest headline in a quarter century. So why was the story killed? What newspaper wouldn't milk that?" Not waiting for an answer, Jack turned and started back to the car. "Ready to leave this place? I could use a big glass of Cassie's sweet tea right about now."

On the drive back to the inn, they road in silence for a few miles. Enid was jotting a few notes in her research folder. "I want to talk to the coroner," she said.

"Then we should have dropped in on him while we were at the church."

"You mean he's dead?" asked Enid.

"About five years ago." He paused. "What are you looking for in the report?"

"I don't know exactly. Just anything that might help us."

"There's no telling where the coroner's files are now. South Carolina coroners are often part-time people who serve several counties. A coroner might be the local vet or a retired accountant. Their files are usually kept in a county coroner's office. When a coroner dies, his files are supposed to be sent to a county courthouse or another county office for safekeeping. But sometimes, files just disappear. At any rate, since this is an open case, even if we find the report, they're not going to hand you a complete copy of the file, only what's public information." Jack looked in the rearview mirror and then slowed to pull off on the road.

"Why are you stopping?" asked Enid.

Jack turned slightly in his seat so he could face Enid. "Go home."

"What?"

"You need to drop this story," said Jack.

"I don't understand."

"You told me you wanted to write about Rosie and how she was a lost soul looking for something she never got. You think her family and everyone else let her down."

"And?" asked Enid.

"Now don't go getting mad at me, but I think you're trying to pay penance for all three of us by writing this story."

"I don't understand. Who are the three?" asked Enid.

"Me, for bowing to pressure and dropping the story. And Cade, because Rosie was his family and he let his mother talk him out of digging into it."

"And the third person?"

Jack pointed his finger at Enid. "It's you. You need to move on," said Jack. "Either it's as simple as a young girl getting killed for her drug stash or for stiffing a dealer. Or … it's bigger than you want to know." Jack started the car and continued up the road. "Either way, you're putting too much on the line for this story. Your marriage, your relationship with your mother-in-law. And worse, you may be putting yourself in danger."

"You think Chief Jensen is involved, don't you?" asked Enid.

"I don't know, but he killed the story for a reason. And I have to assume that he wants it to stay dead."

"I'll think about it."

A few minutes later, they pulled into the inn's parking lot and stopped beside a black car. Enid read the white lettering on the door: "Madden Police Chief." She looked at Jack. "Can I put my notes in your trunk for now? I have a feeling Chief Jensen isn't here to join us for a glass of Cassie's tea."

CHAPTER 22

When Enid walked into the inn's entrance foyer, Chief Jensen was sitting in the living room with Cassie. He was tapping his heel and playing with the edge of his wide-brimmed police hat. Cassie was sitting in a chair across from him and stood up when Enid came into the room.

"Chief Jensen is here to see you," said Cassie. "I was just keeping him company until you returned."

Jensen rose halfway from his seat and bowed slightly. "Ms. Blackwell, I'd like to have a word with you."

Cassie looked at Enid and motioned toward a chair. "You can sit here." Cassie looked at Jensen. "Unless you need me, I'll just be in the office taking care of some paperwork."

"Always a pleasure to see you, Cassie," he said.

After Cassie left the room, Enid looked at Jensen. "How can I help you?"

"I was under the impression Jack Johnson was with you."

"He just dropped me off."

"Well, I'll catch him later." Jensen laid his hat on the sofa and put his hands together, interlacing his fingers. "Ms. Blackwell, I thought we discussed the fact that Rose Marie Garrett's murder is an open case."

"Yes, Chief, you told me. Is there a problem?" Someone must have told Jensen about their visit to the dump site.

"I just want to make sure we *don't* have any problems," he said.

"I'm afraid I don't understand what you're implying."

"Actually, I think you know exactly what I'm saying, with all due respect." Enid noticed his left heel was tapping the floor again. Jensen waited for her to reply, but Enid sat with her hands in her lap. "I've been getting reports that you're going around town asking a lot of questions and digging into things that don't concern you."

"With all due respect to you, Chief, I told you I'm doing research for a story on Rosie's life and her death. She was my husband's cousin, and I have both a journalist and a familial interest in learning more about her life. How can I gather the information I need without asking a lot of questions? Besides, don't you want to close this case? I might find out something helpful to you."

Jensen's leg stopped tapping the floor. "You being new around here, I can understand why you might have misunderstood our earlier conversation. But I felt sure Jack and I had a clear understanding, so I'm surprised he's involved in all this." Enid started to speak but he held up his hand. "No need for you to speak for Jack. We'll have a little chit-chat later. You know, man to man."

Enid weighed her options and decided on the most efficient, but most provocative, path. "I assume you're referring to the fact that you, or at least your family, made him drop the story ten years ago," she said.

Jensen stared at Enid, and she could see the muscle in his jaw twitch slightly.

"How well did you know Rosie?" he asked.

"I didn't, and I thought I made it clear that I was to learn more about her."

"You know, Ms. Blackwell, Madden is a great little town. My family has lived here for generations. And the whole town, well, we're like family. We take care of each other."

"And Rosie didn't fit into your little picture-perfect town, is that what you're telling me?"

"She was troubled, and Myra couldn't handle her. Honestly, I'm not surprised that she fell in with the wrong crowd and got herself killed," he said.

"That's the second time you've made it sound like she was responsible for her own murder," she said. "And wasn't your son, Ray, part of that *wrong* crowd?"

Jensen rubbed one leg with his hand, studying the back and forth motion before he looked up at Enid again. "I don't know what you're trying to prove by digging up ancient history, but I think you need to reconsider this mission you're on."

Enid couldn't help but smile. "Are you trying to run me out of town?"

Jensen picked up his hat and stood up. "On the contrary, Ms. Blackwell. You are welcome to stay in Madden as long as you like. Just keep your nose out of open police cases." He leaned down slightly to straighten the crease in his pants. "I'm sure Cassie enjoys the female companionship." He walked to the door of the living room and put on his hat. When he got to the hallway, he turned halfway around and tipped his hat to Enid. "A pleasure, ma'am." He walked out the door, slamming it harder than necessary.

Cassie walked back into the living room. "I thought I heard him leaving. Are you okay? You look a little pale."

"I'm mad as hell, but, yeah, I'm fine." Enid stood up and reached down to get her tote bag before remembering she had left it with Jack.

"I didn't mean to eavesdrop, but I heard most of the conversation, I'm concerned about you. And about Jack." Cassie walked over to Enid and gave her a hug. "I've just got a little more work to do, and then we can talk more. I'll make a light supper and we can eat on the porch and have a glass of wine." Cassie smiled. "Or two."

Enid laughed. "I could use it."

When Cassie left the room, Enid reached into her pants pocket and got her cell phone and punched Jack's number. "Hi, this is Enid. When you get this message, call me. Jensen is probably headed your way about now, and he's not happy." She added, "Oh, and I need to get my tote bag and notes back from you."

She ended the call and started up the stairs to her room when she heard the hinges squeak on the inn's massive oak door as it opened. Thinking that Jack had been waiting nearby for Jensen to leave before he returned, she expected to see Jack.

"That was quick," she said turning around. When he saw the man standing in the doorway, her smile faded. "Cade, what . . .? What are you doing here?"

Cade came in and shut the door behind him. "You left your contact information with our neighbor. She told me where to find you." He clenched his hands and then released them. "We need to talk."

CHAPTER 23

Enid walked down the stairs and hugged Cade. "It's good to see you. It's just, well, this is a total surprise." Enid pulled back from her embrace. "Are you alright? Fern?"

"Everyone is fine."

Cassie came out of the office. "Hello, I thought I heard someone come in." She put out her hand to Cade. "I'm Cassie, the innkeeper."

Cade shook her hand. "I'm Cade, Enid's husband."

"Nice to meet you. You look hot and tired. How about some iced tea and cookies? They were baked fresh this morning." She studied Cade's face.

"Sure, that would be nice," said Cade. He looked down at the floor and shifted his weight.

"Yes, that would be great," said Enid. "Can you bring the tray to my room? Cade and I need to catch up."

"Yes, dear, of course. You go on, and I'll be up in a minute."

In Enid's room, Cade went to the bathroom and threw cold water on his face and neck. "It's hot as hell down here."

"The capital city's marketing slogan is 'Famously Hot,' and you can see why." Cade dried off with a towel and sat in one of the chairs at the small table by the window overlooking the lake. He sat silently, looking across the water.

Cassie's voice followed a light knock on the door. "The tray's here on the hall table. Just call if you need anything else."

Enid got the tray and brought in to her room. In addition to sweet iced tea, there were cookies and cheese straws, the kind with a hint of red pepper that had become one of Enid's favorites during her stay at the inn. Enid poured tea in the glasses and handed one of the small napkins to Cade.

"I'm not sure what I like the best about this place, the view or Cassie's treats." Enid sipped her tea, but Cade left his untouched and watched her.

"Why are you here?" he asked.

"I told you I was here doing research on Rosie."

Cade took a sip of tea, frowning. "This tea is really sweet."

"You get used to it after a while." She reached out to take his glass. "Here, I'll pour that out and get you some water."

"No, it's fine." Cade put his glass back on the table. "This isn't just any story and you know it. This is my family you're digging around in."

Enid brushed crumbs from her hands. "Not long ago you would have said she was *our* family."

Cade shifted in his seat. "I'm going to take the job in Montana." Condensation from the cold glass had dripped onto his pants leg and he brushed it away. "I start in two weeks."

Enid wiped her hands slowly with a napkin, giving herself a few moments to collect her thoughts. "How am I supposed to respond to that? I thought you said you wouldn't make a decision until we had a chance to discuss it." She was determined not to become emotional.

Cade raised his voice slightly. "Like you included me in your decision to come here?"

Tears ran down Enid's cheeks, and she quickly brushed them away. "This story is important to me. I thought you, of all people, could understand that." They sat in silence for a moment, each looking away from the other.

"I thought you'd poke around a little and come home. I didn't realize you had become fixated on Rosie's story. Have you talked to Mother?"

"Not since I returned the news clippings to her."

"Did you tell her you were coming to Madden?"

"No."

"I'm sure she's not going to be happy that's you're here. Besides, I had hoped our marriage was more important to you. I want you to come with me."

"To Montana?"

"Yes. It'll give us a chance to make some changes and start a new life."

Enid went to the bathroom for a tissue and came back to her chair. "I'm sorry. It's just that this a lot to take in."

Cade reached out and took her hands in his. "Oh, baby. I'm sorry we've come to this."

Enid nodded. "Me, too."

"I'm going to Montana on Monday to start looking for a place to live. Will you come with me? I want you to help find us a home."

"And what about my work here?" she asked.

"I thought you wanted to leave the bank anyway."

"I meant my research. I want to finish it and maybe do a story on Rosie."

Cade turned and stared out the window at the lake. A heron swooped down on the water, hoping to grab a fish. He turned back toward Enid. "You can find another story to write. I'll help you find one, and I'll use my connections to help you get back into journalism. If that's what you really want to do."

"It's just that . . ." She got up and threw her tissue in the small trashcan under the sink. She ran cold water on a washcloth and wiped her face while looking in the mirror. A rash of fresh freckles had developed on her nose and forehead since she had been in Madden.

Cade came into the bathroom and stood behind her, putting his arms around her waist. He kissed her neck and looked at her reflection in the mirror. "I love those freckles. Don't try to rub them off."

Enid turned around to face Cade and kissed him. "I've missed you." She ran her finger across his lips. "You seem so far away at times."

Cade released her waist. "Come with me." He kissed her neck again and then her lips. "Please." He made an exaggerated sad face, and Enid laughed. She took his hand and led him to the edge of the bed and motioned for him to sit beside her.

Cade put his hand on her back, stroking it slowly. He closed his eyes and leaned his head against hers. Enid took his face in her hands and began kissing his nose, his eyes, and then his cheeks. Cade closed his eyes and made a small contented murmur.

Enid dropped her hands. "But you're a journalist, not a media relations person. Why are you taking this job? And what about Fern? Are you just going to leave her alone in Charlotte?"

Cade stood up. "I think you'll agree I'm qualified to deal with reporters and the media on behalf of the mining company." He walked back over to the chair and sat down. "And Mother has a gaggle of ladies in the garden club to take care of her. When I'm gone, they'll dote on her, and she'll love it."

Enid walked over and sat across from him. "You really want to make a change, don't you?"

"That whole thing with the exposé on the senator taking bribes just took everything out of me. I'm tired of fighting newspaper executives who are paper pushers, not journalists, who make decisions based on profit and power." Cade reached out and stroked her face with the back of his hand. "That's not what we dreamed about when we wanted to be journalists. We wanted to go out and expose the truth, no matter what the cost. But that's not the way the world works." He tapped the tip of her nose with his finger. "Yes, I want to start a new life—with you." He reached down and took Enid's hand and led her back to the bed.

CHAPTER 24

Enid opened her eyes and squinted at the bright morning sun peeping in around the edges of the window shades. She looked down at her naked body and remembered Cade's warmth and the cool breeze of the ceiling fan on their damp bodies. She also remembered the promise she made to him about returning to Charlotte today.

Enid swung her legs off the bed and sat there, trying to get the cobwebs out of her head. She noticed a handwritten note on the bedside table. "Hurry back home. Love you. Cade." He left early that morning to wrap up a few things in Charlotte before leaving for Montana.

Enid showered and then packed her bags. Part of her was anxious to leave Madden and its secrets behind her. Maybe she and Cade could start over. She packed her suitcases and left them at the foot of the bed. She desperately needed a cup of tea, and she needed to let Cassie know she was leaving.

Halfway down the long stairway, she inhaled the smell of hickory smoked bacon that filled the inn. Yes, she would miss Cassie's cooking. And, she would miss Cassie. Enid had grown fond of her, and they had developed a close relationship. At times, Cassie reminded Enid of her mother, especially when Cassie fussed over her and tried to protect her.

Cassie met her at the bottom of the stairs. "Hey, sleepy-head. Didn't think you were going to get up this morning. Breakfast is out on the library porch. It's such a beautiful morning, I thought you'd like to enjoy it." Cassie scurried back to the kitchen, calling over her shoulder. "Go on out. I'll be there in a minute."

* * *

Enid was looking out across the lake when Cassie brought out a tray of scrambled eggs, bacon, and blueberry scones. When Cassie finishing laying out the food, Enid asked, "Do you have a minute to sit and talk while I eat?"

"Of course." Cassie got herself a cup of tea from the big mahogany sideboard in the library and returned to sit with Enid. "I just love this amaretto rooibos blend, don't you? It's so soothing."

Enid smiled. "Yes, it's delicious." She picked a few crumbs from the napkin in her lap and put them on the tray. "I need to tell you something."

Cassie put her cup down and looked at Enid. "You're going home, back to Charlotte, aren't you?"

Enid nodded.

"Your husband must have left pretty early this morning. If I had known, I would have given him some coffee and muffins for the road."

"Cade is taking a job in Montana and wants me to go with him."

"Is that what you want?" asked Cassie.

Enid thought before she replied. "I want to save my marriage."

Cassie looked down at her hands and appeared to be studying a piece of loose cuticle on her finger. "I'm torn about what to say to you."

Enid reached out and patted Cassie's hand. "I know. I'll miss you, too."

Cassie put her hand on top of Enid's and smiled. "Yes, but that's not what I meant."

"What is it then?" asked Enid.

"An innkeeper never talks about her guests, especially to other guests. But I feel like you've become more than that." She paused. "Last night, when your husband came in, I thought I recognized him."

"How could you possibly know Cade? We were living in Charlotte by the time you came to Madden."

Cassie got up and went inside to the library and opened the middle desk drawer. She returned to the table with a photograph and handed it to Enid. "Last night, I looked through some photo albums until I found this. It was taken almost ten years ago at one of our annual picnics. I'm good at remembering faces and placing them, but not so good with names."

Enid studied the photograph. Cade was standing by the lake with a glass in his hand. He was with an attractive brunette, and they appeared to be laughing together.

"Who is that woman?" asked Enid, pointing.

"She's Chief Jensen's niece, an attorney in Columbia. The picnics are an open invitation. My guests attend, but we always have others who come from the town and elsewhere."

Enid put the photograph down and looked at Cassie. "Are you saying she was here to see Cade?" Her mind was racing.

"She came here several times to talk to Cade, but I assumed it was business. They always looked serious when I saw them talking, but not intimate. Although, they were somewhat secretive, too. You know, they stopping talking when I came around."

"Was Cade a guest here when this photo was taken?" asked Enid.

Cassie nodded her head. "As I recall, he stayed at the inn for nearly a week."

Enid was replaying conversations with Cade, trying to remember if he ever mentioned staying at the inn. "Was that for Rosie's funeral?" As Enid recalled, Cade had gone to Rosie's funeral and was back at work the next day.

Cassie twirled the corner of a napkin with her fingers. "No, this was a year or more after that. When I saw Cade last night, I tried to remember our conversations. Of course, that was a lot of years and a lot of guests ago. I'm pretty sure, though, he told me he was checking into a family matter." She put the napkin back on the table. "Of course, since I didn't remember his name, I had no way of connecting the two of you when you showed up. Not until I saw him."

Enid picked up the photo again. "May I keep this a little while? I'll mail it back to you."

"Of course, keep it if you like. It has no meaning for me. I just snap a lot of photos for the scrapbooks in the library. Guests seem to like seeing them, especially my repeat guests who show up each year."

"I remember Cade saying he did some checking into Rosie's death, so perhaps that's why he stayed here." Enid looked down at the photo again. "I don't know why he didn't mention it last night."

Cassie stood up. "Well, I just wanted you to know, but I think you're making the right decision to try to make your marriage work. If you love him, hold onto him." She leaned down and hugged Enid. "I'll help you get your bags down."

CHAPTER 25

Enid looked around the large oak-paneled entrance foyer for the last time before heading back to Charlotte. She said goodbye to Cassie, with a promise to stay in touch. Cassie opened the front door and put one of the suitcases on the porch. "Just drive up to the front door so we can load your bags."

Cassie picked up a package wrapped in brown craft paper on the porch near the door. Across the top of the package was a note written with a black marker: "To Enid Blackwell—Personal." Cassie handed the package to Enid. "This is for you."

Enid took the package, which was about the size of a man's shoe box, and looked at it. "This must have been delivered last night or very early this morning. There's no postage or mailing label on it. I wonder what it could be?" She put the box on top of her suitcase. "I'll open it when I get to Charlotte. Maybe it's from Jack."

Cassie put her hand to her mouth. "Oh, I forgot to tell you, Jack called and said he would drop your tote bag and notes off after lunch today. I'll ship it to you, but you need to tell him you're leaving." Cassie looked at the box again. "That's not Jack's handwriting."

"Then I think I'll see what's in it before I leave." Enid sat in one of the big upholstered chairs in the entrance hall. After loosening the heavy twine holding the paper wrapping, she examined the small wooden box inside. The initials RMG were crudely carved into the cover. Enid ran her hand across the letters and looked at Cassie. "Rose Marie Garrett."

Enid walked into the library and sat at the big table. She opened the box and carefully removed each item so as not to tear the brittle paper. Surveying the contents spread out on the table, she saw several documents, an envelope, a bus schedule, and two photographs. She opened the envelope, which contained $200 in five, ten, and twenty dollar bills. She put the cash aside and unfolded the first document—Rose Marie Garrett's birth certificate from Mississippi. Rosie would have been twenty-seven if she were still alive. Wynona Garrett was typed in the space for the mother's name, but the father's name had been left blank.

Enid folded the birth certificate and put it aside. The next document she picked up was a handwritten letter signed "Mom." As Enid read the letter, her eyes kept drifting back to one line: "I'm sorry I let them tell you I was dead."

"Oh, my," Enid said aloud. She massaged her temples with her fingers and took a deep breath before picking up the bus schedule, which listed the dates, times, and fares from Columbia, the nearest city with a Greyhound bus terminal, to Jackson, Mississippi. According to Wynona Garrett's letter to her daughter, she was a prisoner at the Central Mississippi Correctional Facility.

Enid examined the last items from the box—two photographs. One showed a woman holding a small baby. The other was a photo of a man. His clothing and hair style dated the image to at least twenty years ago. He had dark hair and a boyish grin, with a cleft in his chin. He reminded Enid of John Travolta in a vintage costume.

She turned the photos over. "Wynona and Rosie" was written on the first. On the second one someone had written "Frank" in pencil.

Enid pushed her chair back and massaged her neck. She sat for a minute and then repacked the items in the box.

Enid jumped at a knock on the library door.

"Are you alright?" asked Cassie.

"You startled me."

"I called out to you but you didn't respond," said Cassie.

"I'm sorry, I didn't hear you."

"You look like you've seen a ghost," said Cassie.

"I didn't see a ghost, but I think she may be trying to talk to me."

"Who are you talking about?"

Enid closed the box. "I may not be leaving right now after all. Would that be a problem for you? I don't want to impose on your hospitality."

"No, of course not. You're welcome to stay as long as you like." The crease on Cassie's forehead deepened. "But what are you going to tell Cade?"

Enid stood up. "Honestly, I don't know. Right now I need to talk with Jack."

Upstairs in her room, Enid punched Jack's number into the cell phone. After the beep, she left him a message. "Jack, this is Enid. We need to talk. Call me as soon as you get this message."

CHAPTER 26

A loud knock on Enid's bedroom door pulled her from her thoughts. When she saw it was Jack, she motioned for him to come in. "Thanks for coming over. I thought we could talk here at the table by the window. Unless you'd rather go downstairs to the library."

"No, this is fine if it's alright with you." Jack handed the tote bag to her. "Here's your bag." He sat down and glanced out the window. "I never get tired of seeing this view." He looked at Enid's suitcases at the foot of the bed. "You taking off? Is that what this is all about?"

Enid has not even noticed that Cassie had brought her bags back up to the room.

"No. I mean, I was." She sat down across from Jack and told him about Cade's visit and her decision to leave. She then went to her bed and brought the box to the table. "This is what I want to talk to you about."

"Where'd you get it?" he asked.

"Cassie found it on the front porch this morning as I was leaving."

"Any idea who left it?" he asked.

"I have an idea, but I'm not positive. There's only one person I know of who was close enough to Rosie to have her keepsake box."

Jack opened the box, and Enid watched silently as he examined the contents. Like Enid, he read the letter twice that was from Wynona to her daughter Rosie. "Damn," he said softly. "Poor kid."

"We've got some work to do," said Enid.

"Whoa, there. I thought you promised Cade you were going with him to Montana to look for a house."

Enid stood up and paced across the room several times. "This changes everything," she said.

"How's that? This doesn't tell us anything about how or why Rosie got killed."

"No, but it helps explain why she became so rebellious. How could she trust anyone when they all lied to her about her mother being dead?" she asked. "Even her own mother was in on the scheme."

"But Wynona wrote that letter to Rosie trying to make things right. It's too bad Myra never gave it to Rosie."

"Can I borrow this photo?" Jack was holding the picture of the man presumably named Frank. "I'd like to ask around, see if anyone knows him."

"Sure, but he could be just a family member or a friend."

"Or maybe he was Rosie's father," said Jack.

Enid massaged the side of her neck and top of her shoulder trying to get the tension out. "Maybe." Enid looked up and saw that Jack was staring at her. "What?"

"I hate to see you throw away your marriage for the sake of a ten-year-old story that may not even have an ending." He leaned back in his chair. "Are you sure this is what you want to do?"

Enid put her hand on the box and stroked her hand across the top of it. "I won't let Rosie down. She deserves better." *And this story isn't to blame for my marriage failure.*

"Alright, then. It's your decision." He walked toward the door and then turned around. "Media Relations Specialist in Montana?" He shook his head. "What was Cade thinking?"

After Jack left, Enid walked down to the lake and sat in one of the turquoise-painted Adirondack chairs by the edge of the water. She leaned back in the chair and let the sun shine on her face, listening to the water slapping gently against the shore. After a few minutes, she pulled her cell phone from her pocket and called Cade's number, hoping he didn't answer. A few rings later, she heard his familiar voice.

"Hi, babe. Are you in Charlotte yet?"

CHAPTER 27

Searching for words she knew would be inadequate at best, Enid picked at a piece of peeling paint flaking off the arm of the chair by the lake. "No, I'm still in Madden."

"Why? Are you alright?"

"Cade, I'm sorry, but I can't go with you to Montana." There was so much more that needed to be said, but Enid couldn't bring herself to say it. Since her mother died, she had problems opening up to people. Keeping everything inside wasn't healthy, but it protected her from more hurt. At least temporarily.

Cade exhaled deeply into the phone. "I'm not sure what to say. I thought we agreed. I wanted you to help me look for a house." He paused briefly. "A home. For us."

"I need to stay." Enid couldn't get the rest of her words to come out.

"Why did you change your mind?" he asked.

Enid watched a weathered plastic soda bottle bobbing in the water like a miniature ship in a storm. "I need to stay here. For a while anyway." She watched the soda bottle drifting further out into the lake. Enid listened to Cade's breathing as the bottle disappeared from sight. "I'm sorry. I know you're disappointed in me."

"You think I'm disappointed? Is that all you think this is? A minor disappointment?" His tone was sharp.

"No, that's not what I meant." Enid stopped to consider her words. "I love you, but I don't want to live in Montana. And no matter how foolish you think I am, this story is important to me. Rosie has become important to me, and I want to finish it."

Cade cleared his throat and coughed slightly, something he did when he was upset. "I guess there's nothing else to say then, is there?"

"You can't just expect me to drop my life and follow you to a place we've never thought of living, where you will be doing a job that you're probably going to hate pretty quickly." She sighed "And then what do we do?"

"Ah, so that's what this is. You don't have any confidence in me making this change."

Enid looked over the water and saw the bottle bobbing its way back toward her. "As much as I hate to say this, I think you need to figure out what you really want before you drag me along with you."

"This is not about me trying to figure out my life. The company is a hundred years old, very reputable. One of my college friends is a senior officer there, and he offered me this chance to build a new career. But what about you? Do you know what the hell you want?" He coughed again. "This is about your willingness to throw away our life together to chase something, but I'm not sure what."

Enid remained silent, stung by his words. He was right, at least partially. In the beginning, Rosie's story was about breaking away from the bank and fulfilling the promise to return to writing. She could have chosen another story if she had really wanted to save her marriage. But somewhere along with way, Rosie had become more than just another story to her. *Am I choosing Rosie over Cade?*

"Look, I've got to go. I love you, and I'm sorry that . . . I wish things were different. Just be careful down there."

After Cade hung up, Enid stared out over the lake, trying to decide how she should feel. Angry? Relieved? Most of all, she felt responsible. And empty. She had traded her marriage for a dead girl's story that no one else seemed to care about.

When her cell phone rang again, she assumed it was Cade calling back, but a glance at the screen told her it was Jill, her boss at the bank. Enid considered letting the call go to voice mail. She had been intending to call the office but had put it off. Now she was embarrassed for not checking in sooner.

"Hi, Jill, how are you?" She forced herself to be cheerful. For the next few minutes, she listened to Jill talk about the bank merger and all the employee changes that had taken place. Her last comment was what Enid had been dreading, yet expecting, to hear. The new position was given to someone else.

"What does that mean, exactly? For me, I mean." Enid knew the answer wasn't going to be good, and it wasn't. "Of course, I understand. Thanks for letting me know." Enid tried to focus on the conversation, but she just wanted to hang up. "Yes, let's keep in touch. Drinks after work would be nice. Thanks for calling." She ended the call feeling numb. Her job had been eliminated and there was nothing else available for her at the bank. The words from the song "Bobbie McGee" popped into her head. *"Freedom's just another word for nothing left to lose."*

Enid stared out over the water and tried to get her thoughts together. First Cade, now her job. Suddenly, she felt foolish for chasing a pipe dream and trying to revive her journalism career. Mentally, she began calculating the amount of their savings and how long it would last. Not long, especially now that they would have two households. Or a divorce. She needed to talk finances with Cade, but not today.

She leaned her head back and shut her eyes to block out the world, when Cassie's voice quickly brought her back to attention.

"Enid?" Cassie called out as she walked down to the beach area where Enid was sitting. "I just wanted to make sure you're alright."

"I'm fine. I just came out here to clear my head. Sorry, I didn't hear you."

"There's a storm coming. Don't stay out too long."

"I'll be in shortly."

Cassie started to say something but hesitated. Instead, she walked up the path toward the inn. Enid glanced up at the sky. Dark clouds were moving toward the lake. The bobbing bottle had disappeared completely and small whitecaps were forming on the water. Flash lightning lit up the sky, not in a streak but in an all-over flash, as though someone were trying to take a photo of the whole world with a giant camera. Shortly afterward, a rumble of deep thunder shook the earth.

How many times had she sat with her mother during a storm when her mother counted the seconds between the lightning and the thunder? Each time, her mother would tell her that the sound of thunder traveled about a mile in five seconds. Together, they would count right after the lightning flash. One one-thousand, two one-thousand, three one-thousand, until they heard the thunder. Not missing an opportunity to make the weather a math lesson, as well as a science one, her mother would ask Enid to calculate how far away the storm was from them. Enid smiled as she remembered her mother's praise after Enid proudly announced that fifteen seconds between the lightning and the thunder meant the lightning was three miles away.

The sky lit up again and Enid counted five seconds before the earth shook again. The storm was getting closer and heavy drops of rain began to fall. Enid got up quickly and walked back to the inn, thankful the rain had washed the tears from her face.

CHAPTER 28

The next morning while Enid was having breakfast in the library, Jack walked in. "Cassie told me you were in here." He reached over and pinched off the end of a croissant. "Um, that's good." He licked his fingers and then sat down at the small table. "We need to find out who Frank is."

Enid wiped her mouth with the napkin from her lap. "And just how to do you propose we do that?" She laughed. "Wait, let me guess. You have a contact that can help us."

Jack grinned. "Something like that. You look tired. Everything okay?"

Enid sighed. "Not really, but I don't want to talk about it. Not now, anyway."

Jack cocked his head and smiled slightly, putting his hand on top of hers. "When you're ready, I can listen pretty good."

"Thanks." Even though she appreciated the offer, Enid pulled her hand away and focused on the task at hand. "So who and where is this contact of yours?"

Jack stood up. "At the paper. She's a gal who's been there forever. Knows everybody and everything worth knowing." Jack pushed his chair under the table. "You up for it? I can go myself, or we can wait 'til later."

Enid put her napkin on the table and stood up. "No, getting out will be good. Just let me run upstairs and get my things."

* * *

"You smell that?" Jack walked into the Madden Gazette and inhaled deeply. "That's what heaven must smell like."

"You mean newsprint and printing press lubricant?"

Jack made a face at Enid and walked up to the counter. Slamming his palm on the top of the bell sitting there, he called out, "Hello, anybody here?"

A young woman walked down the hall. "Can I help you?" She chewed vigorously on a wad of gum as she stared at Jack. "I know you." She walked over and pointed to one of the photos on the wall. "That's you, isn't it?"

Enid walked over to the photo and looked at the caption beneath it: "Awarded to Jack Johnson for Excellence in Journalism." A younger Jack in the photo was smiling broadly and holding a large plaque in one hand and shaking hands with an older man.

Jack cleared his throat. "Yep, I'm the guilty party. Got that when I worked at the Tribune in Chicago, but my editor here wanted to show it off, so I let him." He hung his head. "I had forgotten that thing was still hanging up there."

"They still talk about you, you know." She grinned. "You must have been a hoot back then."

Jack looked at the photo. "Yep. Back then, I was definitely a hoot. Is Helen here today?"

"Yeah. She's always here. You want her?" She popped her chewing gum.

"That would be nice." Jack walked toward the hallway and motioned for Enid to follow him. "Alright if we wait in the conference room down the hall?"

The girl shrugged. "No problem."

* * *

The real-life Helen was nothing like the image Enid had envisioned from Jack's comments. Enid was certain Helen
would be a plump, old woman with gray hair. Instead, the
woman who walked into the conference room was tall and
elegant, with dark brown hair, just slightly tinged with grey.
She swept into the room as gracefully as a swan.

"Jack, darling, how are you? And where have you been?"
The woman hugged Jack and then turned to Enid. "Hello,
my dear, I'm Helen. And who are you?"

Enid introduced herself and then the three of them sat
down at an old wooden conference table that had seen better days. Jack and Helen reminisced about old times for a
few minutes. Jack appeared to be enjoying it, so Enid just let
them talk until they ran out of steam.

"As much fun as this is, I doubt you came by just to
chat." Helen was a woman who clearly liked to be in control. She turned to Enid. "So how can I help you?"

"We're hoping you know who this man is." Enid slid the
photo across the table in front of Helen. "Apparently, his
name is Frank."

Helen put on the reading glasses that were hanging
around her neck on a chain with amethyst stones in it.
"Frank, huh?" She stared at the photo. "I may have seen
him." She looked at it again. "Well, no, I'm not sure. I don't
think he lives in Madden."

"So you don't know who he is?" asked Enid.

Helen took off her glasses. "If you'll let me copy that photo, maybe it'll come back to me. I'll also ask around."

"Thanks, we'd appreciate that," said Enid.

When Helen returned from the copier, she slid the photo across the table to Enid. "Why do you want to know who this man is?"

Enid placed the photo in the folder. "That's a fair question." She told Helen about Rosie's murder and box of mementos left at the inn. "They told Rosie her mother had died, but she was in prison for killing Rosie's father. Rosie was about two when her mother was incarcerated in Mississippi. That's when Rosie came to Madden to live with Myra. When Rosie was sixteen, she discovered a letter her mother had written her from prison. That's when she realized her mother was alive, at least at that time. Rosie was saving money to go to Mississippi to see her mother when Rosie was killed."

Helen shook her head. "Poor kid. No wonder she had problems. I thought Rosie was an orphan when she came to Madden. I heard that her mother had lived in Madden but moved away before Rosie was born. No one here knew about Rosie until she came to Madden to live with Myra."

"I hate to admit it, but I didn't dig too deep on Rosie's father before the story got shut down," said Jack. "He had been dead almost seventeen years by the time Rosie was killed. Several people made vague references to her father being from another state. I accepted the story that Rosie's mother was dead. I had no idea she was in prison for killing Rosie's father." He paused. "Damn."

"Don't beat yourself up. I know you got pulled off the story rather abruptly," said Helen. She turned to Enid. "I can tell this story is important to you. Where do you plan to sell it?"

"I really hadn't thought about it. I've been out of journalism a while, and I've lost most of my contacts."

"I'm sure between the two of us, me and Jack, we can find someone who's interested in it. In fact, I'd love to run it here at the *Madden Gazette*, but it would never get past our owner." She stood up. "Nice to see you again, Jack, and nice to meet you, Enid. Good luck. I'll ask around discreetly, and if I find anything about this Frank fellow, I'll be in touch."

CHAPTER 29

After they left the newspaper office, Jack drove for several miles in silence.

"You're not driving toward the inn. Do you mind telling me where we're going?" asked Enid.

"You said you wanted to find the coroner's full report and notes on Rosie. I'm hoping his file on Rosie is at the courthouse over in Camden." He glanced over at Enid. "It's not far from here."

Enid put her head back and closed her eyes. The warm sun was making her sleepy, so they rode in silence. She must have dozed off because Jack was shaking her by the arm.

"Wake up, sleepyhead. We're here."

Enid pulled down the visor to check her makeup. She got a tissue from her bag and wiped a smudge of mascara from under her eye.

"You're beautiful already. Come on," said Jack. Looking a bit embarrassed, he got out of the car and waited on the sidewalk.

The Kershaw County Courthouse was a relatively modern looking brick, two-story building on Broad Street in the quaint little town of Camden, South Carolina. They parked on the street and walked into the front entrance.

Inside the courthouse, they went through the metal detector and one of the deputies on duty directed them to the Clerk of Court's office. After they explained what they needed, the young woman told them the coroner's records would likely be filed at the courthouse since he had died. She gave Jack and Enid a request form to fill out and told them she would see what she could find.

After completing the form, Enid discreetly motioned her head toward the door. Jack didn't understand at first, so Enid nodded again.

"I've got phone calls to return. I'll be downstairs," said Jack as he left the clerk's office.

Enid focused on the young woman. "I know you have rules you have to follow, and I don't want to get you into trouble. But I want to explain to you why we need to see that file." Enid proceeded to tell the clerk about Rosie's murder and the lack of information available. "Rosie had dreams, but she was killed before she even had a chance to fulfill them. If she were alive today, she'd be about your age. Will you help me?"

"My name is Maggie, by the way," said the clerk. "The coroner was my daddy's fishing buddy. He was a good man, and he was thorough. I've heard the county solicitor say he was an excellent witness in court, because he kept such good notes. If we have his file, I bet it could help you find that poor girl's killer. I remember hearing my grandmother talk about her murder. So sad." The clerk motioned to a chair against the wall. "You wait here. Let me see what I can find."

* * *

When Enid left the clerk's office, she found Jack near the water fountain in the lobby, studying the oil portraits along the wall. She called out, "Hey, you ready to go?"

"What was that all about? Why did you motion for me to leave?"

"I just wanted to make sure she understood the significance of our request," she said.

"And?"

"Come on, I'll tell you in the car."

While Jack was driving, Enid explained what she had learned from the clerk. "The coroner's records were sent to the courthouse when he retired, just as you said. Maggie found it, but there were no personal notes. She said that was unusual."

"Then why did you look so happy when you left there?" asked Jack.

"During my little tete-a-tete with Maggie, she told me that keeping separate files of notes is against the rules. Notes are part of the official documents and are supposed to be stored in an official place. Maggie suggested we check with the coroner's widow. Maggie said she would call to let her know we're coming." Enid gave Jack the address, and he put it in the car's navigation system.

Jack checked the rearview mirror, and Enid noticed the look on his face. "Anything wrong?" she asked.

Jack didn't respond. Instead, he turned into a Quick Mart and circled around so he could see the oncoming traffic on the road. A green pickup truck drove slowly past them. The driver had a bandana on his head. He looked at Jack and then sped away quickly.

After the truck had traveled down the road and out of sight, Jack backed up and turned around in the parking lot to get back onto the highway. "Sorry, didn't mean to alarm you." He rubbed his chin in the now-familiar gesture. "That truck followed us to Camden and showed up again when we left."

"Did you recognize the driver?"

"Yeah, I know that knucklehead. He's one of Eddie's bikers." Jack checked the mirror again. "He's gone. He knows I saw him."

"Why do you think he was following us?"

"I'm sure it's nothing to worry about."

Enid frowned and then looked out the window, her pulse racing. "I think that's one of the bikers from the cemetery. I recognized him."

"Let's hope he's just out for a ride."

Enid nervously watched the rear mirror as Jack drove in silence for several miles. The truck had not appeared again, but Enid couldn't relax.

After turning onto a narrow gravel road, Jack slowed down to keep from throwing the small rocks against the car. After about a half mile, he pulled up in front of a large two-story brick house and stopped in the wide circular driveway.

"Is this the house?"

Jack smiled. "Yep." He pulled the key from the ignition and opened the car door. "Come on. You said she was expecting us."

CHAPTER 30

Jack pushed the doorbell and melodious chimes announced their arrival. The door opened and a housekeeper in a gray uniform invited them in. Inside, a heavy scent emanated from a large glass container of potpourri sitting on the table in the spacious entrance hall, making the house smell like a florist shop.

Enid glanced around and realized this place reminded her of the small funeral home where her mother's memorial service was held. Other than the cloying smell of flowers, what she remembered most was the oppressive silence, and she was feeling it again now.

Enid and Jack waited while the housekeeper went to find the coroner's widow. After a few minutes, a pleasantly plump woman with silver hair in a pale blue dress appeared. She shook hands, first with Jack and then Enid as they introduced themselves.

"Maggie said you might be stopping by. How may I help you?" Enid glanced at Jack with the mention of Maggie, the clerk from the courthouse.

"We were hoping you might have some of your late husband's files here," said Enid.

The woman seemed reluctant to respond. "Anything that's part of the file would be at the court house," said the woman.

Enid took the lead. "We don't want to get anyone in trouble, but we really need your help. If you do have anything that might not be in the courthouse file, we'd like to see it. Please. It's important."

The woman eyed Enid suspiciously. "Isn't this still an open case?"

Enid put her hand on Jack's arm to signal that she would respond. "Well, yes and no," she said. "It's never been solved, so technically it's still open. But no one, other than us, seems to be looking into it. It's been over ten years, so what could be the harm?"

"I see," said the woman. Her smile was gone. "Maggie said you're both reporters."

"Rosie's not just a story. She's a relative," said Enid. "Jack is helping me with my research in Madden, since he knows the people and the area."

The woman's face softened, and she nodded sympathetically. "A tragic loss of a young life, indeed." She kept nodding, which reminded Enid of a little toy dog with a bobble head her father had given her. Enid remembered tapping its head and watching it bob up and down. The toy was still in her box of childhood mementos.

"As you know, my dear husband's files were taken to the county courthouse when he died shortly after that poor girl was killed. God rest his soul."

Enid nodded. "We have his report, or at least part of it, but are there any other notes your husband may have kept for himself?"

"Maggie said you were looking for any notes about the murder." The woman tucked a stray strand of silver hair back into the neatly coiffed chignon, worn low on her neck.

"If there were any personal notes, the coroner would have included those in his report."

"I'm sure he would have," said Enid. "And we're not suggesting he did anything wrong."

The woman fingered her wedding ring. "If he made notes that didn't go into the file, then he must have had a good reason. As I recall, he did mention to me that he was getting a lot of pressure to finish his report quickly. He was also told not to discuss it with anyone." She looked directly at Enid. "Especially reporters."

"Who told him to keep quiet?" asked Enid.

The woman looked like she was struggling with her conscience, so Enid and Jack remained silent, allowing the widow to think about her response.

"I know this must be hard for you, and I'm sorry we've put you in a difficult situation," said Enid. "But Rosie had her whole life ahead of her, and whoever took that life from her has not been brought to justice. From what you've told me about your husband, the coroner, he was a good man and wanted to do the right thing."

The widow nodded at the mention of her husband. "Yes, he was a good man. God rest his soul."

Enid replied, "As you said if he kept notes separate from the official file, he did it for a good reason. Don't you think he would want you to help us?"

The widow seemed lost in thought for a moment. "Wait here." When she returned, she had a large accordion file in her hands. It was free of dust and in pristine condition, so it must have been carefully preserved. She handed it to Enid. "Here. This is a copy of the official reports ... and his notes.

For that poor girl. Bring them back to me when you're finished."

Enid and Jack said their goodbyes. As they were walking to the car, Jack said, "Hey, that was pretty good the way you convinced her to give us the file. I'm impressed."

"She did what she thought her husband would have wanted. Bless her heart." Enid laughed at herself when she realized how quickly she was adopting the local expressions. "Let's go back to the inn. I can't wait to look through these notes."

CHAPTER 31

Sitting at the table in the inn's library, Enid and Jack opened the brown folder containing the coroner's report and personal notes and spread the papers out on the desk. The first document they examined was the county coroner's report, which listed the cause of Rosie's death as asphyxiation due to strangulation. The manner of death was shown as "homicide" followed by "choked by unknown person." So far, the report didn't contain any information they didn't already know.

The next document Jack picked up was the South Carolina Law Enforcement Division's Child Fatality Report, required for homicide victims under the age of eighteen. The autopsy report described Rosie as a healthy young woman with no signs of abuse prior to death, other than a blunt-force head injury. Since the injury showed no signs of healing, it was classified as peri-mortem, occurring at or near the time of death. The toxicology report showed no drugs or alcohol in Rosie's system. The coroner had noted that the body was found just inside the Madden city limits, so the Madden City Police Department had jurisdiction.

Photocopies of the coroner's photos were attached with a paper clip. Enid picked up one of the photos and examined it. Rosie was lying on her back, fully clothed. A small purse was on the ground near her body. In spite of the brutality of Rosie's murder, she seemed to be resting peacefully on the bed of leaves and underbrush.

Enid picked up the coroner's report and read it again. At the bottom of the form, there was a note, handwritten in pencil: "goat hairs found on the victim's clothing."

"Did you see this note?" asked Enid, pointing to it.

Jack adjusted his reading glasses and took the report from her. "Huh. That's interesting. Don't think I've seen that before."

She handed him another piece of paper. "Look, here's the lab report confirming the hairs were goat." Pointing at the name and address on the invoice, she said, "This lab work was ordered in his wife's name at their home address. That's odd."

"Looks like he wanted to keep the information under the radar."

"Myra didn't have any goats, did she?"

Jack laughed. "No, she lived in the city limits. No farm critters allowed." He handed the report back to Enid.

"I wonder why no one followed up on this information." Before Jack could reply, Enid answered herself. "Never mind, I know why. Same reason nothing else was done."

"You're probably right." He looked at Enid over the top of his glasses. "I don't want to disappoint you, but do you know how many goats there are around here? That's probably why nothing came of it."

Enid looked up from the report. "Are you serious? Why would so many people have goats?"

Jack took off his glasses and put them on the table. "I'll have you know goats are good for a lot of things," he said, pretending to be indignant.

Enid smiled. "Oh, yeah. Like what?"

"Well, for one thing, there's goat milk and cheese. I'm sure you've seen some in the fancy displays at the grocery store under that tacky orange and pink 'Buy local' sign."

"Cassie gave me some the other day on a snack tray with her homemade crackers and some fresh blackberries. It was delicious."

"There, you see." He nodded his head. "Lots of folks around here who have any kind of acreage own goats to keep the kudzu cleared out. Goats will eat anything and keep land cleared pretty good, especially on hills, gullies, and tight places you can't get to easily with a mower or sickle."

"I saw a tiny goat eating grass by the lake one day. Cassie said it must have gotten out of a nearby pasture."

"Probably a Pygmy goat. We've got a few places around here that raise them for pets and sell them all over the world. I've been told that Pygmies have sweeter milk, and better dispositions, than the big ones. And they are especially good as stable companions for horses."

"I had no idea you knew so much about goats. Let me guess. You did an article on them once."

Jack laughed. "I did, actually."

Enid's smile faded. "I thought the goat hairs would narrow our search, but I guess not."

Jack put his reading glasses back on. "It might. Maybe Rachel can help us. She should know where Rosie might have come into contact with goats."

"I don't think she'll talk to me again, but I can try." Enid picked up a handwritten note and read it. "Hmmm. That's interesting."

Jack waited for Enid to continue, but she was lost in thought. "What's interesting?" he asked.

She handed him the note. "The coroner put in his personal notes that he felt Chief Jensen was pressuring him to slant his findings."

Jack was reading the note. "I see here where Jensen told him there had to be drugs in Rosie's system and encouraged him to put that in the report. He also said Jensen told him to wrap the investigation up quickly."

Enid handed Jack another note. "Look at this. The coroner asked SLED for information on Jensen."

Jack looked at the note she had read. "Why would he do that?" He put the note back on the table. "Damn. You're right." He grinned.

"Why are you smiling?"

"Because I know this guy at SLED who may be able to help us." He slapped the table with his palm. "He was a reliable source of confidential information for years."

"How did you meet?"

"On a plane. Both of us were flying from Charlotte to Chicago in bad weather. We had to circle O'Hare a few times, so we had lots of time to talk shop and compare notes. We hit it off, so we kept in touch. He was my go-to guy for anything SLED was involved in. Of course, I was careful never to give away state secrets."

"Will he still help you?"

"I aim to find out." His smile faded. "I'll make the initial contact and try to set up a meeting for the three of us. He could get into real trouble for talking with me, so he may not agree to it."

They went through the remaining documents but found nothing else of value, so Enid put the papers back in the folder.

"I'd like to go through the coroner's notes again before we return it. I'll keep it at the inn, someplace safe."

After Jack left, Enid went to her room and made some notes. In one, she wrote JENSEN in big letters and circled his name several times with her pen. *What were you trying to hide?*

CHAPTER 32

Enid looked at her notes and found Rachel's cell number. After a few rings, a girl's voice answered. "Hello."

"Rachel? Hi, it's Enid Blackwell."

After a brief silence, Rachel responded in a low voice. "Why are you calling me?"

"I'm sorry to bother you, but we need to talk."

Rachel whispered. "I told you I couldn't talk to you no more."

Enid could hear people in the background and assumed Rachel was at her job at the convenience store.

"If you didn't want to talk with me, why did you leave Rosie's box at the inn?" Silence. "Rachel, are you still there?"

"Meet me here at the store when I get off at seven tonight," Rachel said before she hung up.

* * *

Enid sat down in a booth in the snack area of the convenience store. The seat and table were both covered in a nondescript beige laminate. Bread crumbs and a lone, stale French fry littered the tabletop. Enid pulled a paper napkin from the dispenser and was cleaning the table when Rachel sat down.

"Those kids come in here, they never clean the tables," said Rachel. She took the napkin from Enid and threw it in the trash can. "I don't have long. Mama's got dinner waiting."

"Molly seems like a good mother. I'm sure she worries about you."

Rachel remained silent, looking down at the tabletop.

"I want to thank you for giving me Rosie's box. It helped me understand a lot about her."

Rachel looked up at Enid. "How did you know I left the box?"

"You were Rosie's best friend. And I know you left it because you want me to know her." Rachel remained silent, so Enid continued. "You saw the good in her when no one else did. I want others to see the Rosie you knew."

"Nobody told her the truth, about anything." Tears streamed down Rachel's face. Enid reached out to put her hand on top of Rachel's, but Rachel pulled away. "She was my cousin."

Enid wasn't sure she had heard Rachel correctly. "Rosie? She was your cousin?"

Rachel nodded.

"But, I don't understand. How is that possible?" asked Enid.

"Cause her daddy was my Uncle Frank." Rachel looked down again at her hands in her lap. "I didn't really know him. Mama says he was a black sheep."

Enid leaned back in her seat, trying to make meaning of what she had heard. "Frank was your mother's brother?"

Rachel nodded.

"And Frank was Rosie's biological father? The man Rosie's mother killed?"

Rachel nodded again.

"Why didn't Molly mention this when we talked about Rosie that evening at her house?"

No response from Rachel.

"Or why didn't you, when we talked earlier?"

Rachel stood up to leave. "Look, I've done said enough. Please don't tell Mama I told you. I'm not supposed to talk about Uncle Frank."

Enid put her hand on Rachel's arm. "Wait, please let me ask you just a few more questions." Rachel pulled away. "You're one of the few people left who knew Rosie, or who's willing to talk about her. Please, Rachel, it's important."

Rachel slid to the edge of her seat. "Okay, but you've got to make it quick. I can't be seen with you."

"Did Rosie know you were cousins?"

Rachel nodded. "Just before she . . . a year before she died, she found a box hidden in Myra's closet. The letter from Rosie's mother and Rosie's birth certificate was in it."

"That's when Rosie found out her mother wasn't dead."

Rachel nodded.

"Rosie got real mad at Myra for telling her that her mama was dead. Rosie told her she was going to run away and never come back until Myra told her the truth. That's when Myra told her about her daddy."

"So Myra told Rosie her father was Frank?" asked Enid.

Rachel nodded.

"Why wasn't his name on the birth certificate."

"Myra said that Wynona went to Mississippi to live with Frank, and she when got pregnant, he was real upset and claimed the baby wasn't his. Then after Rosie was born, he slapped her every time she cried. One day, he got real mad and hit Wynona hard—broke her nose. He threatened to kill Rosie if she cried again. That's when Wynona got the gun and shot him."

"That sounds like self-defense. A good attorney should have been able to get her off."

Rachel shrugged.

Enid took a deep breath and looked around the snack bar. No one was within hearing distance. "Did Myra give Rosie the photo of Frank?"

Rachel shook her head. "No, I gave it to her. When Rosie told me her daddy was Frank Kelly, I told Rosie he was my uncle. She asked me if I had a picture of him, so I snitched it from Mama's picture album and gave it to her."

"But why keep it a secret? Why tell Rosie her mother was dead instead of in prison?"

"People here can be mean sometimes. Rosie's family thought it would be hard on her if they knew her mama killed her daddy."

When Rachel stood up to leave, Enid said, "Just one more question. What about the letter Rosie's mother, Wynona, wrote to Rosie? Wasn't Rosie just two years old when her mother went to prison?"

"Rosie found that in Myra's closet, too. Myra was supposed to give it to Rosie when she was old enough to understand."

Enid rubbed her temples to alleviate the throbbing in her head. "But she obviously didn't."

Rachel shook her head. "I told you Myra was paid money to tell her that. That's what Rosie said."

"When I asked you earlier, you said you didn't know who paid her." Enid realized she had raised her voice and looked around to make sure no one had heard her. There was a woman at the drink dispenser, texting on her phone.

"I don't know."

Rachel stood again to leave, and this time Enid didn't try to stop her. "Thank you," she called out to Rachel as she walked away. As Rachel disappeared from sight, Enid realized she had been so floored by Rachel's revelations that she forgot to ask her about the goat hairs.

Enid bought a cup of coffee and sat down in the booth again to process the conversation. The coffee was dark and bitter, just like everything she was learning about Rosie's short life.

CHAPTER 33

Enid couldn't wait to tell Jack about her conversation with
Rachel, so she sat in her car, parked at the convenience
store, and pulled out her cell phone to call him. Just as she
retrieved it from the bottom of her tote bag, it rang, and she
saw Jack's name flash on the screen.

"I was just getting ready to call you. You won't believe
it—"

Before she could finish, he interrupted her. "Helen
called, and I know who Frank is."

Enid hid her disappointment at having her surprise an-
nouncement snatched away by Jack's friend at the
newspaper, especially since he sounded so anxious to tell
Enid. "What did she find out?"

"His name is Frank Kelly. She found an archived article
from Mississippi about Rosie's mother killing him. The killing didn't get more than a couple paragraphs under local
news. Just another domestic murder. The *Madden Gazette*
never reported on it, because Wynona wasn't living in Madden, so the family was able to keep it under the radar."

"That explains Fern's donation. It was hush money. Did
Helen give you any more information?"

"According to the article she found, Frank dropped out
of school when he lived in Madden and moved to Mississippi, working odd jobs. He was arrested a few times for

petty crimes. Wynona Garrett was living with Frank when she killed him. She claimed self-defense but was convicted of second-degree murder."

"Did you know Frank Kelly was Molly Anderson's brother?" Enid asked matter-of-factly.

Jack was silent for a few seconds. "What did you say?"

"I said Frank was Molly's brother. That made Rachel and Rosie cousins."

"Well, I'll be damned." Jack laughed. "I saw the article, and there was no mention of Frank's family here. I guess that means your meeting with Rachel was pretty productive. Good job!"

"I wonder why Molly withheld that information about Frank when I had dinner with her?"

"She obviously wanted to keep it private," said Jack. "After all, he was somewhat of a scoundrel. Not somebody you'd jump up to claim as family."

"It just seems odd."

Enid summarized the rest of her conversation with Rachel. "I wonder who paid Myra to lie to Rosie? That seems so mean and unfair."

There was a brief silence before Jack responded. "I really think you need to talk with Cade about all this. There's a lot more to this situation than we thought. It looks like the Blackwell family had its own secrets."

* * *

Enid punched in Cade's cell number for the third time. Twice, she had changed her mind before hitting the green button. This time, she let the call go through.

Cade answered after a few rings. "Hello. Enid?"

The sound of his voice sent a stabbing pain through her heart. "Hi. How are you?"

"As well as can be expected, I guess. Montana is hard to get used to. It's beautiful, but it doesn't feel like home. Not yet anyway." His cleared his throat. "I miss you."

As much as she missed Cade, today he was a source of information. Still, she couldn't stop herself. "I miss you too. Are you taking care of yourself?"

For the next few minutes, Cade told her about the new job and the apartment he had rented. He had decided not to buy a house for now. Enid knew that in personal matters, Cade could be indecisive.

Enid reminded herself why she called. "I need to ask you a few things about Rosie."

Cade let out a long sigh. "I should have guessed that's why you called."

Stay focused on what you need. "Cassie, the innkeeper, showed me a photo of you that was taken not long after Rosie's death. You were at an event at the inn, a picnic or some kind of outing." Enid waited for Cade to respond, but he was silent. "You were with a blonde woman, a Jensen family member."

Cade's raised his voice. "It's not what you think. Yes, I was at the inn, but the woman I was talking to was just someone I was trying to get some information from. Her name is Madelyn Jensen."

"Cassie told me you stayed at the inn and that you met with Madelyn several times." Enid regretted pulling Cassie into the middle of all this and especially hated sounding like a jealous wife.

Cade's voice was more stern this time. "What do you want me to say? I told you I had looked into Rosie's death."

Enid took a deep breath to calm herself. "I didn't call you to argue, but when we talked earlier, you said you looked into it. You didn't tell me you spent time in Madden." *Or that you were spending time with Madelyn.* "If you know something I need to know, please tell me. I'll find out anyway, you know."

Cade chuckled softly. "I'm beginning to see that."

Enid filled Cade in on what she had learned from Rachel about Rosie's mother and father. When she got to the part about someone paying Myra to lie to Rosie, she confronted Cade. "Who would do that? And why? Do you have any idea?"

Cade was silent, and Enid knew from experience he was wrestling with himself about how much to tell her. "I didn't know Rosie's father was related to Molly Anderson. That's good investigative work you did."

Cade's praise spread throughout Enid's body like a warmth, even though she knew that if Cade had looked harder, he would have discovered the same information. "Thanks, but I'm asking you to tell me what you found out. With or without your help, I'm going to do this story."

Cade's tone sharpened. "I can't believe you're doing this. It's not just any story. It's my family you're digging around in."

Enid could feel herself losing control. "Your family? What happened to *our* family? And you've never put a story ahead of me?" She tried to control the quiver in her voice.

"I never had to choose between the two. I just did my job. And I never wrote about *your* family or worked on a story you asked me to drop." Cade paused. "Look, Enid, I don't want to fight with you, but I don't understand your obsession with this story, or with Rosie. Is it just because Mother asked you not to do it? Is that what this is all about? Are you willing to ruin our marriage just to spite her?"

Enid's frustration overcame her. "No, I'm not trying to spite Fern. Don't you care about Rosie? Aren't you the least bit ashamed that everyone in the family has forgotten her? And you, of all people, an investigative reporter. You could have found out what happened, but you dropped it. Why? Are you so afraid of your mother that you walked away from finding out the truth just to keep her happy?"

"Whoa. Hold on. How was it *my* responsibility to write about Rosie? I didn't tell her to get hooked on drugs and shame our family name." He hesitated briefly and then spoke so softly Enid could barely hear him. "Let's not do this to us."

Is there still an "us"? "Don't you understand that if I walk away from this story, I'm selling myself out again?"

Cade sighed. "No, I don't have the foggiest idea what you mean."

"When my mother got sick, I walked away from my dream. I've tried to rationalize it a hundred different ways, telling myself I was being a good daughter, that I did the right thing. The truth is . . ." Enid stopped herself. *Maybe Cade is right. Maybe we shouldn't do this to us.* "The truth is, I resented you for being able to live the life you wanted, doing what I wanted to do." She paused and could hear Cade breathing, but he remained silent. "This time you're moving to Montana to pursue what you want and you're asking me to give up what I want just to keep you happy. Have you thought this decision through?" She paused to compose herself. "This time, I won't sacrifice my own needs again for someone else. Besides, I promised Mother before she died that I would return to what I really wanted to do."

"I never asked you to leave journalism. That was *your* decision."

"No, but you complained that we were using *our* money to take care of *my* mother." *God, I hate the way this conversation is going.* "And you were happy for me to work seventy hours a week doing a job I loathed so we could buy nice things."

"What are we actually fighting about? I don't know any more."

"Neither do I, Cade." She lowered her voice. "Neither do I." Enid had never felt as alone as she did now.

"Ask me what you want to know, and then I never want to talk about this again."

Enid was tempted to tell him to forget it and hang up. *Try to think of him as any other person you're interviewing for information.* She took a deep breath and jumped in. "Who paid Myra to lie to Rosie?" The minute she asked the question, she was filled with a sense of dread. "Do you know who it was?"

Cade said nothing for a while and then spoke softly. "She was doing what she thought was right—for me, for the family."

Enid's mind quickly began piecing the bits of information together. "Wait. Are you telling me Fern paid Myra?" Enid could feel herself getting angry. When Cade didn't answer right away, she added, "Cade, please answer me."

"You know how important family image is to Mother. Her only sister, Wynona, was younger than Mother and always getting into some kind of mess, so Mother covered for her. When Wynona killed Rosie's father, Mother convinced her that Rosie would be well cared for and better off not knowing her mother was still alive. So, Mother paid Myra to take Rosie in and raise her."

"I don't mean to judge Fern, but she didn't have the right to withhold that information from Rosie. I'm having a hard time understanding how protecting an image is more important than doing what was right for Rosie."

Cade exhaled deeply. "I know you're never going to understand why Mother did it, but in her own way, she *was* protecting Rosie, in the only way she knew how. The family's reputation was at stake, and she wanted Rosie to have as normal a life as possible—without the baggage of having a mother in prison. Myra needed money to care for Rosie, and so they made a deal. She paid for Myra to raise and care for Rosie, with the understanding that Myra would never tell Rosie about her Mother being alive. Mother convinced the local news not to report on it. After all, it happened in another state and Wynona wasn't living in Madden any longer." Cade coughed and cleared his throat. "Mother also donated money to the town to renovate a building for the women's club. She wanted the Madden residents to remember her family for something positive, I guess."

Enid wanted to scream at Cade about Fern's insensitivity but decided nothing good would come of it. "So what about the Jensen woman you met with. How does she figure in all this?"

Another sigh from Cade. "Madelyn is the niece of Chief Jensen. I met her at the annual Glitter Lake Inn picnic. That's the photo you saw. When she told me who she was, I told her I was writing an article about small town life. She told me she had moved away from Madden to go to college and then law school. She set up a practice in Columbia and came back to Madden only for holidays and a few birthday parties here and there."

"She must have had something you wanted since she kept meeting with you at the inn." Enid scolded herself for letting her jealousy surface.

"We met at the inn because Madelyn didn't want to be seen around town with a reporter. You know how small-town gossip can be. When Madelyn and I met, she made it clear she had nothing to do with her uncle, the police chief, and stayed as far away from him as she could. In fact, she alluded to the fact that he was into some dangerous and illegal activities."

"So, she just told you all that, on your first meeting with her?"

"After we talked a little while, I told her I was really in Madden to check on Rosie's murder. She told me about the biker gang and that she suspected Uncle Dick was on the take, so to speak. I promised not to use anything she gave without confirming it with another source. I think she wanted someone to expose him for taking money from the gang. And apparently, Uncle Dick had screwed her side of the family out of some inheritance Madelyn thought they were due when her grandfather died."

"Are you saying Madelyn thought the bikers killed Rosie?"

"That was the general impression of everyone in town, according to her."

Enid tried to imagine what it would be like living in a town where you couldn't trust the police because they were being paid off. She then thought of Cassie's son and how, like Rosie's murder, it was not fully investigated. "What did you find out in your research?"

Cade cleared his throat. "I wasn't there to investigate the Madden Police Department or Chief Jensen. If Rosie was buying drugs from the bikers, and they murdered her, then—"

Enid interrupted him. "Are you saying she got what she deserved?"

"No, that's not it at all. At Rosie's funeral, Myra had pulled me aside and told me about her 'arrangement' with Mother. She asked me if she had been right in lying to Rosie. When I got back to Charlotte, I confronted Mother about her role in it. Mother went to pieces and begged me to let it go. After all, Rosie's murder was the second one in our family. She just wanted it all to go away. From that day on, we never spoke of Rosie again."

Until I found the newspaper clippings. "So you dropped your investigation."

"I let it go for a while, and then I started thinking about it again. It was almost a year later when I returned to Madden. That's when I stayed at the inn and met with Madelyn about Chief Jensen."

"When Myra asked if she had done the right thing, what did you say to her? Did you approve of her lying to Rosie and withholding Wynona's letter?"

"Look, I know you're disappointed in me, and I'm sorry I didn't tell you everything. I didn't want you to think the worst about Mother, but I admit she was wrong."

Enid wanted to tell him she was hurt more than disappointed that he lied to her, but decided against it. "Is there anything else you found out that I should know about?"

"Just be careful. I know you've developed some kind of post-mortem connection with Rosie and that you're obsessed with finding out what happened. But, don't you see this can of worms you're opening is causing nothing but trouble?" Cade sighed loudly. "Look, as much as I wanted to put things right for Rosie, I chose to walk away. I didn't want to endanger me, you, or anyone else chasing a story about small town police corruption. This one was too close to home—in many ways." Cade paused. "And you need to walk away too."

"I'm not trying to solve her murder or do an exposé on the Madden police. I just want people to remember a young girl whose life and dreams were taken away from her. You know, one of my human interest stories."

"Please think about what I've said. I've got to go," he said. "Promise me you'll be careful. Rosie's life and her death are interwoven. You can't write about one without the other."

"I promise to be careful." Enid could hear Cade breathing into the phone and was overcome with the memory of his warm breath on her neck when he held her close.

"Come to Montana, Enid. Let's not throw away what we have." He paused briefly. "I love you."

Enid could no longer hold back the tears. "Love you too. Bye."

CHAPTER 34

After a sleepless night, Enid felt an urge to call Cade back and try to repair yesterday's painful conversation. Half hoping and expecting he wouldn't answer, she was startled when she heard his voice.

"Enid?"

She took a deep breath to steady her nerves. "Cade, I'm . . ." The words wouldn't come out, so she tried again. "I'm sorry I've made such a mess of things."

She heard Cade's familiar sigh and waited for him to say something.

"I don't know what to say. We've had this conversation." He paused. "What else is there to say?"

She wished she could throw her arms around him. "You must think I'm awful. I messed up our lives and went after this story even though you asked me not to. I feel selfish and stupid." Past arguments with Cade flashed across her mind. The big ones, the awful ones, always ended the same way, with her crying and Cade being silent. *How did we get to this point?*

She reached into her tote and got a tissue to blow her nose. Finally, Cade spoke. "What do you want me to say?"

Enid got another tissue and wiped her eyes. "I wanted to write about Rosie's life, but all anyone remembers in Madden remembers is her murder. They think I should just forget her too."

Cade was silent.

Enid composed herself. "You knew her. Tell me what you remember about her."

After a brief silence, Cade spoke in a low voice. "She was a good kid, about eight years younger than me. I remember her staying with us some during the summers when she was out of school."

"Was she a good student?"

"She was smart as a whip, caught on quickly. But she was rebellious too. Didn't like teachers or anyone in authority telling her what to do. It got her in trouble a lot."

"Did you get along well with her?"

Enid could hear Cade's heavy breathing for a few seconds before replying. "Yes, I liked her a lot." He seemed to be weighing his words carefully. His voice cracked when he added, "She reminded me of you in many ways."

Enid decided to push ahead with her questions. Other than Rachel, no one else seemed to know Rosie very well. "What about Myra? Did she and Rosie get along?"

"For the most part, yes." Cade paused. "Look, you're a good writer. In many ways, you're a much better journalist than I. You have more heart. Even when you were writing about the banking industry, you managed to bring your stories to life with a human-interest angle. I have no doubt you'll find the truth you're looking for."

But you're not going to help me find it. After they ended the call, Enid fell back on the bed and closed her eyes.

Later, when she heard a knock on her door, she glanced at the clock on the bedside table. She had been asleep for more than an hour. Cassie knocked again and called out, "Enid, are you alright? Enid?"

Enid opened the door and invited her in.

"You look terrible," said Cassie. "Sorry, I shouldn't be so blunt. But I'm worried about you. Would you like to talk? I may not have all the answers but I can sure listen." She smiled at Enid.

"It's just that . . ." Enid hesitated. "I put everything on the line to come here and write about Rosie. Now I'm wondering why it seemed so important." She looked up at the ceiling fan whirling softly overhead. "I'm too rusty. I can't seem to get this story going. I've been away from writing too long. All I've accomplished is to alienate myself from everyone, including my husband."

Cassie went to the bed and sat beside Enid. She hugged Enid and took her hand. "Sometimes we get a tap on the shoulder when there are things that have to be done." Cassie tapped her finger on Enid's arm as she spoke. "A voice from deep inside tells you it's your turn to step up and do this thing. You can fight it. You can even refuse it. But in the end, it's what you have to do."

Cassie's comments reminded Enid of her last conversation with her mother.

Cassie squeezed Enid's hand. "This is your thing you have to do."

"That's what I felt when I had to change careers to take care of my mother." She looked into Cassie's eyes. "Isn't once in a lifetime enough?"

Cassie patted Enid's arm with her hand. "I know it seems unfair in a way." Cassie took a deep breath. "When Mark got killed, I learned that we don't have answers for some things." She smiled slightly. "And life certainly isn't fair sometimes. Things just happen." Cassie stared at the wall in front of her, seemingly lost in her own memories.

Cassie stood up and faced Enid. "Why don't you go to Montana and spend some time with Cade? After all, it's been more than ten years since Rosie's death, so another week or so won't hurt. Might do you a world of good."

"We're past that, I'm afraid. If I'm honest with myself, my pursuing this story isn't what came between us. This wall has been building for years, but I didn't want to see it. Cade is ready for a change. He's ready to move on without me."

"But he begged you to go to Montana with him. He must still love you."

"Yes, he did. But I think we both realized if I had gone, we would just be postponing the inevitable." Enid looked up at Cassie and smiled. "He told me today I reminded him of Rosie. I sensed that part of him wants me to stay after this story. It's just that he's struggling with how to be loyal to his mother and to me." Enid hugged Cassie. "Thanks for listening."

"You'll work through all of this. I'm sure of it." Cassie walked toward the door. "Come on down when you're ready. I'll have us some wine and cheese on the porch."

Enid nodded, but her thoughts had already drifted back to Rosie.

CHAPTER 35

Enid drove to the edge of town and parked in front of a red brick building. A small sign in front of it confirmed it was the home of the Madden Garden Club. She looked in the bottom of her tote for loose change to put in the parking meter and then remembered there were no meters in Madden.

She walked to the front of the building, looking up at its impressive exterior. It was clearly one of the most well-kept, attractive buildings in town. It boasted four Georgian columns, three stories high. Above the columns was a marble nameplate that looked like a scroll. Enid couldn't help but laugh to herself when she read it: "Blackwell Center."

She wasn't sure why she was here, as Cade had confirmed his mother had bought the family's reputation by paying for the building to be renovated. Still, she wanted to see it for herself and convinced herself it was her duty as a journalist to confirm her source's story.

A small plaque on the tall oak door instructed visitors to ring for assistance.

Enid pushed the button and waited. The door opened and a young woman about twenty-five-years-old appeared. "Hello, and welcome to the Blackwell Center," she said, smiling broadly.

"I'm just visiting in town and saw the name on the building. I'm Enid Blackwell."

"Oh, how nice. You must be related to our benefactor." The young woman motioned for Enid to enter. "Please come on in out of the humidity, and I'll tell you the history of the building. Part of this center is the Madden Historical Society, which is where I volunteer." When they were in the large entrance hall, the woman held out her hand. "I'm Betsy, by the way."

Enid thought of her first cat, a big orange male her mother gave her when Enid was ten. Her mother thought it was a female, and Enid named it Betsy, after Betsy Ross, whom Enid was studying in school at the time. Once they learned the truth about the cat's gender, her mother began calling him Betsy Boy. Enid remembered how much he liked to sleep at the foot of her bed. Enid's mother tried to shoo the cat away, but Betsy Boy always found a way to sneak back in.

Betsy led Enid across the waxed, wide floor boards to one of the small meeting rooms on the first floor. Enid sat on the one of terribly uncomfortable antique chairs. Every time Enid made a slight move, her chair wobbled on the uneven plank floors.

"Are you a Blackwell by birth or marriage?"

"By marriage. Fern Blackwell is my mother-in-law."

"I see. Well, our building has quite a history, if you'd like to hear it."

Enid listened while Betsy told the story of the cotton and tobacco exchanges that the old building once housed. Later, when agriculture declined in importance, the building was used as a medical clinic. Not too long ago, it was used for a bingo hall until it was condemned due to the leaking roof and sagging floors.

Betsy finally got to the part Enid was waiting for. "And then our wonderful benefactor, Mrs. Blackwell, brought this old beauty back to life." Betsy beamed and spread her arms out in a well-rehearsed gesture. Betsy reminded Enid of a younger version of Vanna White on "Wheel of Fortune," gesturing to the audience.

"I've never asked Fern about this building. In fact, I just learned of it recently. I'm curious as to why she would make such a generous gift to the town." Enid tried to look only casually interested. "Do you have any idea?"

"That was well before my time here. Perhaps you should ask her." Betsy shifted in her seat. "I understand the Blackwell family was once very prominent in Madden. In any event, we are very grateful indeed for her generosity."

"Yes, I'll have to talk with her about her generous gift." Enid looked around the interior of the house. "You have a lot of rooms here."

"In addition to the Madden Women's Club, the center also houses the historical society, a botanical society, and a bridge club." Betsy raised her hand. "Oh, and I forgot. The Jensen family uses the space for political campaigns and several charity events during the year." There was that rehearsed smile again.

Enid thanked Betsy for the history lesson. She also promised to check out the bake sale being held at the center tomorrow to raise money for new street lights.

"You don't want to miss it." Betsy was clearly in her comfort zone as hostess of the center.

"I won't," said Enid, although she was reasonably sure she would be among the missing.

Betsy opened the front door for Enid, and as Enid was leaving, she gasped. Chief Jensen was in front of the building talking to a woman. Enid walked out quickly and tried to avoid him. As she was near the sidewalk, she heard him call out.

"Ms. Blackwell. Are you looking for something? Perhaps I can help you."

"No, thanks. Just looking around." She walked away quickly, sensing Chief Jensen's watchful eye.

CHAPTER 36

When Enid got back to the inn that afternoon, she saw workers packing up their paint and other gear for the day. Cassie's car was gone. Enid retrieved her key from her tote and went inside. The hall lights were on and Cassie had left a note at the front desk with Enid's name in big letters on an envelope. The note said Cassie would be back late that night and that she had left a tray of sandwiches for dinner.

Just as Enid walked upstairs to her room, her cell phone rang and Cade's photo flashed on her screen. As soon as she answered the call, she knew it was bad news.

"Mother had a severe anxiety attack. At first they thought she had suffered a heart attack. She's resting comfortably now." Cade was in reporter mode, discussing his mother's condition matter-of-factly as a reporter, not as a son.

Fern was in the coronary unit for observation only, and the prognosis was good. Fern was a strong woman, in many ways. While Enid listened to Cade talk, she was mentally planning a return trip to Charlotte to see him and her mother-in-law. "I'm so sorry. I know you're worried about her."

"I think they'll let her go home in a day or so."

"I'll pack now and be there in a little more than an hour." Enid was gathering her things as she talked.

Cade was silent.

"If this is a bad time to talk, just call me back when you're free. I'll be in the car," she said.

"No. I mean . . . I don't think you should come here."

Enid was momentarily speechless. "But, of course, I'll come be with you. Fern and I might have our differences, but she's still family." Enid pulled her suitcase from the closet with her free hand.

"The doctor says she can't have many visitors."

"Well, then I'll just sit in the waiting area. I want to be there for you."

"I just, I mean, I don't think you should be here," said Cade.

Enid felt like someone had punched her in the stomach. She wanted to say something but didn't know what.

After a moment of silence, Cade added, "Look, I'm sorry, but it's just not a good idea."

"I understand." The last thing Cade needed right now was a fight with his wife. She kept her voice calm. "Will you keep me posted on how she's doing?"

"Just before her attack, Mother called me to find out why you were in Madden." His tone had changed.

"Did you tell her I was here?"

"No. I figured someone in Madden must have called her. She still has connections there, you know."

"Are you suggesting that my coming to Madden caused Fern to have this attack?" Enid hated the defensive edge to your voice, but she couldn't help it.

"Look, I've got to go. We'll talk later."

After Cade hung up, Enid sat on the bed a few minutes, deciding whether she should go to Charlotte anyway. Cade was just upset, and when he came to his senses, he would appreciate her being there. If not, well, she would deal with that later. Besides, he was an excellent reporter, but not good at handling family crises and medical issues.

Enid packed a few things, and left a note for Cassie. Black clouds covered the sky, so it was dark when she went to her car to put her suitcase in the back of the SUV.

She had her finger on the keyless ignition, ready to press it, when she heard the roar of a motorcycle pulling into the inn's parking lot. She quickly locked her door and checked the rearview mirror to see who it was.

Suddenly, Eddie, the bandana-man biker from the cemetery, pulled into the parking space beside her. He was racing his motor and glaring at Enid. She saw movement in the rearview mirror. His two companions were behind her, blocking her from backing out.

Hands shaking, she started to call 911. Eddie laughed and banged the handlebar of his bike against her car and began tapping it, harder and harder. Enid was giving the 911 operator her location when the biker took off in a roar. She looked in her mirror and all three of them were headed back down the long driveway to the main road.

She sat in the car, trying to compose herself. A knock on the passenger window made her scream involuntarily. Molly Anderson was standing there, looking in at her. She knocked on the window again.

"You okay?"

Enid unlocked the door and motioned for Molly to get in. She opened the passenger door and sat beside Enid. "You look white as a sheet. What happened?"

Enid locked the doors again and looked around her but saw nothing. "Did you see those bikers? They had me blocked in." Enid clasped her hands together to keep them from shaking. "I'm glad you showed up."

The 911 operator was trying to get Enid's attention. "Ma'am. Are you there? I'm sending someone to you now. Just keep your doors locked."

"Oh, I'm sorry. I'm here. Everything is fine now. Sorry to bother you. Please cancel the call." Enid hung up.

Molly patted Enid's arm to comfort her. "The county deputy will get the call, since we're just outside the Madden city limits," said Molly. She pulled her cell phone from her pocket and called a number. Molly explained to the sheriff's dispatcher that she was with the 911 caller and everything was fine now.

"Thank God you came along when you did," said Enid.

"I saw Eddie and those thugs of his driving off when I pulled in. Don't let them rattle you."

Enid remembered Eddie's warning at the cemetery. *"Later,"* he had whispered in her ear. "This isn't the first time." Enid told her about Eddie's harassing her when she visited Rosie's grave.

"Pinewood is no place to go alone. You're lucky it was only Eddie you ran into."

Enid laughed softly. "Only Eddie?" *What could be worse?*

Molly patted Enid's arm again, comforting her. "You feel like driving?"

"Yes, I think I've finally stopped shaking."

Molly put her hand on the car door handle to open it. "Then follow me. We're going to have us a girl talk. There's a place right down the road where can get a good glass of wine."

Enid was about to tell Molly she was headed to Charlotte, but then decided against a trip alone at night.

As Enid followed Molly down the road, she kept checking the mirrors and looking around for any signs of Eddie. When Molly pulled into the parking lot of a bar, only one other car was there. Enid made sure her doors were locked as she followed Molly inside.

As soon as they sat down and ordered, Enid excused herself to go to the ladies' room. She walked slowly down the dark corridor, giving her eyes a chance to adjust to the dim lighting in the bar. She sat on the toilet lid and pulled her phone from her pocket to leave a message for Cade to tell him she wasn't coming tonight, and then she remembered their conversation. He wasn't expecting her anyway. Not having anyone looking for you, or worrying when you didn't show up, was a strange feeling. With her parents dead, no other close family, and Cade moving to Montana, Enid was beginning to realize just how alone she was.

CHAPTER 37

Inside, the place looked safe enough. On one side of the bar was a restaurant, where several patrons, mostly older couples, were sitting in dimly lit booths eating dinner. On the other side, a handful of single men and women were sitting at the bar drinking. In spite of the "No Smoking" signs in the bar, a haze of cigarette smoke hung in the air.

Molly directed Enid to a small table near the back of the bar. Once seated, Molly nodded to the bartender, who promptly brought a bottle and two glasses to their table. Molly poured each of them a glass of the deep red wine and then held her glass up to toast Enid. "To your escape from Eddie."

Enid took a sip, expecting to taste a cheap red blend. Instead, it was bold and delicious. "This is a great Cabernet Sauvignon."

"Glad you like it. They keep this in stock for me." Molly laughed. "Not that I get to come here that often."

Enid smiled politely, as she recalled the bartender's quick response when Molly walked in.

For twenty minutes or so, the two women engaged in small talk about the town, and about the weather and other mundane topics. When the conversation ran out of steam, Molly put her glass on the table and leaned back in her chair. In the semi-darkness of the bar, Enid could see that Molly had been beautiful in her younger years. A few extra pounds and wrinkles did not obscure her former self.

"Thank you for saving me tonight," said Enid.

"Good thing I happened along when I did. I dropped by to see Cassie. Didn't know she wasn't at the inn." Molly glanced around to see who was in the bar. "I'm going to tell you this for your own good." She glanced around again. "You need to steer clear of Eddie and his gang."

Enid stiffened. "Believe me, I had no intention of getting anywhere near them."

Molly picked up her glass and took a long swallow. "Mind if I give you some background on Eddie?"

Enid relaxed the tension in her shoulders a bit. "Please, do."

Molly leaned in toward Enid. "We have an agreement here in Madden with Eddie and his thugs. We don't bother them, and for the most part, they don't bother us."

Enid shifted her weight, trying to get comfortable on the hard wooden chair seat. "You seem to be suggesting I was bothering them." Enid studied Molly's face for her reaction but there was none.

"Rosie, God bless her soul, was foolish enough to get involved with them. And look where it got her."

"How was she involved with them? You mean buying drugs?" asked Enid.

Molly grabbed a few boiled peanuts from the bowl on the table. She opened the soft shell and put it to her mouth, eating the peanut and sucking the salty brine. She then surprised Enid by throwing the hulls on the floor. When Enid glanced around to see if others were looking at Molly, she saw a man at another table toss hulls on the floor also.

Molly threw her head back and laughed out loud. "You must have thought I was crazy, throwing those hulls on the floor." She pointed down to it, barely visible in the dimly lit bar area. "See, it's the custom here."

Enid squinted at the floor. "Yes, I can see that now."

The smile was gone from Molly's face. "Rumor had it that Rosie paid for drugs in an intimate way, if you know what I mean." Molly wiped her mouth with one of the cocktail napkins.

Enid took one of the boiled peanuts in her hand and rubbed its rough, dimpled surface with her thumb, trying to remember what reaction Eddie had shown when they talked about Rosie in the cemetery. All she remembered was the sneer on his face. She laid the peanut on her napkin. Somehow all those hulls on the floor had diminished her taste for peanuts. "Cassie told me you had mentioned it to her. She also told me the bikers shot her son. Was Eddie the one who killed him?"

Molly's eyes narrowed slightly. "Eddie was just a kid then. His older brother, Sam, was head of the gang, and most folks think he was responsible."

"Was Sam ever arrested for the killing?"

"Sam got killed himself not too long after that. Infighting in the gang, you know." Molly ate another boiled peanut.

"Do you think Sam could have killed Rosie too?" asked Enid.

Molly wiped the peanut brine from her hands with the napkin. "Maybe." She reached behind her for her purse hanging on the back of the chair. "I'd just be careful where you start poking around." Molly's face smiled, but her eyes did not. "Like they say, let sleeping dogs lie."

"Wait. Before you go, I'd like to ask just a couple more questions. I really would appreciate your help."

Molly eased back in her chair. "Sure. I've got a few more minutes. Shoot."

Enid tried to relax and think before she spoke. "I realize you've worked for Chief Jensen a long time—"

Molly interrupted her. "Nearly twenty years."

Enid considered how to continue. "And I know you're loyal to the family."

Molly looked at Enid without expression.

"I need to ask you something. Do you think his son Ray was involved in Rosie's murder?"

Molly continued to look at Enid with an unblinking stare. "No."

Enid shifted her weight on the hard seat. "Can you tell me why you feel that way? After all, he was involved with Rosie."

"I've known Ray since he was a little boy. He's got his father's confidence. Some call it arrogance. Oh, he can get into some mischief, no doubt about that." Molly leaned in toward Enid. "Let's just say I wouldn't take on the Jensen family either, any more than Eddie. I'd be real careful."

Enid looked at the nearly empty bottle, wishing she had another glass to fortify her. "I have to look at everyone in Rosie's life, that is if I'm going to write about her. You understand that, don't you?"

Molly continued to stare at Enid.

Deciding she had nothing to lose by continuing, Enid asked, "I have one more question. I discovered some information about Rosie I'd like to ask you about."

Molly remained silent, and Enid felt the tension between them growing. Enid stayed focused on the questions, trying not to let Molly's stare rattle her any further than what the bikers had already done to her. "I've learned that Rosie's father was your brother, Frank Kelly."

A crease formed on Molly's forehead. "May I ask where you got that information?"

Enid drank the last sip from her glass. "I'm sorry. I can't reveal my sources." *How long it had been since she had said that to someone? She and Cade used to joke about journalist clichés while sitting on a blanket by the riverbank, sipping a bottle of cheap wine that cost a fraction of what she and Molly had been drinking.*

Molly looked at Enid with a steady gaze. "Paternity was never confirmed." She paused. "But there were rumors to that effect. Frank was a trifling, lazy man. Never amounted to anything. Rosie probably wasn't the only bastard child he produced. Although, Wynona Garrett was no saint herself."

"I didn't mean to upset you. Please understand, I'm not trying to embarrass anyone. I'm just trying to understand why Rosie was . . . why she led the life she did."

"Some people are just born into trouble. I just can't see where any good is going to come from you writing this story. Some things, and some people, are best forgotten." Those were the same words Fern had used.

"Did you know Myra lied to Rosie about her mother being dead? Were you part of that plan?" asked Enid

"I didn't know anything about it. Not at first anyway." Molly leaned in toward Enid. "Just stay away from Rachel. I don't want her involved. Understand? I'm sure you can appreciate my concern. She's my baby, and I don't want her upset." Molly stood up. "I got to go. You'll be fine going back to the inn." She walked over to the bartender and said something to him that Enid couldn't hear, and then looked back over her shoulder at Enid. As Molly left the bar, she called out, "I'm sure Eddie's long gone."

After Molly left, Enid asked the bartender if she owed anything on the bill. He told her it was taken care of. She tried to tip him, but he waved her away, saying Molly had left a generous amount.

Walking to her car, Enid glanced nervously around the parking lot. She didn't see or hear any bikers, so she got in her car quickly and drove back to the inn. Each time she checked her mirrors to be sure no one was behind her, she cursed herself for letting Eddie play with her head. Cassie had often said Molly was a lifesaver, and after tonight, Enid agreed. She had been lucky Molly showed up when she did.

CHAPTER 38

Enid pulled up in front of the glass and brick building and parked in one of the visitor parking spaces. She pulled down the visor and checked her makeup in the mirror. The freckles across her nose reminded her of Cade. *"I love those freckles,"* he had told her. She pushed the thought away and picked up her tote bag from the floorboard.

Inside the lobby, a lithe blonde woman appeared. "Welcome to OJ Development. How may I help you?" The woman was either blessed with beautiful teeth or she had spent a considerable portion of her annual salary for top-notch dental work.

"Hi, I'm here to see Ray Jensen." Enid offered her business card.

The woman glanced at the card. "Is Mr. Jensen expecting you?"

"No, but I only need a few minutes. Can you help me get in to see him? I'd really appreciate it." Enid showed the woman she, too, could flash an impressive smile.

"Have a seat here in the lobby. I'll see what I can do."

Enid walked around the lobby looking at the portraits on the wall. Apparently, Otto Jensen was the CEO of the company. Several other portraits hung on the wall. At the far end was one of a handsome young man with sandy hair and large

MURDER IN MADDEN · 181

blue eyes. Enid looked at the name plate: "Ray Jensen, Marketing Manager." She saw the family resemblance to Chief Jensen.

The sound of high heels clicking on the marble floors made Enid turn around. The woman walked over to her. "I'm sorry, but Mr. Jensen is not in the office today."

"I see. When do you expect him back?" Enid was careful not to challenge the woman's role as gatekeeper. She no longer had Enid's business card in her hand.

"Actually, Mr. Jensen doesn't work out of this office very often. He travels a lot." The woman pulled her shoulders back and pushed her breasts forward.

"I read your company website this morning, and I was under the impression OJ Developments purchased local farms for resale."

"Yes, that's right. But Mr. Jensen is involved in a number of other activities and committees that involve travel."

"I'd like to make an appointment to see him. When he returns, that is."

"You would have to talk with him about that, but I'll have him call you." Her smile had disappeared.

* * *

Shortly after leaving OJ Development, Enid heard a short burst of siren and then saw the flashing blue light in her rearview mirror. She glanced at the digital speedometer. *Thirty-five miles an hour.* She kept driving, assuming the officer was going to pass her and pursue the red Lexus that had just gone by at a high rate of speed. To Enid's surprise, the police car was right behind her and the driver motioned for her to pull over.

Enid looked in her tote bag for her driver's license. When she pressed the button to lower the window, she saw a familiar face. "Well, hello, Chief Jensen."

Jensen tipped his hat. "Ma'am."

"Since I wasn't speeding, I assume I must have a broken taillight or something."

Jensen leaned into the window, his jaw clenched. "Damn it! I thought I told you to stay the hell out of my open cases. What part of that didn't you get?" Drops of spittle clung to his lips.

Enid clasped her hands to keep them from shaking. "I'm not interfering with anything. As I told you before, I'm just asking about Rosie's life." A car passed them and Jensen threw up his hand at the driver before turning his attention back to Enid.

"I've got a good mind to throw your ass in jail." Jensen hit the car door with the palm of his hand.

Enid could feel a trickle of sweat between her shoulder blades. "I'm not breaking any laws. And what are you so worried that I'll find?"

Jensen glared at her.

"I know you're getting paid to look the other way while the bikers transport drugs through Madden."

Jensen looked her in the eye and then straightened up. He stood erect beside her car. "You get the information you need about Rosie's *life* and then get the hell out of Madden. And I mean quickly. Her *death* is a police matter. You are not to interview my family or my employees. Is there anything I have said that is unclear to you?"

Enid clenched her fists in her lap. "I understand. Completely."

Jensen tipped his hat again and then took several long strides back to his car. Enid was still shaking, now from anger, when he sped away from the shoulder of the road, throwing gravel into her car and leaving a cloud of dust behind him.

As she looked to see if the way was clear to pull out onto the road, a charcoal-colored Mercedes drove past her. The driver looked at her briefly, just enough for her to recognize Ray Jensen from his portrait in the lobby at OJ Development.

CHAPTER 39

Cassie and Jack left early that morning to go to Columbia, and Cassie had mentioned something about "taking care of business." Cassie, ever the attentive innkeeper, had left fresh muffins and scones, but Enid decided to go into Madden and have breakfast at the diner.

After eating a hearty meal of eggs, maple-cured bacon, and toast, Enid felt better but still suffered the effects of staying awake half the night. She decided to go back to the inn, as it was pouring rain, and she didn't want to be out in the weather. The inn would be quiet with Cassie gone and the construction work on hold. She could catch up on her research notes after a brief nap. Enid looked forward to curling up on the sofa in the library and pulling one of the cozy throws over her before dozing off to the sound of the rain on the roof.

The drive back to the inn took more time than usual because of the storm. Small tree limbs had fallen across the road, forcing Enid to navigate around them. She turned on the radio, and the announcer said heavy rain was likely all day. She hoped Cassie and Jack would have a safe trip home late this evening. They had planned to eat dinner at Al's Upstairs Italian, one of Cassie's favorite restaurants, so she didn't expect them until late.

Enid parked her car at the inn and fumbled in her tote to find the key to the front door. She decided not to worry with an umbrella since she would stay in the rest of the day, so she ran from the car to the front porch. She put the key into the lock, opening the inn's massive oak door.

Enid took her shoes off and left them by the front door before walking upstairs to change into dry clothes, something comfortable to lounge in. When she got to the top of the stairs, she stopped in her tracks when she saw the door to her room standing wide open. She had never felt the need to lock her room door, but she always kept it shut. After a moment's hesitation, she decided she must have left it open when she left this morning.

The first thing Enid saw when she walked into her room was her suitcase in the middle of the floor. The drawers of the tall cherry chest were pulled out and her clothes were strewn on the floor and bed. The mattress had been moved off to one side, as though someone had looked under it. After checking to see if anything obvious was missing, Enid reached into her tote for her cell phone. She knew the inn was not in the Madden city limits, but she decided to call Molly. She would know what to do.

Trembling, Enid looked in her contacts and called the number to the police station. A man answered.

"May I speak to Molly, please?"

Molly was out of the office running an errand for Chief Jensen, but the man told her he would notify the sheriff's office. He told her to go to a safe place in the inn and lock herself in until help arrived. Ignoring the officer's instructions, Enid ran down to the library and looked around. Nothing seemed to be disturbed. Enid pulled a chair over to the tall bookcase and felt her hand on top. Rosie's box and the coroner's file were still there.

Enid sat down on the sofa in the library and waited. A few minutes later, she heard the big brass lion's head knocker on the front door. A deputy sheriff's car was parked in front of the inn.

The deputy walked around inside the inn with Enid by his side. He knew Cassie and, in fact, had been a friend of Cassie's son, Mark. Enid told him she didn't think anything had been taken, but told him Cassie would have to do a thorough check when she got home.

As the deputy was finishing his report, Molly knocked on the front door, which was partially open, and came inside. "Enid, it's me, Molly."

Enid ran to Molly and, without thinking, threw her arms around her. "Oh, Molly. I'm glad to see you."

"I got a call from the officer at the front desk. He told me you had reported a break-in, so I got here as quickly as I could."

Enid filled her in on what had happened while the deputy finished his report. Molly assured the deputy she would make sure Enid was alright before leaving her alone.

"I don't understand what they were looking for," said Enid. "I don't have anything of value, at least not to anyone else."

Molly surveyed the room. "Perhaps you showed up before they found something worth stealing. Cassie's got some nice things here."

"Who would try to steal this heavy antique furniture?" asked Enid, gesturing around her.

Molly shrugged. "Who knows. May have just been some kids looking for money or other valuables they could sell.

Anyway, why don't you come down to the station and stay with me until Cassie gets home."

"No, but thanks. I need to call Cassie and let her know what's happened. I'll be fine here until she and Jack get back tonight." Because of Molly's loyalty to Chief Jensen, Enid decided not to tell her that the last place she wanted to be was anywhere near him or his jail. She also decided not to tell Molly that Chief Jensen had threatened to lock her up.

"I've already called Cassie. She and Jack are headed back now." Molly walked toward the door. "If you change your mind, you're welcome to hang out with us at the station."

* * *

A few hours later, Cassie and Jack arrived at the inn. Cassie immediately began fussing over Enid, who assured Cassie she was fine.

"What do you think they were after?" asked Cassie. "Everyone around here knows the inn is closed for renovations, so we don't have any cash. In fact, even when we're open, we rarely have anyone pay in cash these days."

Jack looked at Cassie. "Don't you think we need to tell Enid about our trip to Columbia?"

Puzzled, Enid looked at Jack, who was standing at the kitchen counter munching on a muffin and drinking a Diet Pepsi, and then at Cassie, who was sitting across from her at the kitchen table.

"I just feel so bad about what happened," said Cassie. "Something told me not to leave you here alone."

Enid slapped her hands down on the table. "Will someone please tell me what's going on."

Jack pulled a paper towel from the holder and wiped his mouth, and then he sat down at the table with Cassie and Enid. "We weren't intentionally keeping you out of the loop. Well, I guess we were, but our intentions were good. I hope you'll understand that."

Enid looked at Jack, more puzzled than ever.

"When you came to town and started looking into Rosie's murder, and then when Cassie told you about Mark's murder, she realized how much she regretted never pushing the police on Mark's investigation," said Jack. "So Cassie asked me to start doing some digging around about the Madden Police Department."

Cassie put her hand on Enid's. "I want to know why Chief Jensen never arrested the bikers for what they did. They killed Mark, plain and simple." Cassie's voice wavered. "Jack has a good friend who works for SLED, and he asked him to do some checking on the chief."

"Why didn't you tell me this when we talked? Were you afraid I'd say something?" asked Enid.

Cassie put her hand to her throat. "Oh, no. It's just that I didn't want to influence your research or pull you into my problems. Jack was afraid you might jump to conclusions about Rosie's murder if you learned that the chief was taking bribes. After all, it may or may not have anything to do with Rosie."

Enid looked at Jack. "You don't have much faith in my journalist objectivity, do you?"

Cassie jumped to Jack's defense. "I insisted that Jack not tell you about our own little investigation." Cassie wiped a tear from the corner of her eye. "The truth is, your determination shamed me into doing something about Mark's murder."

Enid walked over to the sink and looked out the window at the dark clouds still overhead. "Do you have hard evidence that Chief Jensen took a bribe from the bikers?"

"My contact at SLED has done some off-the-record checking, but if anything is really going to be done, it has to become an official investigation. I'm not sure we have enough information to get them to open a case against Jensen."

Enid walked back to the table and sat down beside Cassie. "Who knows about what you and Jack are doing?"

Cassie and Jack looked at each other. "No one, that I'm aware of," said Jack. Cassie agreed.

Jack pushed his chair back from the table and stretched his legs. "I know what you're thinking, but I don't think the break-in had anything to do with our trip. Besides, it was your room they tossed."

"My office was messed up some too," said Cassie. "But, other than someone going through my file cabinet, very little was disturbed and nothing taken that I can tell."

Enid rubbed her temples to ease the tension. "I think someone wanted to know what I've learned about Rosie."

Jack pulled his chair back up to the table. "You could be right, but it may be something less sinister."

"I need to find out what's going on," said Enid.

Jack slapped his leg with his hand. "No, *we* need to find out. That is, unless you've fired me as your assistant."

Enid pointed her finger at Jack. "No more secrets. Understand?" She then looked at Cassie. "You too, understand? There's enough of those in this town without you two adding your own."

Cassie nodded. "I promise. But you need to be careful. If Chief Jensen has been taking bribes from the bikers all these years, then you need to stay away from them … and him."

"Don't worry. I'm doing my best." Enid shivered as she thought about her encounters with the bikers and the chief.

"Cassie told me she gave you a gun," said Jack. "You need to carry it in that big tote of yours you live out of."

Enid nodded. "I left it on top of the bookshelf in the library, next to Rosie's box and the coroner's report."

"Well, it won't do you much good there. Get it now and keep it with you … just in case." Jack stood up. "I'm going to check around, make sure everything is locked up tight before I go. Maybe we're all getting paranoid and it was like Molly said, just kids seeing what they could find."

Cassie walked up to Jack and kissed him on the cheek. They reminded Enid of how much can be said between people who care for each other without saying a word. Enid felt a wave of sadness and loneliness wash over her.

CHAPTER 40

When Enid went down for breakfast, Cassie had already set a place for her on the library porch. Enid envied Cassie's cooking skills and vowed to cook more when she returned to Charlotte. The thought of home saddened Enid, and she longed for her old life, even if it hadn't been ideal. She and Cade had been happy once. Or at least she thought they had been. When did they begin to drift apart?

Her mother's illness had certainly put pressure on their relationship. Cade resented having to spend most of their savings for medical bills and private nurses. And then Enid gave up her career and starting working at a bank job she hated. While no one was to blame, the damage had been done. Somewhere along the way, Enid had lost herself. Learning about Rosie's murder had triggered something inside her—a desire to reclaim something that was missing in her life.

Cassie walked out onto the porch. "I hope you like the granola. It's a recipe Molly gave me. After Mark's funeral, well, you know how it is. You get lots of casseroles and chocolate cakes. Don't get me wrong, I was grateful. But I was especially thankful when Molly brought me a big container of homemade granola. It seemed to be the only thing I had an appetite for at the time. Later, I asked her for the recipe, and I've been offering it for breakfast at the inn ever

192 · RAEGAN TELLER

since. In fact, I named it Molly's Grand Granola in the welcome packet where guests pick their breakfast choices."

"Molly seems like the quintessential mother hen." Enid ate one of the juicy strawberries on top of the granola.

Cassie sighed. "Yes, she was a blessing. Still is, for that matter. In fact, I'm going to stop by and ask her to have one of the county deputies check on the inn while I'm gone to Charleston. I think those guys would do anything for her. She mothers them too."

"I hope you're not doing that on my account. I feel safe here while you're away." Enid wiped a drop of milk from the tabletop with her napkin. "The more I think about the break-in, the more I think it was just kids. Since mine was the only guest room occupied, it would be natural for them to go through my things. Besides, you're only going to be gone for one night."

"Oh, I know you'll be fine. I just feel bad about leaving you here alone, but this trip has been planned for a while. I'm looking for a few things for the inn, and Jack offered to go with me."

Enid smiled. "Ah, so Jack's going with you."

Cassie blushed slightly. "Oh, stop. It's just a shopping trip. You know, business. He's got some friends in Charleston who invited us to dinner, and I thought, well, you know, that it would be fun, since we'll be there anyway."

"I think that's great. Please go and have fun. Don't worry about me at all. I promise I'll be fine."

Cassie leaned over and hugged Enid's shoulders. "Just the same, I'd feel much less guilty if one of the county deputies at least drove by tonight."

Not for the first time, Enid was thankful the inn was in the county's jurisdiction, not Chief Jensen's.

* * *

Enid tossed and turned, unable to sleep. It was one of those nights that Cade used to describe as "all the snakes slithering into your head." Random thoughts kept popping up. And then she began to think about Cade and wondered if they could ever repair their marriage.

She tossed a while longer and tried all the tricks she knew for overcoming insomnia. First, she counted backwards from one hundred, but after two rounds, she decided that method wasn't going to work tonight. Another often-used trick was to name everything she was thankful for. Usually, the positive thoughts made her relax and go to sleep. Tonight, it was hard for her not to focus on Cade and what they had lost.

After another hour of tossing, she considered going downstairs for a cup of tea but decided against it. Around 3:00 a.m., she heard a car on the gravel driveway in front of the inn. Since her room faced the lake, she went out into the hallway and looked out a front window. A county police car was sitting there. He got out of the car and walked around the house before leaving a few minutes later.

Enid smiled at Cassie's fussing over her. Cassie reminded her so much of her own mother before she became too ill to worry about anything other than fighting for her own life. And then Enid thought about Fern. She was just as protective of Cade, but in a different way. Fern worried about image and appearances, not so much about his physical or emotional needs. Enid wished she and Fern could have been closer, but sparks had flown between them almost from the day they met, and the tensions had never eased. They had different values and different perspectives on what was important.

Enid crawled back into bed and finally dozed off.

The next morning, the sound of rain hitting against the windows woke Enid. She got out of bed and looked outside. It was pouring, and she heard thunder in the distance. The clock by the bed indicated it was nearly eight o'clock, so she must have gotten at least several hours of sleep.

Cassie had left Molly's Grand Granola and some muffins for Enid, but Enid decided to go into Madden and eat at the diner. With Cassie and Jack in Columbia, she was on her own. Today, she felt the need to be near people.

* * *

By the time Enid dressed and left the inn, the rain had stopped. The sky was still dark with heavy clouds, but at least it wasn't raining. Enid went out the front door and around to the side of the inn where her car was parked. The snakes were gone from her head this morning and she was ready get back into her research. Enid pulled out onto the highway and headed toward Madden. Driving down the two-lane road, she thought of Rosie and what kind of woman she might have been today if she were alive.

A short distance later, Enid noticed a dark green pickup truck following her. It never got close enough for her to see the driver, and after several miles, the truck pulled into a driveway, turned around, and headed back in the direction it had come. *Don't jump to any conclusions. There are lots of green pickups around here.*

CHAPTER 41

Enid walked into the diner and sat near one of the windows. A few older men in overalls sat at the table behind her, arguing about the reliability of the Farmer's Almanac predictions. A television was playing at the back of the dining area, and a newscaster from Columbia was talking about the danger of being outdoors during a thunderstorm.

After the waitress took her order, Enid stared out the window. Few people were out this morning. It was a workday, and in Madden, most people ate breakfast at home. Unlike Charlotte, where there was a Starbucks, Panera, or a fast-food place on every corner, Madden had one diner.

From where Enid was sitting, she had a clear view of the street in front of the police station. She was staring at it, lost in thought, when the door opened and the man she recognized as Ray Jensen came out and started walked briskly down the street. She watched as he walked in the direction away from town. The paved sidewalk ended about a block past the police station, so Ray walked on the shoulder of the road.

The waitress delivered a steaming plate of grits and scrambled eggs. Before Enid could stop her, the woman refilled Enid's cup with coffee.

Enid smiled at her. "That's tea."

"Oh, honey. I'm so sorry. I'm not used to anyone drinking anything but coffee." She picked up the cup and saucer. "I'll bring you a fresh cup."

Enid took a bite of the buttered grits and was amused at how her eating habits had changed since she had been in Madden. In Charlotte, she would have ordered a bagel and espresso at the coffee shop. Part of this change was her trying to blend in with the local culture, but partly it was because she had to admit she had been ready for changes in her life, even if it was only what she ordered for breakfast. Her marriage was in danger because she had foolishly thought only of what she wanted, without including Cade's needs. Isn't that what she had accused him of doing?

"Here, honey. Here's your hot tea." The waitress set the cup on the table. "You really like that stuff? I mean, I drink iced tea and all that, but I never had hot tea. Well, I take that back. I do sip it hot when I'm brewing a pitcher, just to see if I've got enough sugar in it. Know what I mean?" She smiled. "Enjoy."

Enid called out to the waitress as she was walking away. "Excuse me. May I ask you a question?"

"Sure, shoot." The attractive, thirty-something waitress put her hand on her hip and cocked her body slightly to one side.

Pointing to the town's main street, Enid asked, "What's down that road, past the police station?"

"Well, let's see. Nathan's Body Shop is right there past the station. And, well, that's about it. Funny, I never really go down that way much." She leaned in toward Enid to whisper. "Not the kind of place a lady goes unless she wants some real body work." She winked at Enid. "You know what I mean, 'hon?"

"Thanks. I appreciate the information."

* * *

After leaving the diner, Enid decided to drive past the police station to the edge of town, in spite of the waitress' comments. After all, it was broad daylight, and she was just going to ride by. Besides, even though Madden was small, she was still learning all the little side roads and shortcuts the locals knew so well, and she was just curious.

A little way down the road, a small frame house had several wrecked cars sitting in the yard. On a metal building next to the house, a wooded sign with crude white lettering confirmed it was Nathan's place. She drove past Nathan's, and on the next block was an abandoned brick building. The windows were boarded shut, and knee-high weeds were growing in front. A weathered sign painted on the side of the building indicated it had once been Jensen's Feed and Seed.

Enid drove past the building on the narrow two-lane road and passed a large oak tree that had apparently been hit by lightning, considering the long scar in its bark running nearly the entire length of it. The familiar tree reminded her that his was the road Jack had turned down when they went to see where Rosie's body had been found.

Glancing around to see if she was alone, Enid turned down the dirt road she and Jack had taken. After driving a short distance, she stopped suddenly. A dark green pickup with a rusted fender was parked in the same area where Rosie's body had rested. Two men were sitting in the truck talking, but Enid could only see the backs of their heads.

Suddenly, one of the men, the one in the driver's seat, saw her in the rearview mirror and turned to look at her. She was close enough to recognize Eddie, the biker. He started to get out of the truck when the second man in the truck turned to look at Enid. It was Ray Jensen. The shock of seeing Ray with Eddie momentarily hijacked Enid's attention, and she didn't notice that Eddie was out of the truck and walking toward her. When Enid saw him approaching, she put her car in reverse and backed up quickly. Eddie pointed his finger at her, pretending to shoot a gun.

Enid was shaking as she pulled back onto the main road and sped away. She kept looking in her rearview mirror to see if she had been followed when she realized that the biker knew exactly where to find her if he wanted to. She steadied her breath and tried to relax. *Just stay calm. Nothing happened.*

On the way back to the inn, Enid tried to listen to soothing music, but one thought kept popping up. *Whatever Eddie is up to, Ray Jensen must be involved.*

CHAPTER 42

The next day, when Jack and Cassie returned from Charleston, Enid pulled Jack aside to tell him about seeing Ray's secretive meeting with Eddie. Jack suggested they talk at the diner rather than discussing it in front of Cassie. With all that was going on, Jack was concerned about Cassie's emotional state.

They rode into town in silence. Enid thought about Cassie and her son, while Jack appeared to be lost in thoughts of his own. When they walked into the diner, the waitress that had served Enid breakfast yesterday approached their table. She recognized Enid and greeted her. When the waitress returned with a glass of iced tea for Jack and a cup of hot tea for Enid, she pointed to Jack's glass and grinned. "Now that's how you supposed to drink it 'round here." She looked at Jack and winked. "Right, Jack?"

After the waitress left their table, Jack leaned in toward Enid and spoke in a low tone. "What the hell were you doing following Ray Jensen?"

Enid explained what had happened. "I guess it was foolish of me to go down that road."

"You're like a moth drawn to fire. I worry about you."

"I'm sorry. I don't want you, or anyone, to worry about me. But the truth is, I'm tired of being bullied by Chief Jensen. I think he uses intimidation to get his way. Even if he was involved in Rosie's murder, or in covering it up, he's not going to go after a journalist, especially since he knows Cade's family has ties here. That would bring down his little empire."

"Maybe the chief wouldn't, but if the bikers got you, he could always say he warned you. Which, I might add, would be true. But Ray's a different story. I thought he had left his wild days behind him. After all, he's a leader in the community now, and I can't imagine he would risk his reputation being associated with Eddie."

The waitress reappeared with their food, so Jack waited until she was out of earshot before continuing. "One thing I do know is that whatever is going on is bigger than your story. I think it's time for us to see my friend Dan at SLED."

"You think we're in over our heads?"

Jack chuckled. "Definitely." He put two fries in his mouth and chewed vigorously. "I'll call him when we leave and see if he can meet with us soon."

CHAPTER 43

The rain sloshing through the roof gutters woke Enid. She got up and looked out the window. Dark clouds hovered over the inn. After showering and getting dressed, Enid sat at the small antique desk by the window and looked at her notes. Since coming to Madden, she had created more questions than answers.

She put her papers back in the large leather tote and went downstairs. Cassie was in Charleston again today to finish the shopping trip that had been interrupted by the break-in and wouldn't return until late afternoon. Jack had flown to Chicago for his sister's wedding. It was her third, but Jack said she seemed to be just as excited as a first-time newly-wed. Since the workers had finished the inside work, they wouldn't be able to work outside in the rain, so Enid was alone for the day.

She sat at the big table in the kitchen and nibbled at the edges of a blueberry muffin Cassie had left. The rain was still coming down steadily while Enid contemplated on how she would spend the day.

After finishing her breakfast, Enid took her notes to the library. Might as well make good use of the time. Otherwise, it would be a long, boring day. Her conversations with Cade nagged at her. Not just because of the tension between them, but something about his meeting with Madelyn Jensen worried her.

Using her iPhone, Enid searched for Madelyn Jensen online. Numerous hits were returned, showing Madelyn speaking at conferences, meeting with the head of a new women's center in Columbia, and other public appearances. Madelyn had even addressed the women's club at the Blackwell Center in Madden. Enid searched for Madelyn's law firm and got the address and phone number in Columbia. Enid glanced at her watch. It was probably too early for the office to be open, but she decided to try it. On the third ring, a woman answered. Caught off guard, Enid stammered. "I'm trying to reach Madelyn Jensen. Is this her law office?"

"Speaking."

Enid hadn't fully thought about what she would say, assuming she would just leave a message. "My name is Enid. Enid Blackwell." She heard a soft laugh on the other end.

"I was wondering how long it would take you to call me."

Enid wasn't sure whether to be surprised or angry. Obviously, Cade had called her about their conversation.

"Enid, are you there?"

Enid cleared her throat. "Yes. Sorry. I was wondering if I might, that is if you could—"

Before she could finish, Madelyn interrupted her. "Yes, I'll be happy to meet with you." She paused. "But not in Madden. And I won't talk on the phone."

"Then I'll be happy to come to Columbia if you tell me when it's convenient for you."

"How about today? I'm meeting with a client this morning, but my afternoon appointment just canceled. I'm free for lunch around 12:30."

"That would be great." Enid groaned silently at the prospect of driving in the pouring rain, but she didn't want to miss this opportunity. They made arrangements to meet at a restaurant.

* * *

Bourbon was a cozy restaurant just a block from the state capitol building in Columbia and known for its Cajun food. The place was packed. While they waited for a table, Madelyn talked to almost everyone who came in. She was obviously a regular here. When they were seated, each ordered a bowl of gumbo with andouille sausage. Looking around the restaurant, it reminded Enid of places where she and Cade had eaten in Charlotte. She pushed the thought from her mind.

Enid wiped the condensation dripping from the bottom of the glass with her napkin. "I really appreciate your meeting with me, especially on such short notice."

Madelyn pulled at the lapel of her jacket to straighten it. "Let's just get one thing out in the open." She paused, no doubt for a dramatic effect she had practiced in the courtroom many times. "No, I didn't sleep with Cade." Madelyn stared directly at Enid long enough to make her uncomfortable.

"I'm not sure how to respond to that." Enid despised herself for feeling diminished by Madelyn. "Cade said the same thing."

Madelyn sipped her water. "And did you believe him?"

Enid wasn't sure what she believed at this point and was uncomfortable with the way the conversation was going. "The reason I'm here is that I'm doing research into Rose Marie Garrett's murder."

Madelyn laughed. "He said as much. I think he said something like you were going to finish the job he started."

Enid was annoyed with Madelyn's familiarity with Cade. "Look, I'm not here to talk about Cade." As much as she hated to admit it, Enid could understand why Cade would be attracted to this woman. She was smart and attractive, in a disarming sort of way. "I want to write about Rosie's life, not solve her murder."

Madelyn looked at her intently. "Really. And how do you separate the two?"

Enid recalled similar words from Cade. She forced herself to relaxed the tension in her shoulders a bit. "I admit, it's not as easy as I'd hoped. I want to show what kind of person she really was, not the one portrayed in the articles and in Madden gossip."

A tall man walked over to their table and talked to Madelyn about a court date, so Enid tasted her gumbo. It was delicious. Knowing how much Cade liked gumbo, she wondered if he had been to this restaurant with Madelyn.

After the man left, Madelyn turned her attention back to Enid. "Sorry for the interruption. Where were we? Oh, yes. You were telling me you're your own woman, and you aren't trying to show Cade up." Madelyn laughed. "I'm sorry for being such a bitch. It just comes naturally in my line of work."

Enid smiled. In spite of herself, she was beginning to appreciate the woman's straightforward manner. Out of habit, Enid glanced around to see if she recognized anyone sitting nearby.

"Don't worry," said Madelyn. "You're not in Madden. You can relax."

"Until this minute, I hadn't realized how nice it was to be away from all the problems there."

"It's a great little town, or at least it could be, in spite of my family's influence." Madelyn gracefully tucked her hair behind one ear. Somehow she made such a simple gesture look seductive. While Madelyn was aware of her own beauty and used it to her advantage, she did not appear to be vain at all. "I understand why you are disappointed in Cade. I admit, I was too." She looked directly into Enid's eyes. "But he had his reasons. Let's face it, we all do things in the name of family that we wouldn't otherwise do."

"Cade mentioned that you felt your uncle, Chief Jensen, might be involved with the bikers."

"I'm sure of it. I'd rather not go into detail, but just trust me on this one."

Enid wasn't sure she was ready to trust Madelyn completely. She reminded herself that Madelyn, like most good attorneys, was persuasive.

They finished the meal talking about their favorite restaurants. When the waiter left the bill on the table, Madelyn put her credit card on top of it. "Lunch is on me." She waited until they were alone again before continuing. "May I ask why my uncle's involvement with the bikers is of interest to you?" Her tone was Madelyn-the-attorney again.

"Everyone seems to be convinced that Rosie was buying drugs from the bikers and that they killed her, yet the autopsy didn't show any drugs in her system. She was a healthy young woman."

Madelyn studied Enid's face. "And what do you think?"

Enid weighed just how much she wanted to open up to Madelyn. "I honestly don't know at this point. What I do

know is that Rosie became disillusioned with her family—
for good reason. After she was killed, her family just wanted
to forget about her. I think she deserved better, no matter
what happened."

"I heard about the Blackwell family making a big donation to the town to buy back their reputation." Madelyn
paused and then leaned forward, speaking softly. "Uncle
Dick is paid by the bikers to look away from their drug business. I know it, and I'm pretty sure I can prove it. As you
know, I'm an officer of the court, so I'm in a difficult situation, both legally and with my family." She leaned back and
shook her head. "But I'm not getting involved. I promised
my mother I'd leave him alone. That's why I turned to Cade.
He may be able to do what I can't."

"Are you convinced the bikers killed Rosie?"

Madelyn stared at Enid as if sizing up a witness on the
stand. "Actually, no. I'm not." She smiled. "Does that surprise you?"

"Nothing about this mess surprises me anymore." Enid
hesitated. "I know you need to get back to your office, but
I need to ask one more question."

Madelyn remained silent but nodded consent.

"What about Ray Jensen?" asked Enid.

"What about him?"

"Is he corrupt too?"

As a good attorney would, Madelyn avoided Enid's question and responded with her own. "Are you aware Ray was
in love with Rosie?"

"I knew they were close friends, and that he sometimes
supplied drugs for Rosie."

Madelyn signed the charge slip and put her credit card back in her purse. "Maybe you need to talk with Ray yourself. I'd rather not speak for him. In fact, I assumed you already had."

"I tried." Enid wiped her mouth with the napkin from her lap. "Maybe you could set something up with him. For me to talk with him, I mean."

Ignoring Enid's request, Madelyn stood up and flashed her attorney smile. "It was great meeting you. Good luck with your story." Madelyn walked over to another table and spoke to an older man there and then left abruptly.

CHAPTER 44

The next morning when Enid woke up, the sun was shining and the workers were back at work on the inn's renovations. She could hear hammering outside beneath her window. She checked her phone messages. Jack had decided to extend his trip to visit a cousin he had lost contact with, so he would be in Chicago a few more days. Before showering, she called Cade to ask about Fern's condition. She left a voice message and went downstairs.

"Hey, Sunshine," said Cassie. She gave Enid a hug. "Sorry I was so pooped last night. I wasn't much company." Cassie returned from Charleston late last night, exhausted from driving in heavy rainstorms that had now moved east, toward the coast.

"I was tired too." Enid decided not to tell Cassie about going to Columbia to meet with Madelyn. No sense in worrying her needlessly. Cassie was only a little older than Enid but had assumed the maternal role in their relationship. Her protectiveness reminded Enid how much she missed her mother.

Trying to sound casual, Enid asked Cassie, "Do you by chance know Ray Jensen, the police chief's son?"

Cassie sat down in the chair across from Enid. "Why do you ask?"

"He was close friends with Rosie, and I've been trying to talk with him."

"I see." Cassie studied Enid's face, as if looking for more information. "Well, of course, I know who he is, but I don't know him. At least not well enough to get you a meeting with him." Cassie stood up and walked back to the stove for more hot water. "But I know someone who can help you."

"Who would that be?"

"Molly is like a part of that family. I'll be glad to ask her to help you. Or you can ask her yourself."

"I don't think Molly appreciates me asking a lot of questions around town. She may not want to help me."

Cassie smiled. "Oh, of course, she will. That's just Molly being Molly. Like me, she's a bit overprotective at times, and she can be a bit grumpy. But I assure you, she's harmless. I'll ask her for you."

"I would appreciate it. Thanks." Enid put her dishes in the big farm-style sink. "I've got some things to do today, so I'll see you later this afternoon."

As Enid was walking away, Cassie called out to her. "Oh, wait. I forgot to give you something." Cassie walked into hallway and returned with a large FedEx envelope in her hand. "This must have come for you yesterday. It was on the porch when I got in last night."

"Thanks. It must have come while I was out." Enid took the envelope upstairs and sat at her desk to read it. She studied it twice to be sure she understood it. The message was clear. She and Cade were several months behind in their mortgage and the bank was giving them notice of possible foreclosure.

Enid stared out the window at the lake. She had lost her job and her husband. Now she was going to lose her house.

Why had she assumed Cade was taking care of all the finances? She'd call him later. Right now, she couldn't bring herself to have that conversation.

Enid heard a knock on her door, and then heard Cassie call out. "Enid, I've talked to Molly. May I come in?"

Enid forced a smile as she opened the door and offered Cassie the seat at the window. "That was quick. Your contacting Molly, I mean."

Cassie was sitting on the edge of the chair. "Molly said she was glad to help you, but Ray has left town. She wasn't sure when he'd be back. Some kind of committee meeting in Raleigh, North Carolina. That's too bad, I don't guess you'll be able to talk with him. Not right away, at least." Cassie stood up to leave. "Well, I'll let you get back to whatever you were doing." She glanced at the papers on the desk and walked over to Enid. Putting her hands on Enid's shoulders, she squeezed affectionately. "Everything will work out. You'll see."

After Cassie left, Enid sat on the bed and considered her next steps. The path she was on had cost her a lot. Or maybe these changes had been inevitable, and she had just hastened the process. At any rate, she now had to deal with the fallout sooner rather than later. She rubbed her temples to ease a throbbing headache.

Reluctantly, she picked up her cell phone and called Cade. His familiar voice mail message only worsened her sense of doom and failure. "Cade, it's me. Call me. We need to talk." She then added, "It's about the house." She threw the phone on the bed and lay down, tempted to pull the covers over her head as she had done as a child when she was afraid of monsters lurking in her bedroom. Her mother never tried to tell her the monsters weren't real. Instead, she encouraged Enid to "be brave and don't let them scare you." Looking back, Enid realized her mother was talking as much to herself as to Enid. When did her mother become so fearful of everything? The only thing she didn't appear to be afraid of was her own death.

Enid resolved to stop worrying about the foreclosure, her job, their marriage, and everything else that was on her mind. Instead, she decided to go into town. She dressed and was headed out the door when the phone rang. It was Cade. For a moment, she was tempted to avoid him and then realized how foolish that would be.

"Hi. Thanks for calling me back. First, how is Fern?"

"She's doing much better."

"Tell her I asked about her. Or maybe I'll give her a call.

"I'll give her the message."

"The reason I called is that I got a foreclosure warning on the house."

Cade remained silent.

"Cade? Did you hear what I said?"

"Yes, I heard you. The problem is we don't have enough savings to catch up our mortgage. Enid, look, I'm . . . I know you're . . . Damn! How did we get so screwed up?"

Enid laughed softly, in spite of the ache in her heart. "Yeah, we really messed it up this time." She added in a more serious tone, "You were handling the bills. Why didn't you tell me we were behind? Maybe we could have done something."

"I didn't want to worry you or make you feel even more trapped in your job. I never said anything to you, but I knew you weren't happy at the bank."

"Okay, look. I'll call the bank and see what I can do." She stopped herself. "But what is the point? I mean, if you're in Montana, and I don't have a job." *Or a husband.* "I'll call them. Maybe we can at least salvage our credit. A foreclosure would keep you from buying a place there."

Cade said softly, "You're not coming here, ever, are you?"

Before she lost her composure, Enid replied, "I don't think that's the solution. Goodbye, Cade."

CHAPTER 45

Enid heard the phone ring somewhere. It sounded like it was underwater. She pushed the duvet away that had been covering her head and reached over to retrieve her phone from the bedside table. Dried tears caked her face. She reached for a tissue and blew her nose.

"Hello?"

"You sound like you were asleep. Did I wake you?" asked Jack.

"I was just taking a nap."

"At two o'clock in the afternoon? You've gotten lazy while I've been gone." When Enid didn't reply, he added, "Are you alright?"

"I'm fine."

"I just got back from Chicago last night, and I talked with my friend Dan at SLED this morning. He can meet with us this afternoon if you're up to a little road trip." He added, "I'll even throw in dinner."

Enid ran through a list of excuses she might use, but none seemed plausible. Catching a glimpse of her face in the mirror, she cringed. "Okay. I should be ready by the time you get here."

* * *

The drive to Columbia was short and there was little conversation. Jack pulled into the parking lot at the Lizard's Thicket restaurant on Broad River Road. "We're meeting him here since this conversation is off the record."

As soon as they sat down at a table inside the restaurant, a friendly blonde waitress appeared. "What y'all having?"

"We'll have two teas. One sweet, one un," said Jack. A tall man in khaki pants and a light blue shirt walked in and sat down. "Add another unsweet," he said.

Jack introduced Enid to Dan and then they talked about the USC Gamecock's fall season for a few minutes.

Dan turned to Enid. "Jack told me you were writing about Rose Marie Garrett. You were related to her somehow?" He glanced around the room, which was practically empty this time of day.

Enid nodded. "Yes, she was my husband's cousin."

"I see," said Dan. "But you wanted to talk about Police Chief Dick Jensen, is that right? And this is somehow related to your story?"

Enid gave Dan a brief summary of what they had learned about Rosie's death, while he listened attentively. At the end, she said, "When I began this story, it was about her life. I assumed the killer was dead or long gone by now."

"And what do you think now? Do you think Chief Jensen was directly involved in Miss Garrett's death, or you do think he merely botched the investigation?"

"Before I answer that, can I ask you a question?"

Dan remained silent, waiting for her to continue.

"Is Chief Jensen under investigation?" she asked.

The waitress appeared to provide drink refills, so everyone was quiet until she left. A man came in and sat down in the booth behind them. Dan glanced back to see who it was and then leaned in to reply in a low voice, directing his comment to Jack. "You know I could lose my job for talking to two reporters."

Jack grinned. "You're safe, since neither of us are reporters any longer. I'm sort of retired, and Enid doesn't work for a newspaper."

"That's not very reassuring" said Dan, looking at Jack. "I trust you, but this conversation is way, way off the record, okay?"

Both nodded in reply.

"Chief Jensen has been on our watch list for a while. He, well, let's say, we haven't caught him red-handed, but he appears to skirt around the edges of the law. We had an informant tell us he paid the chief to look the other way. This was about five years ago. We snooped around a bit over there but found nothing solid to substantiate that allegation."

"Are you still investigating him?" asked Enid.

"Not actively, but his name comes up from time to time, so we have an active file on him." Dan shifted his weight to get more comfortable on the hard plastic seat. "You've got to understand, though, in small towns, especially where the family is as entrenched as the Jensen family is, they play by different rules. Things that we may consider out of line are often routine in places like Madden. For example, I can't accept a fruit basket at Christmas from a grateful family, but Jensen probably gets a dozen pies during the holidays. It's all relative and it may not seem fair, but unless we can prove Jensen actually took money from someone doing something illegal, then we've got nothing."

Jack leaned forward. "Who supposedly paid off Jensen? One of the bikers?"

Dan wrapped a paper napkin around his glass to absorb the moisture and then took a sip. "I'd rather not confirm any specifics, but that wouldn't be a bad guess."

Enid responded to Dan's earlier question. "I think Jensen knows who did it. The popular vote around Madden is that one of the bikers killed Rosie during a drug buy."

"But you don't believe that?" asked Dan.

"Rosie was a troubled kid. She was disillusioned and felt betrayed by everyone close to her. She may have played around with drugs a bit, but there were none in her system, according to the coroner's notes. She was never arrested or treated for addiction, and I think the family, my husband's family, would have intervened if she had a drug habit."

"That still doesn't implicate Jensen," said Dan.

Jack jumped in. "No, it doesn't. But he's pushing that story awful hard. Too hard, if you ask me. What have you heard about Ray Jensen, the chief's son?"

"Ray refused to say anything. He said he didn't know anything and didn't want to get involved."

"Did you believe him?" asked Enid.

Dan shrugged his shoulders in reply and glanced at the time on his phone screen. "I've got to get back." He put his phone back in the case on his belt and looked at Enid. "If you have specific information that he was involved in Miss Garrett's death or that he deliberately misdirected the investigation, we want to know about it. You, or anyone else, can give us an anonymous tip." He stood up to leave. "But I need specifics."

Jack left money on the table for the teas, and he and Enid followed Dan out to the parking lot. Jack shook Dan's hand and thanked him. Dan appeared to be uncomfortable talking outside, and quickly got in his car. "Don't forget Garrett's murder is still an open case. As civilians, you don't need to be sticking your nose in it." He held up his hand to keep Enid from speaking. "I know—you're just writing about her life." He put the key in the ignition and started the car. "And don't misunderstand what I said about small town law enforcement. Underestimating Chief Jensen because he's a small-town cop would be a mistake. The less involvement you have with him, the better."

After Dan drove away, Enid said to Jack, "That meeting wasn't very productive."

"I know it seems that way, but Dan plays everything close to the cuff. He'll go back and document everything you said, as coming from a confidential source, and add it to Jensen's file. If Jensen is dirty, they'll get him eventually. In the meantime, he's right about staying as far away from Jensen as you can."

After Enid and Jack got in the car, and Jack looked at the time on the car radio. "It's a bit early for dinner, but we can hang around Columbia for a while. There's a great little Italian Restaurant, the Villa Tronco, where we can eat dinner later."

Enid focused on checking the text messages on her phone. "Sure, sounds good." One, in particular, caught her attention. "On second thought, I'm a little tired. Can we do dinner some other time? I'd like to get back to Madden."

"Sure." Jack sounded disappointed. "Everything okay?"

Enid nodded. The message from Ray Jensen was clear:

"I'll be in touch. Don't tell anyone about this message."

Thanks, Madelyn. You came through for me after all.

CHAPTER 46

Cassie walked into the inn's library where Enid was staring at her laptop screen. "You working?" asked Cassie.

"Just checking on a few things." Enid closed the laptop.

"I called Molly again to see if she had any more news on reaching Ray Jensen. She said he's hard to reach these days, but she'll see what she can do." Cassie sat down in the chair across from Enid. "She said she was worried that you're getting yourself in too deep with this story about Rosie."

"In too deep? What exactly does that mean?" Her tone was harsher than she intended.

Cassie's face showed her concern. "You keep saying you're writing about Rosie's life, not her murder. And I realize the two are inseparable in many ways. But it does seem like you're playing detective." Enid started to speak but Cassie held up her hand. "I know you're tired of everyone telling you to be careful. But we care about you."

Enid stood up and gathered her tote bag. "You're right. I'm tired of people telling me to be careful. I know what I'm doing." Enid saw the hurt on Cassie's face. "Look, I appreciate your concern. But it's time for the truth to be told. And it's time for me to do what I think is right. I've been playing it safe all my life. I took a better paying job to make life easier, or so I thought. I watched Cade's journalism career progress while I focused on taking care of Mother." And to take care of Cade. She stopped to gather her composure. "I don't regret any of it. I did what I thought was right at the time. But now, I'm going to give Rosie a voice and make sure she's heard."

"Are you sure you're doing this for Rosie and not for you?" Cassie's expression reminded Enid of her mother's when Enid had tried to convince her mother she had taken the job at the bank to advance her career. Her mother knew, in the way mothers know these things, that Enid was making a big sacrifice to take care of the mounting medical bills. *"Are you sure you're not just doing this for me?"* Her mother had asked with the same anxious expression Cassie had now.

Enid stood up again to leave. "I appreciate your concern, and your friendship. But if you can't support me, at least don't try to stop me." She walked out of the room, sorry that she had been so abrupt with Cassie.

Half way up the stairs, she heard her cell phone ring. She tried to retrieve it but couldn't reach the bottom of her tote without losing her balance. At the top of the stairs, she dug down into the large bag and felt the now-silent phone in her hand. Checking the missed calls, she saw a local number she didn't recognize.

Enid went in her room and dropped off her things at the desk by the window. She called the missed number and it rang repeatedly, but no answering message kicked in. She was about to end the call when a male voice answered. "Hello." He spoke softly, with a refined Southern accent.

"This is Enid Blackwell. I believe you just tried to reach me." After a moment of silence, Enid assumed they had been cut off. "Hello. Are you still there?"

"I understand you've been trying to reach me," he said.

Enid was annoyed at the secrecy. "Who are you and what do you want?"

"My name is Ray. Ray Jensen."

Enid sat on the bed. "Ray?" She was momentarily speechless. "Thanks for calling."

"Madelyn asked me to call you."

Enid was struck by his obedience to Madelyn. She gathered her thoughts. "I'd like to meet with you."

"What do you want from me?" He didn't sound too happy.

Enid was afraid he was going to hang up. "I assume Madelyn told you that I am writing a story about Rose Marie Garrett, about her life." No reply from the other end, so she continued. "I understand you two were close friends."

"I'll meet you at the old tobacco farm on the south side of town. I'll text you the directions. Six o'clock this evening. And come alone." Before the call ended, he added. "Don't worry. I'm not the person you need to be afraid of."

Enid held the phone in her hand, trying, but failing, to take comfort in those last words. She was tempted to ask Jack to go along and hide in the backseat, but decided against it. She didn't want to do anything to jeopardize the chance to talk to Ray.

She decided to leave a note on her bed before she left. At least, if something happened, Jack and Cassie would know where she had gone and who she was meeting. She pushed her worry aside and focused on what she wanted to ask Ray. She'd have to keep it simple and short, as this might be her only opportunity to talk to him. *He knows something.*

CHAPTER 47

At this time of day, there's usually plenty of daylight left. This evening, the dark clouds overhead made it seem more like twilight. The old tobacco barn where Enid had agreed to meet Ray Jensen was leaning slightly to one side, its brown weathered siding hanging loose in places. Enid glanced around but saw no cars or sign of anyone. The car clock showed 6:05. Maybe he had already left, but surely he would have given her a few minutes' leeway.

By 6:15, the gathering clouds made it almost as dark as night. The wind had begun to whip the trees in the approaching storm. Enid started the car and was putting it in reverse to leave when she saw a vehicle driving up behind her. Her survival instincts kicked in, and she looked around at her escape options. The only way out now was going through the open field beside the road. She kept the car running until the man she recognized as Ray climbed out of his car and walked toward her. Because of the heat, her car window was down. As a precaution, she raised it slightly but left enough space to carry on a conversation.

Ray rapped his knuckles on the car window. "Get out and let's talk. Unless you want me to get in with you."

Enid turned off the engine and opened the car door slowly.

Ray must have sensed her reluctance and stepped back away from her car. "You wanted to talk to me, remember?"

Feeling a bit foolish, Enid got out and shut the car door behind her. Ray had his hands in his pockets and looked harmless enough.

"Can we talk over by the barn?" he asked. "There's an old bench over there we can sit on. This place belongs to my uncle. I come here sometimes to clear my head."

Enid looked behind Ray and saw an old wooden bleacher that appeared to have been on a high school football field. It was sagging in the middle, and whether it could hold both their weights seemed questionable. Ray surprised her when he took a cloth handkerchief out of his pocket and laid it on the rough wooden plank for her to sit on. "Don't worry. It's clean—the handkerchief, I mean."

Enid relaxed a bit and sat down on the neatly pressed white square. "Thanks," she said. Ray sat slightly away from her but close enough to carry on a quiet conversation. "I appreciate your meeting with me." Even though she was becoming more comfortable with Ray, she kept her tote close by, taking comfort that the gun Cassie had given her was in it. She mentally calculated how long it would take her to reach into the bag and grab the gun if she had to.

Forcing herself to breath normally, Enid turned slightly on the bench to face Ray. "Do you mind if I get my pad and take a few notes?"

A bolt of lightning illuminated the sky. Ray looked up at the clouds.

"Looks like we're going to get a storm." He leaned forward, resting his forearms on his legs and putting his hands on the back of his neck. He massaged the base of his skull a few times. "Madelyn says you're writing an article or something about Rosie. I don't want to be a part of it, but I'll tell you what I can. But only off the record." He pointed to Enid's notepad she had pulled out of her tote. "I'd feel better if you wouldn't write any of this down."

Enid had always admired Cade's ability to remember long conversations without notes. After years as an investigative journalist, Cade had honed this skill, but Enid had trouble remembering a grocery list unless she wrote it down. Hopefully, with practice, she'd at least regain what recall abilities she had at one time. Enid smiled inwardly when she realized the irony of not being able to remember any of the mnemonic techniques her journalism professor had taught her.

"Alright, that's fine." Enid's mind was racing. Should she start out with the easy questions to build rapport with Ray? But maybe he would only answer a few questions so she needed to jump right to the meaty ones. *I hate being rusty. Just relax.*

"What was your relationship with Rosie?"

"We were . . ." He seemed to be looking for the right words. "Special friends." He looked away toward the dirt road leading to the barn.

"I'm not sure what that means. Were you platonic friends?" She paused. "Or more special than that?"

Ray continued to stare off into space, lost in a world that didn't include Enid. She waited until he spoke. "We were more than just friends. At first, we were just two kids pissed off with our families. That was our common interest." Even after more than a decade, he appeared to have difficulty characterizing his relationship with Rosie.

He continued, "I guess you know all about that crap her family pulled on her—telling her that her mother was dead."

Enid nodded.

226 · RAEGAN TELLER

Ray wiped the dust from the soft leather of his brown loafers. Enid recognized them as Bruno Magli only because she and Cade had looked at them in a store and laughed, wondering who would pay that much for a pair of shoes. Cade ended up with a pair of knockoffs at a third of the cost.

"We never had sex." Ray smiled slightly. "Not because I didn't want to. But she needed a friend more than a tumble in the hay." He paused. "I guess I loved her. In my own way."

The wooden bench was getting harder by the minute, and Enid shifted her weight trying to get some relief. "I know Rosie did drugs. And I've been told the two of you used together—that you supplied her."

"We were kids, experimenting, trying to forget. We got caught a few times. My dad threatened to send me to a military boarding school if I didn't stop seeing her. One time, Molly caught me and Rosie in the barn on their farm. Rachel was there too. I've never seen Molly that mad. She was sure me and Rosie had gotten Rachel hooked on drugs." He slapped at a bug that had landed on his arm. "Goes to show how much Molly knew her daughter. Rachel was always telling us to straighten up and quit. She fussed over us like a mama hen."

"Where did you buy the drugs?"

"At first, I got weed from a friend of mine. That was fine for a while, but then Rosie wanted something stronger. I only used drugs a few years, and then I quit. I tried to get Rosie to quit too, but when she found out about her mother, she became self-destructive." His cleared his throat. "Then one day I found her in the tool shed behind Myra's house. She had passed out. I couldn't get her to wake up and got scared. I ran in and told Myra to get her to the emergency room." His voice cracked. "Rosie wouldn't speak to me after that, because she got in big trouble with Myra. Rachel later told me Rosie had started buying the hard stuff from Eddie. You know, from the biker gang. I went to see Rosie a few times, to tell her to be careful, but she refused to see me. Myra was really worried about her. I was too." He wiped his eye with the back of his hand. "Then one day, out of the blue, Rosie came to see me and asked me to take her to a job interview. I was supposed to pick up her the day she was … you know, the day she disappeared."

Enid pulled a tissue from her tote and handed it to him. "What happened that day? Did you see her at all?"

He shook his head. "I was supposed to pick her up at the corner, but I was running late. When I got there, I didn't see her anywhere. I drove around trying to find her, and then went to the insurance agency where she was supposed to have the interview. They said she never showed up. I waited there for over an hour and then went back to Myra's to see if she was home. I never saw her again."

He turned his back slightly to Enid and cried softly. She wanted to comfort him but decided to leave him alone with his memories of Rosie.

After a few minutes, he turned back to face Enid. "I figured she had blown off the interview. I was mad at her for being irresponsible." He blew his nose with the tissue. "Sorry. I guess I had a lot bottled up inside. I should have trusted her and realized something was wrong. Maybe I could have done something to save her."

"I'm sure there was nothing you could have done. And please don't apologize. I'm sorry this interview is painful for you." Enid hesitated. "Do you feel like a few more questions?"

He nodded.

"I need to ask you the most obvious question." She looked at the sad young man sitting beside her, and her heart ached for him. So much for journalist objectivity. "What do you think happened to Rosie? Who killed her?"

Ray just sat there, and she wondered if he had even heard her.

"Ray?"

He started to say something but stopped. Instead, he shook his head. "I don't know." Ray was beginning to fidget.

"Do you think your dad, the chief, knows who did it?" *Did your father kill Rosie? Is he protecting someone?*

Ray stood up just as a few drops of rain began to fall. "Let's just say he knows more than I do." After he had taken a few steps toward his car, he turned back to Enid. "He sure as hell didn't lose sleep any sleep over Rosie's murder." Ray clenched his fists a few times before turning away again.

Enid called out after him. "Ray, wait. Please." She grabbed the handkerchief on the bench as she walked toward him. "Here, this is yours," she said as she held it out toward him.

"Keep it."

Enid decided to press him further or lose the opportunity forever. "I think Eddie killed Rosie and that your father was paid to turn his back." She waited for him to react but he just stood there, silent. "Why did you meet secretly with Eddie at the old grain store the other day?"

He hesitated before replying. "Eddie and I went to school together. For a while at least, until he got kicked out.

He's had a tough life and had to fend for himself. I hate that he turned to the gang and selling drugs, but he's not a bad guy." Ray laughed. "I can't believe I'm standing here defending Eddie."

"Are you saying he didn't kill Rosie?"

Ray kicked at a rock, stirring up dust that eventually settled on his shoes. "He swears he didn't touch her."

"And you believe him?" The rain had started.

Ray stuck his hands in his pocket and rocked back on his heels. "Yeah, I do, actually."

Enid's mind was swirling with a million things she wanted to ask. "The autopsy report said Rosie had goat hairs on her clothing. Where was she exposed to goats?"

He looked surprised and started to say something, but stopped and kicked at a rock. "I appreciate what you're trying to do, but you need to forget about her." He stiffened and spat out his next words, "Go home, Ms. Blackwell. You don't want to tangle with my father, and certainly not with Eddie. He's not a monster, but he'll do what he has to do to protect his business interests. Don't mess with him."

He walked briskly back to his car, started the engine, and drove away, spraying loose gravel in his wake. Enid stood in the rain watching the one person whom Rosie had loved and trusted drive away.

CHAPTER 48

Enid pulled into the inn's parking lot and saw Jack's car. She decided to go in the back entrance to avoid questions about where she had been. When she opened the back door, Jack and Cassie were sitting at the big kitchen table eating one of Cassie's famously good omelets.

"Jack, I'm surprised to see you here." She then said to Cassie. "I'm sorry I didn't let you know I was going out. Don't let me interrupt anything—I'll just head upstairs."

Jack stood up and pulled out a chair for Enid. "Oh, no you don't. You're going to sit down right here and explain yourself." Both Cassie and Jack looked at her with serious expressions.

Enid set her tote on the floor and sat in the chair. "Well, okay. But I'm not sure what I need to explain." *This is not going to be a good conversation.*

Cassie held up the note Enid had left on her pillow. "Maybe this will jog your memory. I found it when I went in to turn down your bed."

Enid sighed. "I didn't mean to alarm you, but I wanted to let someone know where I was."

"Dammit, do you have a death wish or something?" Jack shook his head. "I can't believe you went out to meet Ray Jensen alone, especially in an isolated location." Jack made a noise that reminded Enid of a horse exhaling air when it was being saddled. "Damn foolish, even for you."

"I'm sorry I worried you." Looking at Cassie's face, Enid's heart ached for her. "I can only imagine how you must worry because of what happened to Mark." Enid turned to Jack. "And, I know you lost someone close to you too. You don't know how much I appreciate the fact that you two care about me." She paused briefly. "But you're interfering with my work."

Jack said somberly, "Is this one of your 'I'm a serious journalist' speeches?"

Enid laughed, mostly at herself. "Yes, I am a serious journalist, and I was out doing journalist stuff."

Cassie walked to the stove. "Then I'll get you a cup of tea and you can tell us what you found out. Unless this is a private conversation. Maybe I should let the two of you talk."

"No, of course it's not private. Please stay." Enid filled them in on her meeting with Ray. "Ray confirmed Rosie got drugs from him and then later bought them from Eddie. In spite of what Ray said, I think Eddie, or perhaps one of his bikers, did it. Ray's perception of Eddie is from high school, and I think Ray might be blind as to who Eddie has become. He's more hardened that Ray described." Enid recalled Eddie's earlier warning at the cemetery. *Later.*

Cassie nibbled on a shortbread cookie. "Where does that leave Chief Jensen? Do you think he's involved?"

Jack had been silent but jumped back into the conversation. "Before we answer that question, I think you need to rethink the lead for your story. You keep saying you're writing about Rosie's life. But I think you are writing about her murder." When Enid started to speak, he held up his hand to stop her. "And I think you want to solve it."

Cassie stood up and went to the sink with her back to the table. "I can't watch another person I care about get killed by those bikers. I won't."

Enid turned to Jack. "I'm haunted by Rosie. I see her face in my sleep. When I think of how she must have felt, the fact that she couldn't trust her family any longer. I keep seeing her body in the woods." She cleared her throat. "I won't turn my back on her, too."

Cassie walked away from the sink and stood behind Enid, putting her hand on Enid's shoulder. Enid looked up at Cassie. "I'm going to find another place to stay. My being here has reopened old wounds for you. That was insensitive of me."

Cassie sat back in the chair and put her hand on Enid's arm. "No, you're not going to move out. My pain is not your problem." She squared her shoulders. "Besides, I'm the inn-keeper, not your mother. If you want to put yourself in danger, I can't stop you."

Jack stood up. "I can't stop you either, but I hope you'll reconsider. We don't know the bikers killed Rosie. Hell, it could have been anyone. And that person may or may not still be in Madden." He added, almost as though he were talking to himself. "But something's not right. We should be getting answers, not more questions." He looked at Enid. "You still got that gun Cassie gave you?"

Enid pointed to her tote bag. "It's right there."

"Good. Keep it handy. 'Night, ladies. I'm headed to the barn." He started to leave, then stopped. "Oh, by the way, I've got to go back to Chicago to take care of some family business."

After Jack left, Enid reached out and took Cassie's hand in hers. "I'm glad you're more than just the innkeeper. You remind me so much of my mother." She cleared her throat to keep from choking on her words. "Tomorrow is the anniversary of her death."

Cassie dabbed at her eyes with her napkin. "I'm so sorry, honey. You miss her don't you?"

Enid nodded. "I hate to admit it, but there were times when I resented her for getting cancer. I hated that I had to leave journalism and spend our savings on her medical bills." Her voice trailed off and she blinked away the tears. "But researching this story has made me realize that I can't rewrite the past, as Cade has accused me of doing. I have to own it and admit that I stopped writing because I didn't think I was good enough." She stared at the wall in front of her. "Cade is so much better than I could ever be. He was my role model, my idol."

"And now you resent him for giving up the life you wanted," said Cassie. "Your hero fell, and then he left you."

Enid buried her face in her hands and sobbed, releasing years of pain, sorrow, and confusion. Cassie brought her a box of tissues and set them on the table in front of her. "Turn out the lights when you go up. Good night, honey."

As Cassie was leaving the room, she turned back to Enid. "I want you to remember something. One of the reasons I've been so concerned is that I know you *have* to write this story. It found you, not the other way around. Maybe Cade is a better reporter than you are, but he doesn't have your heart. He could walk away—but you can't." She smiled and cocked her head to one side. "And don't you forget it. Me and Jack are both scarred—we're still healing too. But in a different way from you. This story is your way of healing. I see that now, and I know Rosie is up there smiling down at you," she said, pointing above. "Sleep tight."

And don't let the bedbugs bite. Enid's heart ached recalling the phrase her mother used to whisper in her ear each night.

CHAPTER 49

Cassie was going to be busy all day meeting with contractors about the finishing touches to inn's renovations, and Jack was flying to Chicago later, so Enid had the day to herself. She realized she had never asked Rachel about the goat hairs. Today would be a good day to tie up that loose end.

When Rachel answered her phone, her tone was sharp. "Why are you calling me? There's nothing else I can tell you."

"Rachel, wait. Please don't hang up," said Enid. "I just have a one question I forgot to ask you earlier." Enid could hear people talking in the background. "Are you at work?"

"Yes, and I need to hang up. My boss is going to be furious if he catches me talking on my cell."

"Okay, I'll be quick. Where could Rosie have come into contact with goat hair?"

"You mean a live goat, or like a sweater or something?"

Enid tried to remember the details of the coroner's report. She didn't recall anything about dyes or chemicals on the goat hairs. "Live goats, I think."

"I'm coming," Rachel yelled to someone. "Sorry, I really gotta go. There's a lot of goats around here, you know."

"So I've heard. But was Rosie around goats? Please just tell me."

Even though Rachael was anxious to hang up, she took a long pause before replying. "If I think of anything I'll call you." Rachel hung up, and Enid mentally filed the conversation away in her nice-try-but-this-was-a-dead-end box. Still, there was something about the conversation with Rachel that bothered her.

Enid thought about the local goat cheese Cassie often served. She jumped up and ran to the refrigerator. Pushing aside a carton of milk and a container of eggs, she found a small plastic container with a handwritten label on the top. "Spicy Goat Cheese." Enid remembered the tangy taste and how good it tasted with Cassie's homemade crackers. Enid pulled the container out to look at it. On the bottom of the container, a small printed label read "Robinson Goat Farm" but gave no other information.

Enid opened her laptop and did a search for the goat farm. Nothing came up. She tried several other combinations of words and phrases. *Who doesn't have a website these days?* Frustrated, she dug down into her tote and pulled out Helen's business card from the *Madden Gazette* and called her number.

After a few rings, Helen answered. Enid reminded her they had met with Jack to talk about Frank.

"Of course, I remember you. Did Jack give you the information on Frank ... what's his name?"

"Frank Kelly. Yes, thanks. That article you found was helpful." Enid resisted telling Helen about Frank's relationship to Molly, at least until Enid could make more sense of it. "I'm calling because I'm trying to find a goat farm, the Robinson Goat Farm. According to an article I found, I think the owner is Toby Robinson. Have you ever heard of the farm or know where I can reach the owners?"

"May I assume this has something to do with your story about that Garrett girl?"

"Maybe. I'm not sure at this point. I'm hoping the owners might be able to help me with a few questions I have."

"Hold on a minute." Enid heard the sound of typing on a keyboard. A moment later, Helen returned to the call. "Robinson Goat Farm is a subscriber, but the address is the Gazette's private information. I'm not sure how I can help you."

Enid tried to think of what Jack would do to get Helen to give up the information. He wouldn't have to do much, because Helen clearly worshiped him. "I understand. I'll just tell Jack you weren't able to help us. Thanks, and sorry to bother you."

"Now wait a minute. Did I say I wasn't going to help?" She made a slight grunting noise, and Enid smiled to herself. "Just don't go making headlines about where you got this information, that's all." Helen gave Enid the address of the farm and then gave her directions on how to get there.

"You've been a great help. I'll be sure to let Jack know."

"You tell him to come thank me personally." Helen chuckled and hung up.

* * *

About 20 minutes later, just outside of Madden, Enid saw a sign for Robinson Goat Farm beside the road. The sign was leaning and looked like a car had hit it while turning onto the narrow road. She was glad Helen had given her directions, because she doubted her GPS would have found this place. A white wooden fence separated the farm from the highway. The big white gate was open, so Enid drove through it. A short distance up the gravel driveway, she saw a woman walking from one of the well-kept barns. Enid parked the car and got out.

"Excuse me, ma'am. I'm looking for Mr. Robinson." The woman looked at her as if she had not heard Enid, so Enid walked a little closer.

"He's not here." The woman hesitated. "I mean my husband's dead." She held out her hand. "I'm Bonnie. Can I help you?"

"I'm sorry. I didn't realize he was deceased." Enid shook her hand. "Pleased to meet you, Bonnie. I'm Enid Blackwell. I'm a guest at the Glitter Lake Inn. You may know Cassie. She serves your goat cheese often."

Bonnie seemed to relax at the mention of Cassie. "Yes, I know Cassie. She's one of my best customers." Bonnie invited Enid to join her for some refreshments.

Enid followed her to one of the four rocking chairs overlooking the front lawn. The gray paint had peeled off the arms of the chair and weathered wood exposed years of wear. She envisioned Toby and Bonnie sitting out here for hours, talking about their little farm.

Bonnie returned to the porch with a pitcher of lemonade and small sandwiches made with cucumber and goat cheese on homemade rye bread.

Enid took a bite. "Oh, my. This is delicious."

"Thanks. That blend of cheese is, or was, Toby's favorite." Bonnie looked over toward one of the barns as if she expected to see Toby come walking up to the porch.

After a few minutes of small talk, Enid put her glass on the little table between them. "Of course, I'd like to buy some of this wonderful cheese while I'm here." She paused. "But I'd also like to ask you for some information."

"I'll be glad to help if I can. I think the world of Cassie."

Enid felt slightly guilty for leveraging Bonnie's friendship with Cassie in order to get information. But, as Cade had reminded her many times, a journalist does whatever it takes to find the truth. "I need information about goat farms in this area. Is there a list somewhere? Do all of you belong to an association or something?"

Bonnie wiped her hands on a napkin and brushed some bread crumbs from her lap. "Well, some of the dairy farmers, you know, the ones who produce cheese and milk, belong to the American Dairy Goat Association. But there are other associations some belong to, like the American Goat Federation."

Enid cleared her throat and jumped directly to the point. "I'm writing about Rose Marie Garrett's life. And about how she died. Did you know Rosie, by any chance?"

Bonnie instinctively put her hand to her neck and looked uncomfortable, reminding Enid that Rosie had been strangled. "I knew of her, but didn't know her personally. Poor girl." She dropped her hand from her neck. "I'm sorry, but what's that got to do with goats?"

Enid quickly debated with herself how much information she should give Bonnie and decided to be straightforward. "The coroner's report showed goat hairs on Rosie's clothing, and I was just wondering how she came into contact with them."

Bonnie studied Enid's face as if she were trying to read her thoughts. "Wouldn't the police have checked that out? It's been a good many years back, as I recall."

"Yes, it's been over ten years." Enid hesitated. "But the police apparently didn't spend a lot of time tracking down goat hairs."

Bonnie was quiet for a moment. "Me and Toby bought this place about a year after that girl, Rosie, got killed. It was already a goat farm when we bought it from Otto Jensen."

Enid felt the hairs on her neck bristle at the mention of Ray Jensen's employer. "You mean OJ Development Company?"

Bonnie nodded. "Yes, that's him." Bonnie pointed toward Enid's glass. "Can I get you a refill?"

"No thanks." Enid's mind was racing. "Did Otto work the farm himself before you bought it?"

Bonnie smoothed the legs of her mud-stained coveralls with her hands. "No, he was just the broker. The previous owners had leased the farm to another family. Mr. Jensen told us if we had any questions about running the place, we could talk to them. Mr. Jensen knew we had never owned a goat farm and probably figured we'd need the help. But we never had to. Toby did his homework before we invested in this place." Bonnie's eyes drifted back to the barn again. "He was a good man."

"I'm surprised you stayed after Toby died. It must be a lot of work for you. Alone, I mean."

"It's home." She paused and appeared to be composing herself. "I'll get you a list of the local dairy goat farmers if that would help you, at least the ones I know. Although, like I said, not all goats are dairy goats, and not all goats are on farms. You probably saw a few goats here and there while driving over here. It's not unusual to have goats in rural areas, especially if you need to keep an area cleared out. They'll eat anything, and I mean *anything.*" She laughed. "One time when Toby was alive . . ." She stopped and looked out across the big front lawn where several goats were chewing vigorously on something. She smiled. "I love these goats. I know that sounds silly, but they're my family now."

"That's not silly at all." Although, Enid couldn't imagine getting attached to a goat. "Can you also give me the name of the previous owners? They may be able to help me."

"I'll get that information for you, and the cheese you wanted."

Bonnie went inside, and Enid finished her snack while she watched the goats chew contentedly. *What a peaceful life this must be.*

When Bonnie returned, she gave the cheese to Enid but refused to take any payment. "Here, it's on the house. Besides, it was nice to have the company." She took a piece of paper from the pocket of her coveralls and handed it to Enid. "When you introduced yourself, I didn't connect your name with the previous owners."

"I'm sorry, but I don't understand."

"I checked the folders all our property papers are in and found the name of the previous owners. I didn't recall their names, because they didn't come to the closing, and we never met them."

Enid looked at the note Bonnie had given her and felt like someone had punched her in the stomach. The previous owners were Samuel and Fern Blackwell.

CHAPTER 50

"Hi, sleepyhead," Cassie called out when Enid walked into the kitchen the next morning. "Hope the workers didn't wake you." Cassie's face lit up. "I'm so excited. The renovations will be finished next week and we can reopen the inn."

Enid poured herself a cup of coffee and stumbled to one of the kitchen chairs. "That's great. I know you'll be glad to have all this construction work behind you." She carefully took another sip from the steaming cup. "How was your shopping trip?"

"Good. I found the new linens I wanted." Cassie brought a cup of hot tea to the table and handed it to Enid. "Here. I saw you making a face trying to drink that coffee. You look tired."

Enid put the coffee cup aside and picked up the teacup. "Thanks." The welcome bergamot scent of Earl Grey filled her nostrils. "I didn't sleep well last night. Too many snakes in my head again."

Cassie sat down at the table. "Anything I can do to help? I listen pretty good."

Enid smiled at Cassie. "Thanks, but I just need to talk to Cade about something that's come up." Enid looked down into the cup and saw her own reflection. "You're so good to me. I'm going to miss you when I go home. Though I'm not sure where home will be."

"Things have a way of working out. You'll see." Cassie patted Enid's hand gently. "Besides, I expect you to be a regular guest. You'll get the family discount, of course."

"Do you know when Jack will be back?" asked Enid

"Oh, sorry, I forgot to tell you he called and left a message. He's helping his sister and her new husband move into a new house and won't be back for a few more days. But he will be back in time for the celebration."

"Celebration?"

"Yes, we'll have our usual picnic on the beach of Glitter Lake. We'll have South Carolina, mustard-style barbecue and all the cold beer you can handle. It'll be fun to take your mind off your troubles."

Enid's attention had already drifted back to the conversation she needed to have with Cade. "I'm sure it will be." Enid stood up. "I'm going to take one of your scrumptious Morning Glory muffins upstairs to my room."

* * *

Upstairs, Enid put the tray on the small desk by the window and pulled the note from her bag that Bonnie had given her at the goat farm. No matter how many times Enid read it, "Fern and Samuel Blackwell" was still unmistakably printed in Bonnie's child-like handwriting.

Enid tapped on Cade's number from the list of favorites in her cell phone. Cade's voice mail message said he was in meetings all day and would return all calls within twenty-four hours.

"Cade, it's me. We need to talk. Call me as soon as you can." Enid ended the call and stared out the window. The morning sun was glittering on the lake. *Dammit, Cade. What else haven't you told me?*

Her cell phone rang, and thinking it was Cade, she answered quickly without checking the screen. "Hello."

"Hi, it's Molly. Molly Anderson."

"Hi, Molly." Enid hoped her disappointment wasn't reflected in her voice. She liked Molly but just wasn't in the mood for chit-chat this morning. "This is a surprise. What can I do for you?"

"I was hoping we could get together. I may have some information for you."

"About Rosie?"

"Let's not talk about it over the phone. Can you meet me at the snack bar at the Exxon station on the edge of town?"

Enid remembered that's where she had met Rachel. Was this Molly's way of letting her know she knew about Enid's meeting with her daughter? "Yes, I'm pretty sure I know where that is. What time?"

"I get off work at eight tonight. Would that be too late for you?"

Enid remembered Cassie's son had been killed at night at that station. "Well, I . . ."

As though Molly sensed Enid's concern, Molly said, "I know you're worried about Eddie, but I doubt he's foolish enough to bother you again. See you then."

Molly hung up at the same time Cassie knocked on the door and called out, "Can I come in for a minute? There's something else I forgot to tell you."

Enid opened the door and offered a seat to Cassie. "What did you forget?"

Cassie looked at Enid's teacup. "I'll bring you a fresh, hot cup."

"Is that what you forgot?" asked Enid.

"No, sorry. Occupational hazard of being an innkeeper. You're always looking to see what people need. What I forgot to tell you is that Bonnie left me a message yesterday afternoon while I was driving back. I let the call go to voice mail because the traffic was bad on I-26, and I didn't want to get distracted. I forgot to check messages until late last night. By the time I got her first message, she had left a second one. She said you were really nice, and she enjoyed your visit. But after you left, she starting wondering if you were who you said you were. She mentioned something about the previous owners' name, but I didn't follow what she was saying. Anyway, poor Bonnie has been a fraidy cat ever since Toby died. Thinks everybody is trying to con her." Cassie shook her head. "Bless her heart. Anyway, after she couldn't reach me, she called the Madden Police to see if they knew who you were."

"Oh, great. Just what I need. Chief Jensen will probably arrest me now for harassing the locals."

Cassie laughed. "No, you're in luck. Molly answered her call and assured her you were really Enid Blackwell and that you were my guest."

"That's funny, Molly just—" Enid heard a knock on her door and saw the construction foreman standing in the open doorway.

"Miss Cassie, I need to you look at something downstairs if you don't mind." He looked at Enid and tipped his hardhat. "Sorry for the interruption, ma'am."

Cassie stood up and said to Enid, "Anyway, I just wanted to tell you about Bonnie's calls. Got to run." Cassie scurried off with the construction foreman.

Bless your heart, Bonnie. Enid suddenly remembered she had left the goat cheese in the car overnight and hoped the smell wouldn't be too awful.

CHAPTER 51

The road leading away from Madden, where the Exxon station was located, was nearly deserted. Most of the traffic during the day came from commuters who worked in Columbia and other nearby areas. Once the work traffic died down, few people came into town, or left it, at that time of night. Other than the Exxon station, there wasn't much around except thickets of pine trees. At late summer, the days were getting a bit shorter, and the new moon didn't provide much light.

Enid was beginning to reprimand herself for agreeing to this meeting. After all, what could Molly have to say? Maybe she had found out Enid had talked to Rachel. If Enid was going to get scolded, she'd rather hear it over the phone.

The interior of her car was suddenly illuminated by the headlights of a vehicle behind her. It must have pulled from one of the side roads because she had just checked her rearview mirror a moment ago. Enid turned up the volume slightly on the radio to hear the national news. Lately, she had been so absorbed in local happenings that she felt isolated from the world she once knew.

Suddenly the vehicle behind her sped up and rammed into the back of her car. Stunned, Enid gripped the steering wheel and tried to maintain control. *Idiot! What are you doing?* Another jarring bump almost knocked her off the road. Her anger quickly turned to fear when the attacking vehicle pulled up beside her. Fighting to maintain control of her car and her emotions, Enid glanced to the side and saw a green pickup truck. In the fading light, she couldn't be sure, but the driver looked like one of the bikers she had encountered in the cemetery. He smiled as he rammed her again from the side. The side airbag deployed just as her BMW went off the road and headfirst into a deep ditch.

The driver's car door was wedged against a huge boulder embedded in the wall of the ditch. Her car was almost on its side. If there was any way out of the car, it would be on the passenger side. Her leg was hurting and the right one was jammed against the console. She managed to free her leg and tried to swing it over the console, with no luck. With the shift in weight, the car moved slightly, so she held still.

Enid wasn't sure which she heard first—the gunshot or the back window shattering. Immediately afterward, she heard herself scream. Another shot sounded like it rico- cheted off the rock right outside the driver's door. She instinctively covered her head and crouched down as much as she could.

Where was her cell phone? It had been in the cup holder before the crash. She eased her hand out, careful not to show much movement in case someone was looking into the car. Her fingers came up empty. Slowly, she put her hand on the floorboard and reached around trying to find her cell phone. She touched something but before she could pick it up, the sound of tires peeling rubber stopped her. The loud noise of the pickup's engine was faint now as it traveled away from her. After she assumed the assailant had left, fear overcame her. Her hands shaking, she groped around in the darkness trying to find her phone. She froze when a beam of light shone in the car. Someone with a flashlight was standing on the edge of the road looking down into the ditch at her car.

Enid twisted around and sat up. She looked up toward the road. She hadn't heard the truck coming back, but fear was causing her mind to play tricks. She felt sick to her stomach and her leg was throbbing from pain. The beam of light moved away from her to the back of the car. The jerky movement of light probably meant someone was climbing down into the ditch. Cursing herself for not bringing her gun along, she prayed that whoever was after her would not rape or torture her. After so much of the life she had taken for granted just a few weeks ago had died, would physical death just be the next step? In an instance, she thought of the things that would be left undone. *Cade, I'm sorry the way things turned out for us.* And then she thought of Rosie. *I'm sorry, I tried.*

The sound of a hand beating on the passenger window made her jump and pulled her back from the morbid thoughts.

"Are you okay in there?" A woman's voice. "Who's in there?" The voice sounded familiar.

"Molly? Is that you? Please help." Enid prayed it was her.

"Enid, is that you? I'm going to break the window. Cover your face."

Enid put her arms across her face. The loud, shattering noise was followed by little balls of glass hitting her head and neck. Enid looked up at the driver's window and Molly was standing there with an emergency glass breaker in her hand. "Are you okay?"

"Yes, I think I'm okay. Did you see that pickup drive away?" Enid pointed down the road.

"No, I didn't see anything. Just your car. I can't get you out, but I'll call the wrecker service. They operate out of the Exxon station, so it won't take them long unless they're out on another call."

"I'm so lucky that you came by when you did. I think I was run off the road intentionally." Enid was shaking uncontrollably.

"I'm sure it was one of the locals who drank a few more beers than he should have." Molly patted her shoulder. "There, there now, you're okay. Molly's here."

CHAPTER 52

Molly poured a shot glass of single malt bourbon for Enid while they sat in the police station. Molly winked. "This is the chief's stash, but I'm sure he won't mind if you have a shot. Not after what you've been through."

Enid didn't usually drink liquor, but tonight was an exception. "Thanks," she said after taking a sip. "I needed that." She tried not to focus on her leg and the side airbag burn on her arm and shoulder. "I want to thank you again for rescuing me."

"Well, I feel bad after I told you it was safe to go out there." Molly put the liquor bottle back in the cabinet. "The chief's coming in to talk to you, but before he does, I feel I need to warn you."

"Warn me? About what?" The warm buzz from the bourbon dissipated.

"You've been poking sticks at rattlers. It's not surprising one of them struck out at you."

Enid wondered who in particular Molly was talking about. There seemed to be a lot of rattlers around. "I'm not sure I'm following you." Enid sipped the last of the bourbon in her glass.

"It's admirable, and all, that you're writing a story about that poor girl. She had a tragic life, even if she brought most of her troubles on herself." Molly's eyes squinted slightly. "This is an open case, and I think you've got what you need for your story. Let the police do the detective work. Anyway, I'm sure you're anxious to get back to Charlotte, especially after what happened tonight." Molly shook her head sympathetically. "I'm afraid you've gotten a bad impression of Madden."

The front door of the small police station opened and Chief Jensen walked in. He took off his wide-brimmed hat and laid it on Molly's desk. "Evening, Ms. Blackwell." He looked at Molly. "Thanks, I'll take it from here. You go on home."

Molly nodded to the chief and turned to Enid. "If you need anything, let me know. And think about what I said." Molly called out as she left, "Goodnight."

For the next hour, Enid repeated the details of what happened several times. The chief rubbed his eyes and looked at the clock. It was nearly midnight. "So you really think you were deliberately run off the road? And that someone shot at you?"

Weariness and bourbon were not a good combination, especially at this time of night. "I don't think so, I know so. Someone deliberately ran me off the road and then shot at me. I'm sure your police department has the capability of finding bullets. There's at least one in my car."

"Your car has been impounded, and we'll take a look at it." The chief appeared to be struggling to hold his anger in check. "When we talked before, I thought we agreed you would leave the investigation of an *open* murder case to the authorities. And yet, here you are running around in the middle of the night chasing leads."

"I wasn't chasing leads. I was going to meet Molly. She called me and wanted to meet, after she left work."

Jensen stopped writing notes and looked up at Enid. "Did you say Molly asked you to meet her?"

Enid nodded. "Yes, she, that is we . . . She asked me to meet her after she left work."

Jensen studied Enid. "She told me you asked to talk with her." He paused. "And she left work around four o'clock this afternoon."

"What does it matter?" Enid made a mental note to follow up with Molly about the mix-up and to find out why she had wanted to meet with Enid.

Chief Jensen ignored her rhetorical question and resumed his questioning. "What about the green pickup truck? Do you know who was driving it?"

"I've seen that truck before. It was parked down the road at that old grain and seed store." After her conversation with Ray, she decided not to mention seeing him there, too. "I think the truck belongs to Eddie, the biker gang leader."

Jensen rubbed his hand on the back of his neck, just as Jack often did. Jensen then stood up quickly and leaned over her, pointing his finger. "I want you out of here as soon as your car is repaired." He hit the table with the tip of his finger. "Is that clear?" Little specks of spittle flew through the air between them.

"And when will you release my car so I can have it repaired?"

The chief picked up his hat and slammed it on his head. "Tomorrow afternoon." He walked to the door and held it open for her. "I've got one of the deputies in his car out front. He'll take you to see Doc Henry first, see if you need to go to the ER in the next town over. He'll make sure you get back to the inn."

"No, thanks, I don't need medical attention. I'm going back to the inn now." Enid limped slightly as she walked out the door of the police station.

CHAPTER 53

Cassie was pacing when Enid walked in the inn's front door. "Where have you been? I've been worried sick."

Enid filled Cassie in on the night's events, leaving out the part about Molly saying the meeting was Enid's idea. She didn't want to cast doubts on Molly's character until she had a chance to talk with Molly to clear up the misunderstanding.

"I really need to get some sleep," said Enid. She said goodnight and went up to her room. But even after a hot shower, she couldn't fall asleep. Her throbbing leg and too many thoughts were competing for her attention. Most of all, she had this overwhelming need to talk to Cade. After tossing and turning but not being able to sleep, Enid glanced at the bedside clock. Three o'clock in the morning, which meant it would be two hours earlier in Montana. She knew he often wrote well into the night and decided to call, even if she woke him up.

Just before she hit the button on her cell phone, she hesitated momentarily. She didn't want to worry Cade or wake him up. Yet, she needed to hear his voice.

The phone rang twice before the call was answered. "Hello," said an unfamiliar female voice.

Assuming she had hit the wrong favorite in her cell phone contacts, Enid apologized. "I'm so sorry. I must have . . ." Enid stopped when she heard Cade's unmistakable voice in the background. She heard movement and a noise that sounded like someone had thrown the phone down on a hard surface.

"Hello." This time it was Cade. When Enid failed to respond, Cade added, "Enid?"

Enid's voice sounded strange, even to herself. "Cade, I'm sorry." Kicking herself for apologizing, Enid recovered. "Who is that woman who answered the phone—at this time of night?"

"Enid, are you alright? What time is it? Where are you?"

"I needed to talk. And I wanted to hear your voice." The events of the day finally overcame her. "You were right. I should have listened to you." All the while Enid was talking, part of her was trying to place the woman's voice who answered. And then she knew. Madelyn Jensen. "What the hell is Madelyn Jensen doing with you at this time of night? You swore to me nothing was going on between you two."

"There's not, I promise." Cade sounded desperate, and Enid wanted to believe him. "We decided to do an exposé on the Madden Police Department. She's got pretty good proof that he's been taking money from the biker gang for years. He's been paid to look the other way while they trafficked drugs." He lowered his voice. "And perhaps worse."

"What are you saying?" asked Enid. "Does this have something to do with Rosie's murder?" She was getting angry again. "And when the hell were you going to tell me about this little piece you and Madelyn are working on, especially since it's connected to my story?"

Enid heard shuffling in the background and Madelyn's voice. "Let me talk to her." More shuffling noises. "Enid, this is Madelyn. I'm not the enemy here, and there's nothing going on between me and Cade. We are just pulling our notes together. With my court schedule and Cade having a new job, we had to meet when and where we could, so I flew up this afternoon. We have separate rooms, in case you're wondering. You can believe that or not, but it's the truth."

Enid didn't know what to believe. "Just tell me if your uncle had anything to do with Rosie's murder."

Madelyn sighed. "I don't know. I honestly don't know. We have pretty conclusive evidence he covered up the death of Cassie's son, Mark. Jack Johnson and I have been talking about it for years. I think you know Jack has been helping Cassie, and I know he's working with you on your research."

Enid was struggling with mixed emotions of jealousy, rage, and curiosity. "Have you talked with Cassie about all of this? After all, it's her son, and she'll be devastated when she learns that you've confirmed her worst fear."

"No, not yet. But we'll talk with her before the piece goes to print," said Madelyn.

Enid noticed she said *we*. "Let me talk to Cade again," said Enid. During the brief period of silence, Enid imagined that Cade and Madelyn were exchanging knowing glances or mouthing messages to each other silently. Enid stopped herself from going further down that road, as nothing could be gained from allowing her suspicions to take over.

Cade took the phone again. "Why did you call?"

For the next thirty minutes, Enid spilled out what she had learned about Rosie's death. She concluded by telling him about being run off the road. "I'm afraid the BMW might be totaled. I'll know in a day or so."

Cade started to speak, but Enid stopped him. "Why now, Cade? You walked away from this investigation a decade ago because you didn't want to upset Fern. Now you join forces with Madelyn and you're ready to forge ahead. What's changed? How do you think Fern's going to react to this story?"

"I'm not going to write about Rosie, so what's Mother got to do with it?"

"Fern has gone to great lengths to protect the Blackwell name in Madden, and Madden is pretty much controlled by the Jensen family. Through her generous contributions, she persuaded the Jensen-owned newspaper not to report on Wynona when she murdered Frank Kelly. And I wouldn't be surprised if she's the one who shut down Jack's articles when Rosie was killed. Whether you are willing to accept it or not, Fern is a player in all this. How do you think she's going to feel when you attack Chief Jensen?"

"You're probably right. I need to talk with her, at least so she won't be surprised."

Enid decided now was not the time to hold back anything. "Do you remember seeing a note on the autopsy report about goat hairs being found on Rosie's clothing?"

"I vaguely remember, but what's your point?" asked Cade.

"The closest goat farm to Madden was owned by your parents. They sold it through OJ Development just after Rosie died."

"Hold on. I really don't like where you're going with this."

"I'm not accusing Fern of anything at this point, but she knows more than she's letting on."

"I think you're jumping to conclusions. Besides, I'm sure there were other goats in town. Did they do any tests to compare the goat hairs?"

"You're kidding me, right?"

Cade didn't reply.

"Even if they had tried, they couldn't have matched the goat hairs, that is unless they had hairs with root bulbs on both samples for comparison."

"You've done your research, I see." Cade's tone sounded a bit softer now. "But the goat connection is irrelevant in a place like Madden. People there keep goats for pets, for Pete's sake, and there are farms everywhere."

"Taken alone, you're right, the goat hairs mean nothing. But given the guilt money Fern paid the town and her insistence that I drop this story, I have to wonder how deep her involvement was. And while she might have thought she was doing the right thing, she took it upon herself to manipulate the truth Rosie was told about her own mother. Don't you see what they did to Rosie? She lost trust in her own family and lashed out by being rebellious and experimenting with drugs."

Cade spoke so softly Enid could barely hear him. "I admit, it doesn't look good."

"I'm going to Charlotte to talk to Fern about the goat farm." Enid stopped Cade from interrupting her. "I know you don't want me to, but I need to find out what she knows." *Or what she did.* Enid knew it was Cade's nature to protect the family, a trait he inherited from Fern. After all, he had been raised to believe that protecting the family name was a matter of defending one's honor—the kind of thing duels were once fought over. Enid's throat constricted, and she felt sick.

"Under the circumstances, I realize I have no right to stop you. But remember, she's my mother, if that still means anything to you. Not to mention, she's already had one anxiety attack, so take it easy." His tone softened slightly. "Please be careful. I don't want you or anyone else to get hurt."

CHAPTER 54

After the two-hour drive to Charlotte in her small rental car, Enid pulled into the driveway of the big brick house with the beautifully landscaped yard. *Fern's domain.* A short Hispanic man was trimming the hedges, stepping back after a few snips to make sure each bush was equal in height.

He never looked her way as she walked to the front door and rang the doorbell.

The door opened and the perfectly coiffed, neatly dressed Fern Blackwell stood before Enid. "Well, Enid. What a surprise." Had Cade warned his mother she was coming to see her? Fern opened the door. "Whose car is that?"

"I had an accident in the BMW. It's being repaired."

Fern stepped back inside and held the door open. "Well, I hope you weren't hurt. Please, dear, come on in."

Enid followed Fern into the living room. Fern sat on the sofa and Enid sat in one of the overstuffed damask chairs across from her. "I'm sorry to barge in like this," said Enid. "But I wanted to talk to you about something."

Fern stiffened. "Well, of course, I'm happy to talk to you anytime." She smoothed a wrinkle from her skirt. "Is this about Cade? I do hope you two can work out your differences."

The housekeeper appeared with a pot of tea and poured a cup for each of them. Fern added milk and stirred a few rounds until she was happy with the way it looked.

Enid squeezed a slice of lemon into her cup. "We've never been good at small talk, so I'll just cut right to it. I'm here to ask you a few questions about Rosie."

Fern took a sip and then set her cup in the saucer on the polished mahogany coffee table. "If I must say so, I don't understand this mission you're on to make our family look bad." Her hands were shaking slightly.

Enid put her cup on the tray. "My intent has never been to make anyone look bad." She leaned forward. "Rosie was family. Your family. I don't understand why you were so eager to sacrifice the truth and then forget her."

Fern's chin protruded slightly. "She was a stain on our family's reputation. I did everything I could to help that girl, but it didn't help. I guess she had Wynona's bad genes. That girl stayed in trouble all her life. I think it's what killed my own mother."

"Did you even know Rosie?" Enid regretted the sharp tone in her own voice.

"Did you?" Fern shot back.

"No, but I've learned more about her in the past couple of weeks."

Fern stared intently at Enid. "Why does this have anything to do with me?" A muscle in her face twitched slightly.

"Why did you pay Myra to lie about Rosie's mother?"

Fern sat erect and raised her voice. "I'm sure I don't know what you're talking about."

The housekeeper came in to see if the teapot needed refilling. Fern assured her they didn't need anything and dismissed her. As the housekeeper was leaving the room, she glanced back over her shoulder at Fern, who nodded slightly to signal that all was well. The housekeeper had been with Fern since before Enid and Cade's marriage. Oddly, while the two woman clearly lived in different social strata, they were more like friends than employer-employee.

"You made sure Frank Kelly's killing was never reported in the *Madden Gazette*. Your sister sat in prison in Mississippi, knowing that her own daughter thought she was dead because you paid Myra to lie."

Fern played nervously with the large diamond ring on her finger. "I did it because they were trash. Both of them—Wynona and Rosie. Trash." Her lip was quivering. "I had Cade to think about and our family name. Cade's father, my beloved Samuel, helped build Madden. He was revered in that town. I'll always regret asking him to leave and come to Charlotte." She sniffed softly. "He never fit in here."

Enid was annoyed at how skillfully Fern had shifted the focus of the conversation to herself. "Wynona wrote a letter to Rosie and asked Myra to give to her when she was old enough to understand. But you made sure that never happened. Rosie found the letter and was saving money to go see her mother in prison. Did you know that?" She watched Fern's face for her reaction but saw none. "Rosie also knew Frank Kelly was her father."

Fern's lip quivered. "I'm not a monster, you know," she said quietly. "I only did what I thought was right for our family. Wynona agreed because she thought it was best for Rosie, too." Fern's chin raised slightly in defiance. "There's nothing a mother wouldn't do to protect her child. But you wouldn't understand that."

"You may have thought you were protecting Rosie, but secrets are like cancer. They feed on the fear of discovery, and small lies metastasize into other parts of your life. Eventually, your soul is consumed by the secrets you tried to protect." Images of Rosie's body at the edge of the woods flashed into her memory. "Was it worth it?"

Fern wrung a napkin in her lap and stared down at her hands.

"Did you own a goat farm in Madden at the edge of town?" asked Enid.

Fern looked up at Enid. "Yes, as I recall, we did. But we owned a number of properties. Why is that important?"

"Did you own it when Rosie died?"

"Where on earth are you going with these questions?" She had regained her composure now and sipped her tea slowly, as if nothing else was more important.

"Did you?" Enid regretted the harsh tone.

Fern set her cup down. "I'd have to check to be sure, but, yes, I'm fairly certain we did own the goat farm at that time."

"Who did you lease it to?"

Fern appeared to be thinking about the question. "I believe, yes, I'm pretty sure I remember now. We leased that property to Molly Anderson. Her family operated a dairy farm there."

"Molly Anderson, the woman who works for the Madden police department?"

"Yes, that's her." Fern's face showed no expression.

Enid stood up and looked down at Fern, who appeared to be getting smaller as she slumped in her seat. "Rosie deserved a better life than the one you and Myra created for her. And she deserves to be remembered."

Fern looked up at Enid. "What would have been better? Letting her know her mother was in prison for killing her worthless father? Subjecting Rosie to small-town gossip? Whether you agree with me or not, I did what I thought was right." She raised her chin slightly. "And I would do it again."

Fern sat stoically as Enid walked out the door.

CHAPTER 55

The vibration of Enid's cell phone on the bedside table jarred her from a deep sleep. The drive back to Madden from Charlotte left her tired, and the conversation with Fern kept playing in her head. Enid didn't fall asleep until after midnight. She glanced at her cell phone. It was three o'clock, and Cade's face was smiling at her from the cell phone screen, a photo from a happier period of life. A call at this time of the morning couldn't be good news.

"Hello. Are you okay?"

Cade seemed to be out of breath. "Mother had a heart attack. She's at the hospital."

"Are you sure it's not another anxiety attack?"

"They put her in intensive care."

"Oh, God. I'm so sorry. Is she going to be okay?" asked Enid.

"The housekeeper called 911 and an ambulance carried her to the emergency room. They admitted her to ICU, and the attending cardiologist called me."

Enid could hear the usual hospital noises in the background, and she recalled the many days and nights she had listened to those noises while visiting her own mother. The phantom antiseptic odors lingered long after her mother's death. "Where are you? I thought you were still in Montana."

"I'm back in Charlotte. You were right about the new job. It was a mistake."

Thoughts swirled in Enid's head. "Well, we can discuss that later. I know you're worried about Fern. Is there anything I can do?"

"The doctor told me she kept mentioning your name. He said she seemed to be upset about something."

Enid felt a knot in her stomach and a growing sense of dread. "I talked to her yesterday, about Rosie, but she was fine when I left. Sipping tea, as a matter of fact."

"Look, I have to go."

"You just focus on taking care of Fern, and we'll talk later." Enid's hands were shaking. "I'm sorry," she said before Cade hung up.

Enid pulled the covers over her head and tried to go back to sleep, but her mind was still racing. *Did I cause Fern to have a heart attack? God, I hope not.* Even though Enid hated to admit it and didn't agree with Fern's actions, she had acted out of motherly love.

Enid got out of bed and sat at the small table by the window. The full moon over Glitter Lake was beautiful. For a moment, she was envious of the life Cassie had created here. It seemed surreal at times, living in a beautiful old inn, and chatting with guests. Enid rubbed her arms and shook herself back into her own world. *What a mess I've made of everything.*

Sitting on the desk was a framed a photo of a Rosie, a smiling teenager. Enid had placed it there as a reminder to stay focused on Rosie's life. If her family had told her the truth and helped her deal with the consequences of Wynona's actions, would it have made a difference?

Enid looked at her calendar. She had been in Madden for a couple weeks and had little to show for it. In spite of her promises to Cade, Jack, and Cassie that she was focusing on Rosie's life, she had gotten caught up in trying to figure out who had killed her. Enid rationalized that she was just thinking like a journalist. After all, murder would make a more compelling story. But Rosie was now much more than a story, and Enid had to admit that bringing Rosie's killer to justice had overshadowed researching her short life.

Enid spread her notes out on the bed and went through each piece of information she had documented. No matter how hard she tried to convince herself she was wrong or push it out of her mind, one nagging thought kept coming up. *I know who killed Rosie.*

CHAPTER 56

Enid had managed to sleep only an hour before Cassie knocked on her door, letting her know breakfast was waiting downstairs. Enid showered and threw on the same clothes she wore yesterday and ran a brush through her hair.

Over breakfast Cassie talked about the reopening of the inn next week. She was excited, and rightly so. The renovations were beautiful, and the new bed linens Cassie had bought in Charleston were the perfect finishing touch to the guest rooms. The opening would coincide with the annual Glitter Lake Inn annual picnic.

"I can't wait for Jack to see the inn," said Cassie. "He promised he'd come back to Madden in time for the reopening."

Enid missed Jack too. Especially now. She needed for him to tell her she was wrong about who killed Rosie. She wanted to be wrong. Desperately.

"I'm looking forward to it, too." Enid took a bite of her muffin. "I'll be leaving afterword."

"Oh. I see. You have what you need for your story then?" Cassie wiped her hands with a dish towel.

Enid looked down at her plate to avoid looking at Cassie. "Pretty much. I need to talk to Jack about the lead, you know, how I want to begin and focus the story."

"Oh, I see," Cassie repeated, as if she didn't know what else to say.

Enid forced a smile. "I'll be back to visit. Often, I promise. It's not like we'll never see each other again." She was sure Chief Jensen wouldn't appreciate her returning later, but after talking to Cade and Madelyn, things could change in Madden. She hoped their investigation into Mark's murder wouldn't distress Cassie further. She didn't need to relive her son's murder, even though Cassie wanted justice for Mark just as much as Enid wanted it for Rosie.

Cassie sat in the chair beside Enid. "I know. It's just that I've gotten used to having you here, and I've enjoyed your company." Cassie walked to the stove where the kettle was whistling. As she looked back over her shoulder, she said, "Oh, I almost forgot. You know that wedding I told you about? The one I said I wasn't going to. Well, I've talked myself into going after all."

Enid felt bad that she couldn't remember Cassie mentioning the wedding. Her mind had been on other things lately.

Cassie sat back down at the table. "It's in Greenville tomorrow. Once the inn's open again, I won't be able to get away, so I decided to go. I really don't have my heart in it, but it's been a while since I've seen some of these people who were Mark's friends, so I feel obligated. But I really don't want to." Her voice trailed off. "Do you know that feeling you have when you know you need to do something but just hate to do it?"

Enid recalled the obligatory visits to Fern's house on Sundays when she really didn't want to go. "But if you haven't seen them in a while and you like them, why not go?"

"I know it's silly. I'm just not the mood for a wedding, I guess. But you're right. I need to go. I'll be leaving this afternoon and staying overnight with a friend. You sure you'll be okay here alone?"

A short time ago, Enid wouldn't have worried about being alone at the inn. But things were different now. Maybe she should stay in a hotel in Columbia while Cassie was away, but Enid didn't want to alarm Cassie, or give her an excuse not to go. "Of course."

"I've already called Molly and asked her to have someone check on the inn tonight. She told me she was glad I called. Seems Eddie and gang have been up to no good again, mostly harassing people. She'll get one of the county deputies to drop by and check on the inn."

Enid felt a knot in her stomach. "You shouldn't have gone to that trouble." She got up from the table and put her dishes in the sink. "I need to make a few calls." She hugged Cassie. "You have a good time at the wedding and don't worry about anything here."

* * *

Upstairs in her room, Enid called Jack in Chicago. As the phone rang, she felt foolish. "Jack, hi, it's me."

"Hey, kiddo. What's up? Everything okay?"

Jack's voice was both comforting and disconcerting. She didn't want to admit to herself how much she had missed him. Her feelings made her feel even more guilty when she reminded herself that Cassie was obviously infatuated, if not in love, with Jack.

"It's good to hear your voice."

"Likewise. I'm coming back for the picnic. I promised Cassie I'd help her get ready for it. Did she tell you?"

Enid tried to keep her voice from trembling. "Yes. She did. That's great."

"You called for a reason. What's on your mind?"

"I'm feeling a bit foolish now for calling you. It can wait until you get back. By the way, I'll be leaving Madden after the picnic, assuming my car is ready."

"Your car? What happened?"

I just got run off the road by someone who wants me to kill me, that's all. "Just an accident. I had a few bruises, but nothing serious." Enid suddenly realized how much had happened since Jack had left for Chicago.

"Are you giving up on the story?"

"No, I found out what I needed to know. I'll fill you in next week." She chewed on her lower lip. "I'm looking forward to catching up."

CHAPTER 57

After talking to Jack, Enid went downstairs to get one of Cassie's homemade gingersnap cookies with lemon frosting. Yes, she would definitely miss Cassie's cooking. The thought of going home to Charlotte filled her with dread. Was Cade staying in their house again? Where would she stay? When would the bank take possession of their house? The questions kept coming, but the answers did not.

She shook off the feelings of despair and tried to focus her thoughts. She needed a sounding board, but Jack was still in Chicago, Cassie had gone to the wedding, and Cade's attention was on his mother who had just had a heart attack—that Enid had likely caused. Unfortunately, Enid was going to have to work her way through this mess alone.

She went downstairs and sat at the big table in the library. She had tried several times to begin writing Rosie's story, but each time, she had struggled with it. Not so long ago, it seemed to be a simple, sad tale of a young woman killed and then forgotten by her family. Now, it was harder for Enid to blame Fern and Myra for their roles in the deception. They did what they thought was right, even if she didn't agree. To complicate things further, Enid had learned who killed Rosie. At least, she was pretty sure she had. *What should I do now? Who should I tell?*

274 · RAEGAN TELLER

Enid looked at the time on the big English wall clock. Chief Jensen would have left the station by now. She rummaged around in the big leather tote and found a crumpled note that had an emergency number for the chief. A few weeks ago, she could not have imagined that she would turn to Chief Jensen as an ally or to ask for his protection. But things had changed.

After three rings, Molly answered. "Hello, this is the Madden Police. How can we help you?"

Caught off-guard, Enid stammered. "Molly, I . . . I was expecting . . . I'm sorry to bother you, I thought this was a private number for Chief Jensen."

"We rotate the after-hours calls to this number. It's my turn tonight. Do you have an emergency?"

"Well, not exactly. But I do need to reach the chief—tonight if possible. Is there another number where I can call him?"

"He's tied up right now. I'll give him a message."

"Please ask him to call me on this cell number. I need to speak with him as soon as possible."

"It might be a couple hours, since you said it's not an emergency." Molly sounded annoyed.

"That's fine. I'll wait."

"Are you at the inn?"

Enid hesitated. "Yes." *Molly knows I'm alone here.*

After ending the call, Enid checked all the windows and doors and read for a while in the library. She picked up the phone to call Jack again, but decided against it. What could he do from Chicago? She sat on the sofa and put a pillow behind her head to ease the pounding in her temples.

* * *

A few hours later, Enid woke up. How long had she been asleep on the sofa? Enid checked the door locks and turned off the lights before going upstairs. She couldn't blame Chief Jensen for not returning her call. After all, their relationship had been contentious from the start. Still, she couldn't imagine that he would ignore her completely. She turned out all the lights and went upstairs to her room.

After a half hour of tossing, her cell phone rang. Thinking it was Jensen, she grabbed it quickly before looking at the screen. "Hello."

Cassie's voice was a surprise. "Enid, I'm so sorry to wake you up. Please forgive me. It's just that I decided not to go to the wedding. I'm coming back tonight and I didn't want to scare you by showing up unexpectedly."

"Why did you change your mind? Are you feeling okay?"

Cassie sighed deeply. "I don't know if I can explain it. I haven't seen some of these people in almost ten years, since Mark, well, you know. Going just to recapture a memory or two about Mark was selfish and foolish. I had dinner with my friend, and we had fun catching up. But I'm leaving now, so I'll be home in a couple hours. The drive has been good for me. I needed the time to think. Besides I have something I want to tell you."

"Well, as long as you're okay, I'm glad you'll be home soon."

"Don't wait up for me. I'll just come in the back entrance and hit the bed. We can talk in the morning."

"Sounds good. Drive carefully." Enid didn't like the idea of Cassie being alone on the highway at night.

"You just get some sleep."

The thought of Cassie coming home helped Enid relax. She would talk to Cassie in the morning and then decide what she needed to do. The fact that Chief Jensen ignored her was annoying but not surprising, all things considered. *Tomorrow, I'll talk to Jack's friend Dan at SLED.* Relieved that she had a plan of action now, Enid pulled up the covers and went to sleep almost immediately.

CHAPTER 58

A noise woke Enid. She sat up in bed and looked at the time on her phone—almost two o'clock in the morning. Then, she remembered Cassie had come in late. The noise she heard was likely Cassie fixing herself a snack in the kitchen. Enid turned over to go back to sleep.

The sound Enid heard next was one of those things that stays with a person the rest of her life. A loud "boom," pierced the silent night. *Cassie!* Enid jumped out of bed and ran to the door. When she opened it, a female voice wailed, "No, no, no" so mournfully that Enid stopped in her tracks.

"Cassie?" Enid called out but heard no response. Enid got the gun her from the bedside drawer and made sure it was loaded before she ran downstairs. There was no smoke or anything to indicate an explosion or fire, other than a faint smell that reminded Enid of the range where she had learned to shoot at Cade's insistence.

When Enid went toward the kitchen, it was dark, but the outside lights provided shadowy illumination. A dark figure bent over a body on the floor in a pool of dark liquid. The kneeling figure raised an arm and pointed a long gun at Enid. She instinctively raised her own gun with shaking hands and fired at the center of the person who was trying to kill her. *Aim for the biggest target.*

The noise and recoil of her own gun firing terrified Enid. The person she shot at was moaning softly and reaching a hand out for her gun that had fallen to the floor. Enid forced herself to break out of her stupor and run down the hallway toward the front door. Just as she tried to unlock it, another loud boom filled the air and small bits of flying debris from the door jamb hit the side of her face and neck. *Don't look back, just run!* She fumbled with the lock and opened the door.

Enid ran across the sprawling front porch and down the brick steps. The damp, cool gravel walkway cut into the soles of her feet. Suddenly, she was blinded by a glare of light, and she heard a car sliding on gravel. Enid felt something warm and sticky on her side. In a half-conscious state, Enid heard someone yell, "No, Mama, don't!" The world then faded to black.

CHAPTER 59

For years after her mother's death, Enid dreamed of being in the hospital again, at her mother's side. Each time, after waking, she would recall the painful memories of watching the woman she loved lose her battle with cancer.

But this time, it wasn't a dream. She was in a hospital. Enid slowly opened her eyes and then shut them quickly, as the bright lights overhead burned into her vision. Through squinted eyes, she saw a woman in a blue uniform standing over her.

"You're safe. Relax." The woman stared at the screen beside Enid's bed, watching her blood pressure and pulse. The woman repeated, "You're safe now."

Enid slowly opened her eyes. "What happened?" Even as Enid asked the question, scenes of the previous night were flooding into her thoughts. *Cassie!* "Where's Cassie? Is she alright?"

The nurse stuck a thermometer in Enid's mouth and then turned around to speak to someone in the hallway. "She's awake. You can come in now."

The unmistakable wide-brimmed hat of Chief Jensen came into view. "Good afternoon, Ms. Blackwell."

Afternoon? How long have I been here? Enid nodded to the chief since she still had the thermometer in her mouth. Jensen sat in a chair in the corner until the nurse removed it. She noted Enid's temperature and turned toward the chief.

"Don't tire her out. She needs to rest. Five minutes, okay?" Before he could respond, the nurse left the room.

Enid tried to remember the details of the shooting, but only bits and pieces surfaced in her memory. She raised her hand, being careful not to dislodge the intravenous needle in her arm, and motioned for the chief to come closer.

Chief Jensen, hat in hand, stepped over to her bedside. "They tell me you will be fine. Just some buckshot in your side and hip. You were lucky. But lost some blood though. Probably why you fainted." He pulled the chair up beside the bed and sat down. The big hat was lying at the foot of Enid's bed. She hated that hat. "Do you remember what happened?"

Enid shook her head, which made her dizzy. "Is Cassie alright?"

Chief Jensen dropped his head and shook it. "I'm sorry. I know you two had gotten pretty close."

Enid's world suddenly spun off its axis. Surely she was dreaming. "What do you mean?" Enid tried to focus on the details of the scenes that kept flashing through her memory. Was that Cassie on the floor? She shut her eyes and squeezed tight, but the tears fell anyway. "Cassie is dead? Who killed her?" Enid remembered firing her own gun. *Oh, God, no!* Had she shot Cassie?

Chief Jensen raised his eyes to meet Enid's. "Molly shot her."

A rush of jumbled thoughts flooded Enid's medicated brain. In the past few days, it had become clear to her that everything she had learned about Rosie's life and death pointed to the fact Rosie had not been killed during a drug buy. Instead, Rosie had been killed by someone close to her. But why?

Enid looked at Chief Jensen. *Did you know Molly killed Rosie? Did you cover it up?* Enid could hear the blood pressure monitor beeping more rapidly, and the nurse came in the room again.

The nurse took Enid's hand and spoke softly. "Do you want me to run him out?" she said with a faint smile.

Balancing her fears with a need for answers, Enid replied, "No, but thanks."

"I'll be right outside at the nurse's station if you need me." She put a box of tissues on the bed near Enid's hand.

As if reading Enid's thoughts, Chief Jensen said, "I had no idea Molly was involved. You probably think you have no reason to, but you've got to trust me on this." The tortured look on his face said it all. She believed him.

"I shot at Molly, but it didn't stop her."

"You hit her in the shoulder. It knocked her down and slowed her up some." Ironically, Enid had shot Molly with Molly's own gun—the one she had loaned Cassie after her son was killed. Cassie's insistence that Enid carry the gun had saved Enid's life, but not Cassie's. A sharp pain of loss shot through Enid. *Cassie is dead.*

Enid struggled again to remember. "Then how . . . Why didn't Molly kill me when I went outside?" Her head was throbbing.

"Rachel found a note her mother had left and put the pieces together. She figured Molly was going after you. She called me first and then drove to the inn to stop her. She got there just as you came out the door and collapsed. Rachel yelled at her mother not to shoot you. Rachel saved your life." He paused briefly to give Enid a chance to absorb what he had said. "When I got there, Molly and Rachel were huddled together on the porch. We took Molly to the hospital, and she's in custody. You don't have to worry about her any longer."

Enid struggled to maintain her composure. "Was Cassie alive when you got there?"

Chief Jensen cleared his throat and shook his head. "She didn't suffer. The shotgun blast to her chest killed her instantly."

Enid took a tissue from the box the nurse had left and wiped her eyes. "It was supposed to be me."

The nurse reappeared and turned to Chief Jensen. "That's enough for now." She handed Enid a little paper cup with a pill in it. "Here, take this."

Before Jensen left the room, he turned back to Enid. "There's a fellow from SLED that will be handling this investigation. His name's Dan Elliott. Said he's met you."

Enid could tell Jensen was waiting for an explanation, but she remained silent.

"Anyway, Officer Elliott will be touch with you soon and take it from there." Jensen stood there, staring at the floor.

"Thanks, Chief." The pill was starting to take effect. "I guess I need to rest now."

"Sure." He looked up at Enid. "I'm sorry about everything. No matter what you think of me, I never wanted anything to happen to anyone."

Enid struggled to stay alert. "Before you go, I have to ask you one thing. Was Eddie involved in Rosie's murder?"

Jensen put his wide-brimmed hat on and tipped it. "We'll talk later. You take care."

CHAPTER 60

The next morning, Enid had a hangover from the medication and her mouth was dry. She leaned over to get the cup of water next to her bed, but a sharp pain in her hip stopped her from reaching it. "Ouch," she said aloud.

"Here let me get that," a male voice replied.

Is Chief Jensen still here? Enid tried to get her bearings. She watched the man step closer to her bedside. "Cade." That was all Enid could get out before a flood of emotions overcame her. He sat on the edge of her bed with his hand resting on her shoulder and kept handing her tissues as she needed them.

"When did you get here?" she asked.

"Late last night. You were sleeping, so I just napped in the waiting room."

"I'm so glad to see you." Enid wanted to cry again, but there was nothing left inside. "Do you know what happened?"

Cade nodded.

"It's all my fault. First your mother's heart attack, and now Cassie." Enid closed her eyes. She couldn't bear to see Cade's face right now. He must hate her.

"Mother is fine. In fact, she asked me to give you her best wishes. She's going home from the hospital. A relative is coming down to stay with her for a few days." He smiled at Enid. "In fact, this whole experience had been good for

Mother, in a perverse sort of way. She's had some time to reevaluate her priorities."

Part of Enid wanted Cade to blame her and get it over with. But the other part of her was grateful for his compassion. This was the old Cade, the person she had fallen in love with years ago. Instead of comforting her, those memories reminded her of another loss she had to bear.

"I know you and Cassie were close. You lost a good friend," he said softly.

A knock on the door announced a young girl with a vase of flowers in her hand. She put them on Enid's bedside table. "These sure are pretty." She handed a small card to Enid. "Here you go."

Enid opened the envelope and read it. "They're from Jack." Another flood of emotion washed through her as she thought of Cassie again. If Jack cared for Cassie as much as she had adored him, he was suffering right now. She wanted to see him but dreaded it too. How could she ever look him in the face again and not feel guilty for what had happened?

"Jack came to see you yesterday, but Chief Jensen said SLED wouldn't let him talk to you until they get a formal statement from each of you. Didn't want you two to compare notes, I guess." Cade smiled slightly. "Jack's a good man. He kept apologizing to me for not being here to protect you and Cassie."

"Yes, he is a good man." Enid blinked away new tears. "I think he and Cassie were more than just friends."

Cade nodded. "He said as much." Cade took Enid's hand in his. "He doesn't blame you. He wanted to make sure you knew that."

Enid laid her head back on the pillow and rested. She was tired and torn between wanting to know more details, yet wanting to sleep and forget escape yesterday's horror.

"You need to rest." Cade released her hand and stood up. "I'll be here until you're ready to go home."

Enid opened her eyes. *Home? Where was home now? And was Cade part of it?* She couldn't handle that conversation right now, so she just nodded and shut her eyes again. "Thanks."

CHAPTER 61

Later in the day, SLED officer Dan Elliott came by the hospital room and took Enid's statement. It didn't take long, as Enid's memory of that night was spotty, as best. The one scene she kept seeing like a movie running in an endless loop was Cassie lying on the floor. When Elliott was convinced she knew nothing more, he gave Enid his card and told her to call if she remembered anything else. *Don't you realize I'm trying hard not to remember?*

As soon as Elliott left the room, Jack knocked on the open door, and Enid motioned him in. Jack sat on the side of her bed and held her hand for several minutes. "I'm so sorry for causing all of this. Cassie is dead because of me."

Jack got up to wet a washcloth in cool water and then handed it to Enid to wipe her face.

"Thanks. I'm sorry to be so emotional."

Jack sat down again on the edge of the bed. "You've been through a lot. I'm so sorry I was in Chicago."

Enid struggled to find the right words. "Cassie loved you, and I took her away from you. I'm so sorry."

Jack smiled, but there were tears in his eyes. "She was pretty special, wasn't she?"

Enid nodded. "She was like my mother and the sister I never had, all in one."

Jack wiped his eyes with the back of his hand. "I had a copy of Cassie's will that she gave me a few years ago. Thank goodness she left instructions for her funeral in it."

"Leave it Cassie to take care of the details so no one else would have to worry. That's what made her a great inn-keeper."

"She wanted to be cremated and her ashes scattered on Glitter Lake. That's where Mark is, you know."

The weight on Enid's heart lifted slightly when she thought about how Cassie would become part of the beau-tiful lake. "She never mentioned that Mark's remains were there, but I'm not surprised."

"I'm planning a memorial service in a few days. The doc says you'll be out of here in a day or so. When you're up to it, I thought we'd have a small service with a few friends, and then you and I will scatter her remains."

Enid just nodded, not trusting that she could speak.

"Dan said he had taken your statement. Are you up to comparing notes? We can wait if you'd rather not talk about it now."

"As I told Dan, I don't remember much. Cassie went to Greenville and then came back to the inn after she decided not to go to the wedding. Everything after that is a blur."

Jack dropped his head. "She called me from her friend's house, said she didn't want to go to the wedding. She sounded so relieved when I suggested she just go back to the inn if she really wanted to. It was like she needed per-mission from someone. If I had only . . ." He paused and sighed deeply. "Before we hung up, she told me how much she was going to miss you when you went home. When I reminded her you would still visit the inn, she said she felt like she'd never see you again." Jack choked up and cleared his throat. "It was like she knew somehow."

Enid wiped her face again with the wet washcloth. "I should have told you when we talked, when you were still in Chicago, that I had figured out Molly had killed Rosie. Waiting seemed like a good idea until Cassie told me she had asked Molly to check on me while she was gone. I tried to call Chief Jensen, but Molly intercepted the call. She had no way of knowing Cassie had returned home, because Cassie's car is usually parked out of sight on the other side of the inn." Enid shuttered involuntarily. "I was the one Molly wanted to kill. Cassie was just an innocent bystander." *Just like her son Mark has been.*

"If you had told me you suspected Molly, especially after Cassie went to Savannah, I'd have flown back immediately. How did you put it all together?"

"When I saw Fern, she said there was nothing a mother wouldn't do to protect her child. That made me start thinking. And then I remembered Ray Jensen telling me how angry Molly was when she caught him and Rosie doing drugs in her shed. Rachel was there, and Molly went ballistic, even though Rachel wasn't doing anything wrong."

"Even so, you took a big leap to assume it was Molly."

"Not really. When you add the fact that she lied about asking me to meet her just before I got run off the road."

"Chief Jensen filled me in. You should have told me."

"I'm sorry, I just didn't want to worry you while you were in Chicago enjoying time with your family. It was foolish of me." Enid looked out the window at the rain that had started to hit the glass. "And then I found out that Molly was leasing the goat farm from Fern at the time Rosie was killed. That explained the goat hairs. They must have been transferred to Rosie's clothing when she was in Molly's car. It *is* all circumstantial, at best, but I was pretty sure I was right."

"Chief Jensen said Molly would have to submit to a psychiatric exam. He admitted she has a hot temper, but no one, especially him, ever thought she'd kill anyone."

"Poor Rachel. I'm sure she's devastated to find out her mother killed Rosie. And now Molly is charged with two murders, so she may get the death penalty." Enid tried not to think about how her coming to Madden had changed so many lives, including her own. "How did Molly kill Rosie?"

Jack stood up to stretch his legs. "I hate hospitals. Seems like there's no way to get comfortable in them." He settled back in the chair beside Enid's bed. "Jensen said that Molly saw Rosie waiting on the corner the day she was going for a job interview. Ray was supposed to take her, but he was late. Molly saw her and stopped to offer Rosie a ride."

"Did Molly plan to kill Rosie?" Enid thought of all the times she had talked to Rosie's killer without realizing it.

"According to Molly's statement, she had repeatedly told Rosie to stay away from Rachel. You see, this was not long after she caught Rachel in the shed with Ray and Rosie."

Enid listened in silence, not wanting to believe any of it had happened.

"Molly said when they were in the car, she told Rosie again to stay away from Rachel. Rosie smarted off, and Molly just lost it. She grabbed Rosie by the back of the neck and slammed her head into the dashboard. Rosie slumped down on the seat, and Molly got scared. She drove out to the edge of town and strangled Rosie with her scarf." Jack took a deep breath. "Just dumped her body and drove off.

Molly said she wasn't even sure Rosie was dead. She went back late that night and checked but couldn't find a pulse. Rosie may have been alive for a while."

Enid couldn't bear the thought of Rosie suffering alone in the woods. "But why did Molly decide to come after me? I hadn't told anyone that I suspected her."

"I asked the chief that same question. Apparently, when Ray Jensen found out you were going around town asking questions, he confronted Eddie. That was the meeting you drove up on, at the old feed and seed store. Ray asked Eddie if he had anything to do with Rosie's murder. Eddie denied any involvement but said Molly hated Rosie enough to kill her. Ray wasn't sure whether Eddie was just mouthing off, or if he knew something."

"Eddie probably told Molly that Ray talked to him. It must have made Molly jumpy."

Jack nodded. "It's a good possibility. According to Chief Jensen, Molly hired Eddie from time to time to do various odd jobs. Those two had a strange relationship. Neither liked the other one much, but they depended on each other. Anyway, Ray got to thinking after talking with Eddie. Ray knew Molly had a violent temper, because Rosie had told him about several times when Molly had lost control. Ray also knew Rosie could push Molly's buttons—and did it intentionally at times."

Enid closed her eyes and rested her head on the pillow. She was overwhelmed trying to absorb everything Jack was telling her, and her head and hip were throbbing with pain.

"It looks like Chief Jensen and Eddie had nothing to do with Rosie's death," said Jack. "That is other than Jensen failing to investigate it properly. And, Molly admitted she paid Eddie to run you off the road to scare you. She wanted you to leave town. After all, she had gotten away with murder for more than a decade."

Enid opened her eyes again. "And then I showed up." She fought another wave of guilt that enveloped her. "What about Chief Jensen taking payoffs from Eddie? And what about Cassie's son's murder? Is Jensen going to get away with both of those?" She rubbed her throbbing temples with her fingers.

Jack shook his head. "After Dan Elliott told Chief Jensen that SLED was investigating him for covering up the death of Cassie's son, Jensen agreed to retire. I don't think there's anything SLED can prove at this point, so dethroning the chief might be the only justice Mark will get."

"I think I need to rest now."

Jack stood up and kissed Enid's forehead. As soon as he left, she rang for the nurse, who arrived promptly. "Could I have another one of those pills?"

CHAPTER 62

Cassie would have enjoyed her own memorial service held at the inn. It was quietly elegant. After the service, Sarah's Tea Shoppe served refreshments by the lake. A cool breeze blew, while the afternoon sun danced on Glitter Lake. Yes, Cassie would have been proud.

A number of people from Madden attended, including several of the Jensen family. Chief Jensen wasn't the same man Enid met a few weeks ago. The man who once stood tall now walked with stooped shoulders. Enid almost felt sorry for him, and then she reminded herself that he had created the mess he was in.

Cade had brought Enid home from the hospital yesterday and stayed for the service. When it was over, he offered to take Enid back to Charlotte, where he had rented an apartment. As a courtesy to Enid, and with her old boss Jill's intervention, the bank had agreed to hold off on foreclosure for a few months to allow Cade and Enid to sell their house. One of Cade's friends had made a rock-bottom offer for a quick purchase, which they accepted to save their credit. Cade had already arranged to put their furnishings in storage temporarily, until they decided what was next. Though the offer was tempting, Enid declined Cade's offer to go back with him to Charlotte.

Fern had sent more than a dozen pots of fall mums for the service. The sea of yellow flowers added to the beauty of the gathering. She had also sent a nice note to Enid, asking for her forgiveness.

In her will, and in one of those if-something-happens-to-me conversations with Jack, Cassie had requested a simple service. She didn't want a minister preaching a sermon and trying to save souls at her expense. Struggling to keep his emotions intact, Jack read from Ecclesiastes:

> *To everything there is a season,*
> *A time for every purpose under heaven:*
> *A time to be born and a time to die …*
> *A time to weep and a time to laugh.*

"Today, we cry for Cassie and for the heartbreak she suffered when her son Mark was killed. She never recovered from losing him, and although she wasn't a religious person, she was certain she would see Mark again in another dimension." Jack stopped to compose himself and then said a few words about what a wonderful, loving person Cassie had been. He concluded by saying, "Rest in peace, my beloved Cassie."

Enid then read one of Cassie's favorite poems, "If Today," written by Jane Marie, a writer and guest who often stayed at the inn. Cassie had been particularly fond of this verse, and Enid liked that Jane shared Rosie's middle name.

> *If today, my absence brings sorrow,*
> *Remember the sun will rise tomorrow.*
> *If today, there are also tears,*
> *Dry them with memories we made through the years.*
> *Our talks, the laughter, those were times well spent,*
> *Hold on to the thoughts that make you content.*

The memories we share, that you hold so dear,
Will be a reminder that I am always near.
No longer will my absence bring sorrow,
Remember the sun will rise tomorrow.

The ache of loss and lingering guilt still consumed Enid. She kept asking herself if she had it to over again, would she have come to Madden? What if she had just ignored those old newspaper articles Jack had written a decade ago? Enid knew she would wrestle with those questions as she tried to rebuild her life.

* * *

Ray Jensen was one of the last guests to leave the memorial service. He walked over to Enid once she was alone. "It was a beautiful service. I'm sure Cassie would have been pleased. I didn't know her well, but the few times we talked, she seemed to be a warm, kind person."

Enid gave Ray an awkward hug. "The copper urn you bought for Cassie was beautiful. That was very generous of you." During the service, when the sun had hit the urn a certain way, it was as if the urn glowed with Cassie's spirit. Now, it was merely cold metal.

"In some way, I felt responsible for Cassie's death," said Ray. "If I had not been late to pick up Rosie, she wouldn't have gotten in the car with Molly that day."

Enid wanted to comfort him, to tell him that life is full of regrets and what-if-I had-done-something-different re-criminations. She also wanted to tell him that she knew firsthand how guilt could eat you alive if you let it. Instead, she remained silent and allowed him time to collect his thoughts.

Ray put his hands in his pockets and lowered his head. "I wish I had pushed my father to do a more thorough investigation of Rosie's murder. Maybe if I had, Molly would have been arrested and Cassie would still be alive. My being late to pick up Rosie set two tragedies in motion—one immediate and one ten years later."

"None of it was your fault." Enid knew Ray needed time and space to work through his role in all of the events that had transpired—just as she did. "Why don't you stay with me and Jack to scatter Cassie's ashes?"

"No, but thanks." Ray lowered his head and walked away.

* * *

The sunlight was fading across Glitter Lake by the time Jack and Enid walked down to the water's edge in silence. There was not much left to be said.

Jack broke the silence first. "Shall we do this now?"

The wind blew and Enid shivered slightly. "Cassie loved sunsets on the lake."

Jack pushed the small rowboat into the edge of the water and then helped Enid get in. He then rowed them a short distance from shore. "I want her to be close to the inn," he said.

Enid nodded in agreement.

Jack took the cover off the urn and waited for the breeze to die down before he leaned over and poured the gray ashes into the water. "Goodbye, my love."

"I'll miss you, Cassie," said Enid, as she watched the ashes floating to the bottom of Glitter Lake.

The last rays of daylight had sunk behind the trees by the time they walked up the path to the inn. Jack put the empty urn on the table in the library. They had agreed to place a memorial bench near the shore of the lake and bury the empty urn beneath it.

"Cassie left me the inn, you know," said Jack.

"I'm glad. What will you do with it?"

"I can't think about that now. There's plenty of time to decide."

"I need to go up and pack my things."

"You can stay at my house tonight," said Jack.

"Are you sure? I can head back to Charlotte tonight. Both Molly and Eddie are in jail, so I'll be safe on the road now."

Jack laughed softly. "Yeah, and I heard Eddie was spilling his guts about paying Chief Jensen to look the other way regarding his drug business. Eddie is trying to cut a deal, or so I heard." Jack motioned toward the porch off the library. "I'll wait out here and watch the sunset while you pack."

Later, as they drove away from the inn, Enid looked back at the dark mansion. If buildings could weep, this one was surely crying for the loss of its beloved owner.

CHAPTER 63

The following week, Rosie's remains were moved from the neglected Pinewood Cemetery to the pristine church cemetery. A dozen or so people gathered for the reburial service. When the wind blew slightly, a few large oak leaves drifted to earth, signaling the early signs of fall. One landed on Rosie's beautiful mahogany casket.

Cade was on the other side of the grave beside his mother. Fern was dressed in the Sunday uniform—a navy sheath and a single strand of pearls. She nabbed at her eyes with a lace handkerchief. Cade looked across the grave at Enid, and for a brief moment they locked eyes.

Rachel Anderson stood behind the others, watching from a distance. Enid could only imagine the emotional turmoil Rachel must be going through.

After the church's minister said a few words over Rosie's grave, Enid walked over to where Cade and Fern were standing. The right words wouldn't come to Enid, so she took Fern's hands in hers and kissed her on the cheek. "Thank you for getting permission from the church to bury Rosie here. I know she's truly at peace now."

Fern's voice cracked as she spoke. "It seemed like the least I could do."

"I'll be happy to help pay for the exhumation and reburial," said Enid. She was broke, but she would find the money somehow.

Cade put his hand on Enid's arm. "That won't be necessary. Mother wanted to handle it herself."

Fern looked at Cade. "I'm tired. Can we please go now?"

"May I have a minute before you go? Enid said to Fern. "We can sit over here."

The two women walked over to a bench and sat, and Cade walked away.

"I'm sorry for the pain I've caused you. Can you forgive me?" said Enid.

Fern pushed away a piece of hair the wind had blown across her face. Her hands were shaking slightly. "My dear, we've both made mistakes we can't undo. There wasn't a day that went by I didn't think of Rosie. I regret that I orchestrated the lies that caused her to mistrust her family. I was wrong."

"I realize now that you acted out of love. You wanted Rosie to have as normal a life as possible."

"I didn't give Rosie enough credit for her strength. She could have handled the truth, if I had let her. That's something I have to live with." Fern patted Enid's leg and smiled slightly. "You're strong, too. I wish I had helped you more with your research. I'd like to contribute what I can. Just come see me, and we'll have a long chat about Rosie and the family. No more secrets."

Enid hugged her. "Thanks. I'd like that."

"I wish you and Cade could work things out. But that's for you two to decide, so I'm staying out of it. Now I'm going to go before we both get too maudlin." Fern motioned for Cade, and he helped her walk to the car. She looked frail.

Enid watched as Cade helped his mother into the black limousine parked at the curb of the narrow road that meandered through the church cemetery. A funeral attendant, dressed in a crisp black suit and standing erect, shut the door after Fern was settled. Cade spoke to the driver and then walked back to the bench where Enid was sitting.

They both started to talk at once. "You go first," said Cade.

"I just wanted to say how sorry I am for all the pain I caused you and Fern. Can you ever forgive me?"

He put his hand on top of Enid's and looked into her eyes. "You always were the troublemaker in the family." He smiled. "Actually, that's one of the many things I love about you."

"You used present tense. Does that mean you still love me?"

He kissed her gently on the lips. "Always." Cade stood up and took Enid's hands in his and pulled her up to face him.

Being this close to Cade, yet so distant, made Enid's heart ache. "Maybe we can try again one day."

He let go of her hands. "One day. Perhaps." He turned and walked back to the waiting limousine.

* * *

After Cade left, Jack walked over to Enid. "You okay?"

Enid forced a smile. "Yes."

He put his hand on Enid's arm. "Let's walk back over to the grave."

Most of the people had left. The casket had been lowered into the cool earth, and grave diggers were covering it with dirt.

"Can you imagine what Fern must have paid for that solid mahogany casket?" asked Jack.

Enid looked down into the grave. "Don't worry. She can afford it." Enid walked over to the tall black granite headstone. She ran her hand across the newly engraved inscription.

Rose Marie Garrett
Gone, But Not Forgotten

Enid buried her face in Jack's shoulder and wept. He pulled a handkerchief from his pocket and handed it to her. "Here, blow your nose before you ruin my only nice suit."

Enid laughed and cried simultaneously. "I seem to be good at ruining things."

Jack put his hands on her shoulders and looked her in the eyes. "Now look here. No pity parties. I won't have it."

Enid pulled away and looked up at Jack. "Rosie is at peace now, but everything else is in turmoil."

"Cassie told me how proud she was that you didn't back down from Chief Jensen when he tried to bully you. She told me you were braver than I was in pursuing the truth. She was right. You are braver." He smiled. "Or at least stubborner."

Enid blew her nose with the handkerchief. "I've even messed up your handkerchief." She folded it into a square. "I'll clean it and get it back to you. Or get you a new one."

"I'll hold you to that."

"Would you and Cassie have gotten married?"

Jack shrugged. "Who knows. We both agreed to take it slow and see what simmered. Or if it simmered. We knew we might be better off as friends than anything more serious." He sighed. "I'd like to think we could have made it, though."

"I appreciate your putting me up, but I'll be leaving tomorrow."

"You going home to Charlotte?"

Enid nodded. "One of Cade's friends is buying our house, so we need to close quickly." She watched the funeral workers take up the folding chairs and roll up the artificial turf.

"Then what will you do?"

Enid watched the workers finish closing the grave. They would dispassionately move on to their next job, but Enid had no idea what the next step would be for her.

"I don't know. We'll see." Enid sighed. "I need to go see Rachel before I leave."

"Want me to go with you?"

Enid shook her head. "No, I need to do this alone." She stepped back away from Jack. "But thanks."

Enid watched as Jack walked back to his car with his head lowered.

CHAPTER 64

Enid didn't want to show up at Rachel's house without notice, but Rachel had not returned any of her calls. Enid couldn't bear the thought of leaving Madden without talking with her, or at least trying to. She also wanted to return Rosie's box of keepsakes to Rachel.

Enid knocked on the front door, its dark green paint peeling in places. Rachel's car was in the driveway but there was no sound of anyone inside the house. Enid knocked again. "Rachel, it's Enid Blackwell. Please let me talk with you, for just a minute." No sound from inside. "I'm leaving Madden today." Enid turned to leave and was walking back to her car when she heard the squeak of door hinges. She turned around and saw Rachel standing in the doorway.

"I can't talk right now," said Rachel.

Enid resisted the urge to walk closer to Rachel for fear she would slam the door. "I understand. But I'm leaving Madden, and I just wanted to talk to you. I promise to be brief."

Rachel opened the front door and stepped aside.

"Thank you," Enid said as she walked up the steps and went inside.

The modest home was clean and neat. Rachel sat in one of the living room chairs, and Enid sat on the sofa, careful not to get too close for fear of making Rachel uncomfortable.

Rachel sat silently with her hands in her lap.

"I don't know what to say," said Enid. "To say I'm sorry seems terribly inadequate. No matter what Molly did, I wish none of this had happened." The dull ache in Enid's heart became a stabbing pain, and she began to question the wisdom of seeing Rachel again. What good could come from it? "Before I leave Madden, I just wanted to see if there is anything I can do for you."

Enid hated how cold and impersonal that sounded, like something you say to people when you don't know what else to say. "And to let you know I've decided not to write Rosie's story. It was a mistake for me to dig up the past." She looked at the young woman across from her, but it was Cassie's face that flashed before her eyes. "In the beginning, I was more worried about reviving my career than I was about Rosie. I'm not proud of that."

Rachel briefly looked up at Enid but remained silent.

Enid continued. "But then I got to know the real Rosie." She handed Rosie's box to Rachel. "Here, I wanted to return this."

Rachel looked at the box but made no attempt to take it.

"In the end, I really wanted everyone else to know the Rosie who was your cousin and best friend. You made the story complete, and I want to thank you."

Rachel continued to stare at Enid without saying anything, so Enid set Rosie's box on the table next to the sofa and got up to leave.

"Wait," Rachel said softly.

Enid eased back down onto the sofa.

"You think I hate you for what happened. But I don't." Rachel clasped her hands tightly in her lap. "I hate my mother for killing Rosie."

Enid wasn't sure what to say, even though a thousand thoughts tumbled around in her head. "I'm sure it was a shock to you. In fact, I can't imagine what—"

"I knew it." Rachel sat up in her chair and pulled back her shoulders. "And Mama knew I knew, but we never talked about it."

Rachel's admission caught Enid off-guard. "How did you know?"

"Right after Rosie got killed, Mama started acting different. You know, all happy-like. Mama told me Rosie got what she deserved, and she was glad she was dead. In my heart, I just knew she did it." Rachel's confession hung in the air like an acrid fog.

Enid searched for words but nothing seemed appropriate.

"I want you to write about Rosie. She deserves it, and I'm glad you stuck with it." Rachel came over to the sofa and sat beside Enid, putting her hands on Rosie's box and stroking it gently. "You keep this. She would want you to have it."

Enid impulsively reached over and hugged Rachel. For a few minutes, the two woman held each other, drawn together by the loss of their mothers, both ravished by cruel circumstances. Enid's mother had been consumed by cancer, her frail body eventually succumbing to the disease inside her. Molly had been consumed by a disease too. Molly's determination to protect Rachel from Rosie, even if her fears were unwarranted, had eventually metastasized into hatred. In in the end, neither Enid's mother nor Rachel's was able to fight off the beast growing inside.

Rachel got up and got a box of tissues and handed it to Enid. "I was ashamed to tell anyone about Mama killing Rosie. I couldn't prove it, but maybe if I had told someone, Miss Cassie might still be alive."

"Please don't think that way. I understand why you didn't say anything." Enid paused. "If I write this story, you'll be in the spotlight again, and you may not want that kind of attention." Enid had learned firsthand what living in a small town was like, and she knew this was the only place Rachel had ever lived. "I don't want you to have to leave Madden."

Rachel straightened up as though she was bracing for what would come next in her already troubled life. "It's over for me here anyway. Just tell everyone Rosie was a good person."

Enid smiled. "I will." Enid studied Rachel's face for signs of reluctance, but all Enid saw was a courageous young woman's determination. "When I write Rosie's story, I want you to read it before I send it in. Is that a deal?"

Rachel smiled slightly for the first time since Enid had arrived. "Okay, if you want me to."

"I do." Enid stood up. "Well, I need to get on the road."

"You going back home, to Charlotte?"

Enid nodded. "I won't be there long, but I'll let you know where I end up."

The two women hugged again before Enid left. As she walked back to her car, she looked back over her shoulder at Rachel, who seemed so much older than when Enid first met her.

CHAPTER 65

Jack helped Enid put the last of her things in the car and shut the rear hatch. "They did a good job on your car." He ran his hand along the side. "You can't tell it was wrecked."

"I'll have to sell it and get something cheaper." Enid opened the driver's side door. "Well, I guess this is it."

Jack held the door for her. "I heard they've got some great handkerchief shops in Charleston. You owe me a new one."

"No one has handkerchief shops, not in this country. Not even Charleston." She searched his face. "What are you saying?"

Jack took her hands in his. "I'm saying that you need to go with me to work on this story I'm doing for the *State* newspaper."

"You're working again? What about the inn?"

Jack rubbed his neck. "Ah, yes. The inn. Well I've never fancied myself an innkeeper." He paused. "Hey, how would you like—

Enid held up her hand. "No, thanks. Don't even go there."

Jack shrugged. "Just thought you might like to make some money, maybe get to keep your car."

Enid just shook her head.

"I do have to decide what to do with the inn. Cassie loved that place so much. I can't bear the thought of selling it.

Madelyn is searching to see if there are any relatives who are more deserving, but so far, she hasn't found any heirs."

Enid shook her head. "Cassie said she had no family. I guess that's one reason we became friends. Neither of us had anyone left."

"Well, unless I can find someone who'll buy it and keep it open, I'll just sit on it for a little while. It's a shame—Cassie worked so hard on the renovations. I've postponed the reopening indefinitely, of course." He kicked at a small rock with his foot. As far as my work, I'm doing some freelance work for some buddies that need a stringer. I'm not ready for the nine-to-five grind again, but I need something to occupy my mind."

Enid put her hand on Jack's arm. "Just remember Cassie's big smile and even bigger heart. And think about the message from her favorite poem I read at the memorial service."

Jack nodded. "I will."

"I can't thank you enough, and Cade too, for convincing the *State* newspaper to run my series on Rosie. But I think Helen and your friends at the *Madden Gazette* will be upset with me for not giving them an exclusive."

"They'll get over it. Besides, you deserve a bigger audience than Madden's weekly newspaper. As your instincts told you all along, the story was more than just one young girl who was murdered. Focusing not just on Rosie but also on the mothers in the story—Wynona, Fern, Molly, Cassie, and even your own mother—is powerful. Cassie would love it." Jack bent over at the waist, bowing to her. "I am humbled by your journalistic instincts."

Enid blushed. "Oh, stop it. I couldn't have done it without you, and you know it."

"I'm serious. You did a great job. When you first came to Madden, I thought you were crazy." He swirled his finger in a circle. "And you were, just a bit. But you were also determined and your compassion for Rosie and her memory inspired me. I think your series will get picked up by the AP and go national." He punched her arm gently with his finger. "In fact, Cade and I are going to lean on our contacts to make sure it does."

Enid looked down at the ground to avoid Jack's gaze. "What happened to Cade's story about police corruption in small towns like Madden—the one he's writing with Madelyn's help?" Enid almost choked saying her name.

"He's going forward with it, but he's going to wait a while so he doesn't take anything away from your series."

Enid watched Jack rub his neck, and smiled to herself. She would miss him and his familiar mannerisms. "That was considerate of him."

"He loves you, you know. I think he hates this split between you two more than you do." He kicked the little rock again with his toe. "Sometimes people just need a change, and they're willing to pay almost any price for it. And, sometimes that price is steep—more than the person bargained for."

Enid wasn't sure if Jack was talking about Cade or her. "Thanks for the offer to go to Charleston, but I need to get these articles written if I'm going to meet my deadline. And I need to have a long talk with Cade. Then I'll figure out where to go from there."

Jack put his hand under her chin and raised her face to look at him. "Don't read anything into my invitation. The only way I can deal with my grief is to stay busy, and I need a work partner, that's all." He tapped the tip of her nose gently with his finger. "We're pretty good at working together, don't you think?"

Enid stammered. "No, I know . . . I mean, yes. Yes, we work pretty good together."

"What I need now is a really good friend, that's all. And I suspect you do too. So, you'll think about it then? If not Charleston, then maybe another story later. The invitation is open—when you're ready. He frowned. "Unless you're thinking of going back to that god-awful bank job."

"I don't think they'd have me."

Jack held the door as she got in. "Their loss indeed."

Enid lowered the car window. "What's your story in Charleston about?"

Jack turned and started walking back toward his house. As he got near the front steps, he turned and called out to Enid. "Come on down and buy me that handkerchief. Then I'll tell you."

Thank you for reading *Murder in Madden*, a fictional story inspired by the real-life murder of Hope Gibson. Like Rosie, Hope is gone but not forgotten

* * *

Please visit Raegan at http://RaeganTeller.com and let her know if you enjoyed the book—or provide any other comments. She would love to hear from you.

ACKNOWLEDGEMENTS

It takes a village to write a book. Without my village, and without their love, support, and encouragement, I would never have published this book.

The chief of my village is my wonderful husband, William Earl Craig. Over the past three years, he has been neglected and subjected to all my writer's moods. He has also helped me work through plot points, create characters, and find errors in my manuscript. He cooked and cleaned when I was too busy to stop working. But the best thing he did was give me a hug when I was discouraged and tell me, "I'm proud of you." In every way, this is "our" book.

My sister, Jane Cook, who writes poetry and stories as "Jane Marie," has also been a big supporter throughout this process. In fact, she wrote the poem for my book, "If Today." Her unwavering confidence in her "little sister" helped me stay focused.

Every writer needs someone who helps her get started. Al Watt of L.A. Writers Lab guided me through the first draft of *Murder in Madden*—and a couple revisions. Most importantly, he helped me dig deep and discover the real story. Every writer should experience working with Al.

After several more revisions, I was nearly finished when I met Bill Looney, author of *Hunting the Storm* and three other suspense novels. Contrary to what he may tell you, I would have finished without his constant nagging. (Okay, so maybe it did help a bit.) Nonetheless, I am grateful for his encouragement, support, and friendship.

The wise woman of my village is Ramona DeFelice Long, my developmental editor. Her patience and encouragement in working with a first-time novelist was appreciated. I am especially grateful for the valuable insights she shared with me that will take years off my learning curve.

I also want to thank our writers group, Indie Authors NE. They have become ardent supporters and good friends. I hope I can make them as proud of me as I am of them.

And my dear friend John Bennett, you have been with me every step of the way. Thanks for your love and unwavering belief in me.

Finally, I want to acknowledge Wilbur Vaughan, a South Carolina coroner; Penny at the American Goat Association; and Dr. Stefanie Oppenheim of UC Davis Veterinary Genetics Lab for their research assistance.

There are many others in my village who provided support and friendship along the way. Please know how much I appreciate all of you for being on this remarkable journey with me.

ABOUT THE AUTHOR

As the saying goes, "you can't pick your relatives." But if you're a fiction writer, you can pick your name. Raegan Teller is the nom de plume for Wanda Bryant Craig, a communications consultant and business writer in Columbia, South Carolina. She has also been a marketing manager, executive coach, and insurance manager—among other things. While working her way through school, she even sold burial vaults at a cemetery. How apropos is that for a mystery writer!

Made in the USA
Columbia, SC
13 November 2018